Beach Wedding Weekend

RACHEL MAGEE

Hallmark PUBLISHING

Beach Wedding Weekend
Copyright @ 2019 Rachel Magee

Print ISBN: 978-1-947892-68-2
eBook ISBN: 978-1-947892-69-9

www.hallmarkpublishing.com

Table of Contents

Chapter One

PAIGE WESTMORELAND WAS ON THE verge of pulling off the impossible. Most of the wedding planners who came before her swore it couldn't be done, and there had been a few times (two particular flaming disasters came to mind) when she'd also doubted its possibility. But here she was, about to manage the perfect wedding.

Pride swirled inside her as she stood in front of the two-story wall of windows and looked out over the manicured gardens the way a painter stood in front of her masterpiece. Sure, it might be a little premature to claim it yet. The bride hadn't even walked down the aisle, for goodness' sake. But she had a good feeling about this one. After forty-seven attempts, this was the first time she'd ever gotten this far without so much as a hiccup. Every single box on her pre-wedding checklist was marked off, the kitchen was fully staffed and running right on schedule, and the bride and groom, along with everyone they considered important to their wedding, were in excellent health and fantastic moods. From where Paige stood, she could almost see the glittering pot of gold at the end of the proverbial rainbow. And since the bride of this particular wedding was her best friend's cousin, it made the victory that much sweeter.

She drew in a deep breath, letting the joy of the perfect day sparkle through her. In her opinion, especially on days like today, she had the best job in the world. Every weekend, and the occasional weekday, she got to see love win. And, as an added bonus, she had the privilege of doing it in Hilltop, the charming resort town nestled in the heart of the Texas Hill Country.

Paige ran through the timeline for this particular wedding in her mind. Ten minutes until the groom and his men took their spots and the wedding processional started. Twelve and a half minutes until the bride walked down the aisle at exactly five o'clock. Which meant...

"I made it." The jovial voice echoed through the otherwise empty room, but even this didn't surprise her. She typed 8:30 into the timer on her tablet and pressed start before she looked up at the latecomer.

Aiden Pierce strolled across the marble floor of Hilltop Resort's famed wedding pavilion, The Chateau. He had the laidback gait and easy smile of someone for whom life always seemed to work out, and the sight of him brightened Paige's already sunny day.

"Cutting it a little close, aren't you?" She gave Aiden a hard time because that's the kind of friendship they had, but inside her pride beamed with such force she wondered if it made her glow. She'd planned this wedding so perfectly that she'd even anticipated his late arrival. Earlier, she'd caught wind that Aiden's golf game on the resort's course was going to be a close finish, and since he was the bride's cousin, she'd prepared a way to sneak him to the front row where his family was seated with minimal disruption.

Aiden tied his sapphire tie as he walked, not bothering to speed up his lazy pace. "The bride hasn't walked down the aisle yet. Therefore, I'm not late."

There was a twinkle in his eye. The same friendly one that won over almost everyone he spoke with. From what Paige had gathered in the eight years she'd known her best friend Ciera's older brother, it was impossible for anyone to be upset with him. Plus he had the kind of charismatic personality that made him instant friends with everyone in the room.

Paige glanced out the window again at her perfect wedding.

Almost all of the two hundred white wooden folding chairs were occupied, but she could see the empty one on the end of the second row she'd saved for him. It just so happened that Aiden's very punctual mama, who was also aware of his tardiness, had chosen the seat right next to it. What could she say? While she could plan for most things, she wasn't a miracle worker.

"I'm afraid I'm not the one you have to convince." Paige pulled a face to show her mock concern.

With his tie in a loose knot, he buttoned the top button of his shirt and ran his hand through his wavy, sandy blond hair in a vain attempt to style it. "Mama talks a big game, but she'll be glad her baby boy's sitting next to her."

Paige tightened his tie for him, smoothing it out against the front of his shirt. This was something she did often because he claimed he liked the way she made it perfectly straight. Perhaps, if he wasn't her best friend's brother, she might've appreciated the way his strong chest felt. But he was, and their relationship, since the day she first visited the Pierce household, was nothing more than friendly.

"Or she'll be wondering why her baby boy couldn't pull himself off the golf course early enough to be here on time."

"Is it that obvious?"

She put her hands on her hips and pretended to examine him with a stern eye. Other than his wind-blown hair and his sun-kissed face, there was no sign he'd been swinging a golf club until less than five minutes ago. In fact, she found it a little unfair that he could look so great with such little effort. "I suppose you'll pass."

Half of his mouth pulled up into a guilty grin and he motioned outside. "With a day like this, can you blame me? Plus, it was more business than pleasure. I had to be there." He adjusted the sleeves under his jacket.

"You know what they say about excuses."

He gave her an apologetic shrug highlighted by his charming

7

grin. Yep, it was true. It was impossible to stay mad at him. She pointed to the door on the far side of the room.

"If you slip out that door you can walk down the side and slide into your seat without anyone but your mom noticing."

"Thanks for having my back, Westmoreland." He buttoned the top button of his jacket. "On the bright side, at least I'm not as late as that guy." He nodded his head toward the main entrance above them.

For the first time during this wedding, Paige felt the slight flutter of surprise. Now that Aiden was here, she thought everyone had arrived. She followed Aiden's gaze up the grand stone staircase to the mezzanine level lobby until she saw him.

At that very moment everything stood still. It was entirely possible even the world stopped turning. Out of all the things she considered that could've gone wrong today, all the contingencies she prepared for, this one never entered her mind. She stood there, stunned.

"Hey, isn't that . . ." Aiden broke her trance.

"Brody Paxton," Paige finished. Her voice had a sort of breathless quality to it that she hated, but she couldn't help it.

Brody stepped up to the railing and paused. Perhaps he had a valid reason for stopping in that particular spot, but as far as Paige could tell, it was only to smolder. Which, by the way, he did so well it made her weak in the knees.

His dark hair was perfectly styled in his signature Ivy League haircut, and his well-tailored suit accentuated his lean, athletic frame. The light flooding through the door cast a halo-type glow around him, making him look like a vision out of a dream. The string quartet behind them picked that moment to reach their crescendo, and she couldn't be sure, but she thought she even heard angels singing. After all this time, her ex-boyfriend was still the most beautiful man she'd ever laid her eyes on.

He slipped off his sunglasses and gazed out the massive windows.

Even from a short distance, she could see the hypnotic sparkle in his cobalt blue eyes, and something inside her fluttered. Was it her or was there a sudden lack of oxygen in the room?

"Didn't he move to Europe?" Aiden asked.

Paige nodded, trying in vain to get her scattered thoughts under control. "His company transferred him to Luxembourg." At least that's what he'd told her thirteen months and eight days ago, when he'd ended their blissful eleven-month relationship with the news that he was moving overseas. Alone.

The familiar ache pinged in her chest.

"Why is he here?" Aiden whispered.

"I don't know." The same question had been swirling around her mind as well. It had been a while since she'd talked to him, but as far as she knew, he was still living in Europe.

Visions of the dismal day she drove him to the airport trickled to the front of her memory. Watching him walk away was one of the hardest things she'd ever done. She knew the move would be good for his career, but it didn't make the ache in her chest hurt any less.

The one thing that had made it easier was hope and a promise. A faint spark of excitement tingled in the tips of her fingers as the pieces of this puzzle started to come together.

On that dreary day in the busy airport, tears had stung her eyes. Brody had told her it wasn't a breakup, just a pause. They weren't saying goodbye, just see you later. His final goodbye kiss still burned on her lips as his airport promise rung in her ears. *Someday, I'll be back.*

She would adamantly deny it if ever asked, but she'd often daydreamed about what their reunion could be like. Maybe she would meet him at the airport with a welcome home sign and a teary-eyed smile. Or perhaps he would surprise her and show up on her doorstep with a bouquet of flowers and, during some of her more hopeful moments, a ring. The setting might have changed, but the ending was always the same; he'd come back, and they'd be together again.

And here he was.

The fingertip-tingles started to work their way up her arms. She hadn't known if it would really happen. Time had a way of changing things, but what they'd shared was special. She'd been certain then he was *the one*, and seeing him now, all of those feelings came rushing back.

She started to call his name, and the excitement flooding into her threatened to launch her up the stairs and into his waiting arms. But as she took the first step, she caught sight of something else. Or rather, someone else.

Brody turned and offered his elbow to the woman stepping through the door. A smitten smile spread across his face. A smile not made for Paige. She froze in her tracks.

"Whoa. Who's that?" Aiden's words didn't help the sucker punch to the gut reality had just dealt her.

An elegant woman stepped up next to Brody. With one hand she tucked a strand of her long, auburn hair behind her ear, highlighting her delicate features, as she slid the other into the crook of Brody's arm. Suddenly the world started to spin again, a little faster than Paige was anticipating, and she swayed on her feet.

The power couple walked the few steps to the grand staircase and paused, as if displaying their beauty and poise for the whole world to see. All the excitement drained out of Paige's body, leaving her limbs feeling limp and heavy. She considered running away. Not to hide, per se, because that would've been juvenile. She liked to think of it as postponing a conversation until she was fully prepared, which seemed rather responsible. And by fully prepared, she meant the ability to speak without sounding like a blubbering idiot.

But it didn't matter if running was responsible or not: her legs wouldn't cooperate. And even if they had, there was nowhere to escape in this otherwise empty, massive room. So she stood there, with no choice but to face him, scattered thoughts and all.

Brody's gaze landed on her. His polite smile turned up the corners of his mouth, accentuating his strong jaw, before he whispered something to the girl next to him. Her gaze drifted to Paige, then refocused on him. Paige's stomach dropped when his intimate look confirmed their relationship was more than friendly.

The girl smoothed the emerald dress that elegantly hugged her curves and then draped her hand over the railing. Then they started down the wide stone steps in perfect unison.

Brody stepped with his usual steady confidence. The girl moved with the grace of a dancer, each of her footsteps skimming the surface of the stairs. The four-inch stilettos at the end of her toned legs seemed to be an extension of her foot, as if she were made to wear them. Everything about her radiated beauty and poise.

Paige glanced down at her own look in comparison. About the only similarity between them was they'd both chosen to wear almost the exact shade of green. Other than their shared penchant for emerald-colored garments, Paige was the complete opposite of the beauty on Brody's arm.

Paige had chosen her loose-fitting A-line knit dress because it had pockets, something she proudly proclaimed to her friends on staff when she arrived earlier. The fact now seemed childish. Her practical dress was paired with sensible ballet flats, which she wore more for function than fashion, and she'd pulled her hair up in a bun about fifteen minutes after she'd arrived at work to get it out of the way. Even if she hadn't, her mousy brown hair would have been hanging in a stringy mess around her shoulders at this point. It didn't matter how many products she armed her hair with, the Texas humidity always won. And although she'd put on lipstick before she arrived, she was positive there wasn't a trace of it left.

Seeing Brody unannounced at one of her weddings with some knockout on his arm was about as far as possible from any of the reunion daydreams she'd managed to come up with over their thirteen-month absence. Every awe-worthy opening line she'd ever thought up—and, embarrassingly, there were quite a few of them—was invalid. To make matters even worse, at the moment her brain seemed incapable of thinking up something new.

Brody reached the last step and his gaze locked with hers.

"Hello, Paige."

The way her name sounded in his smooth voice sent shivers racing down her spine. Although, she had to admit he sounded less surprised to see her than she was to see him, which sent another round of questions swirling through her mind. The girl on his arm smiled.

Paige's mind went blank. She opened her mouth to say something, anything, but nothing came out. Brody either didn't notice or didn't care. The couple glided over and stopped in front of her.

"It's nice to see you." Brody's familiar words caused her heart to skip a beat and his gaze burned into her.

She tried to answer, but since the shock of the situation was still holding her voice captive, she offered a grin instead. Hopefully, it looked more sophisticated-alluring and less lovesick puppy.

An awkward pause filled the air. Aiden cleared his throat and stepped closer to Brody, offering his hand.

"Brody, Aiden Pierce. It's been a while."

Brody held Paige's gaze for another millisecond. Long enough for her to be positive she sensed the air between them crackle. Just like it used to.

Then he grasped Aiden's handshake and shifted his attention.

"Good to see you again, Aiden." He let go of Aiden's grasp and held his hand in front of the beauty next to him, as if to put her on display. "Allow me to introduce you both to Sasha Kane."

The bitterness of jealousy mixed with disappointment rose up in Paige's throat, but she tried to appear delighted to meet someone new. When it was clear that was too tall an order, she settled for an expression she hoped looked pleasant-ish.

Sasha extended a graceful hand to Paige first. "I've heard so much about you."

Now was Paige's chance to offer some clever one-liner that would remind Brody of their times together and remind Sasha whose turf she was on. But nothing even remotely clever came to mind. And even if it had, it wouldn't have mattered because her voice still wasn't cooperating.

So Paige just nodded at her. This was not at all how she imagined their first meeting going. Once again, Aiden stepped in.

"Pleasure to meet you, Sasha." He took her outstretched hand and lifted it to his lips. Sasha appeared to be charmed. Brody glared. The whole situation made Paige feel like she might be sick.

The harsh, screeching sound of a digital alarm echoed through the room and broke up the moment. Everyone stared at the tablet in Paige's hand. Everyone, that was, except Paige, who was still trying to figure out what Brody was doing here. And why was he with *her*? And, for that matter, who was she?

Brody pointed to the tablet. "You, uh, want to get that?"

Paige stared at it for another second, trying to comprehend the sound. Since Brody had walked through those doors, she was having a hard time comprehending anything. 0:00 flashed on her screen.

"The bride!" She bobbled the tablet and fumbled with the off button, trying to get the noise to stop. The heat from her cheeks worked its way down her neck. "I gotta go."

She looked up at the newcomers. An expression of cool acceptance crossed Brody's face. Her already sagging spirit plummeted.

Aiden's hand pressed against the small of her back in a gesture she assumed was supposed to calm her frazzled nerves. "We'll catch you after the ceremony." He winked. Then he looked to Brody and Sasha and held his hand out to the side door. "Shall we?"

The trio crossed the room and exited to the garden. Paige stood frozen in her spot, watching through the windows as Brody and his date claimed the last two empty chairs. Brody undid his jacket and ran his hand through his perfect hair before he settled it on Sasha's knee. Her own knee tingled, remembering exactly how his touch felt.

The string quartet finished their song and silence filled the air. It was the signal for the officiant to lead out the groom. She glanced at her watch, shook her head to try to clear her thoughts, then dashed across the room as fast as her ballet flats could carry her to the bridal suite.

One minute and thirty-eight seconds behind schedule.

So much for pulling off the perfect wedding. Paige plopped down in the empty chair next to her best friend, Ciera Pierce, and let out the long, defeated sigh that had been building up insider her all evening. "I need cake."

Normally she loved wedding receptions, which made her job fun even on the hard days. Being among joyful guests celebrating love was like food for her soul. But right now, a trip to the dentist for a root canal sounded more appealing than being stuck in this room. Too bad she was contractually obligated to be here until the bitter end.

Ciera pushed the plate of half-eaten wedding cake in front of her. "Great job today. The wedding was lovely." She adjusted the strap of her ice-blue dress as she stared dreamily around the room, as if taking in all the decorations.

Paige closed her eyes for a moment and massaged her temples to try to rid herself of the stress headache she'd had since the ceremony. Or, if she was being more accurate, it came on around the same time a certain someone decided to reappear in her life. Blinking her eyes open, she pulled the cake plate closer to her, hoping a sweet treat would help push Brody Paxton out of her mind so she could concentrate on finishing this wedding.

"If you don't count the ceremony starting four minutes late, cueing the wrong song for the first dance or all of the vegetarian meals being cold, then I guess it was okay." She cut off a huge bite of cake and speared it with her fork, perhaps more aggressively than she should have.

Ciera shrugged, causing her tight blonde curls to bounce around her head. "No one noticed those things."

Paige disagreed. She felt sure the seventeen guests trying to force down cold eggplant parmesan noticed, but she didn't argue.

"What everyone did notice were the Longhorn-orange bridesmaids' dresses," Ciera added. She looked out to the dance floor where the bride was dancing among a sea of orange chiffon. "I've never been so thankful to be left out of a wedding party in my whole life."

The thought of Ciera wearing the school colors of her alma mater's number one rival almost elicited a giggle. "They are an unfortunate color. The first time your cousin showed me a picture of them I thought she was joking."

"And you didn't stop her?"

"She said the color signified a time and place that were important to her and her now husband. It's kind of sweet, really." Paige paused and studied the bobbing orange mob. Even with the sweet sentiment behind it, she had to admit the amount of burnt orange when all eight ladies were standing together was a bit much.

"I tried to pick flowers that would tone down the color in pictures." Of course, it didn't help when they were on the dance floor without their bouquets.

"Unless you gave them a bush to hide behind, there aren't enough flowers to mute that distraction down."

This time Paige did giggle, just a little, and she shoveled the giant bite of cake into her mouth before the next catastrophe pulled her away and she missed her chance to eat it.

But as soon as the bite hit her tongue she wished she'd been called away first. Whatever cardboard excuse for white cake had been hiding underneath the chalky fondant icing did not deserve to call itself a treat. She considered spitting it out, but since she didn't have a napkin handy, she forced herself to swallow it in one giant gulp.

"Ugh. This is awful."

Ciera glanced at the offending plate. "Oh right. People noticed that, too." She motioned to all the plates with half-eaten cake on their table then pushed her water glass in front of Paige.

It would take a whole pitcher of water to get rid of the taste in her mouth, but Paige settled for a sip from Ciera's glass. She scanned the neighboring tables for more plates of unfinished cake. As far as she could see, not one person had managed to choke down their whole slice anywhere at this reception. Great. Another thing to add to the list of things that went wrong.

Paige pushed the plate away from her and made a mental note to tell the waitstaff to clear them as soon as possible. Maybe if it was out of sight, the guests would forget how bad it was. One could hope, anyway. "I warned her about the cake. I even told her about the bakery everyone raves about, but she insisted on the one from the magazine layout from the expensive place in the city."

As soon as she said it, the music switched to a slow song. The crowd on the dance floor cleared and couples filled the space. Like a moth attracted to light, Paige's gaze went straight to Brody. He stepped onto the dance floor from the far side, looking dapper as always in his dark suit, holding the new girl's hand. After he spun her once, he pulled Sasha into himself and they glided in perfect rhythm around the floor. Paige let out a long, discouraged sigh. "Everyone wants the pretty cake and doesn't seem to care what it's got going on inside."

Ciera shot her a concerned look. "You okay, sweetie?"

"Brody's back in town," she mumbled without taking her eyes off the couple. She and Brody had looked like that when they were together, hadn't they? All happy and in sync?

"Oh." Ciera screwed her mouth to the side and glanced in the direction of the dance floor, looking more concerned than surprised. "Yeah. I heard that."

"Wait? Heard that?" Paige sat straight up and glared at her best friend. "Like before you watched them walk into the wedding?"

Ciera kept her eyes on the dancing couple and waited a second too long before answering. "Maybe."

"You knew he was in town and you didn't tell me?" Did she have any idea how much humiliation she could've prevented if Paige had a heads-up? The memory of their disastrous meeting in The Chateau caused heat to sear her cheeks. Why would her best friend keep something like this from her?

A pained expression fell over Ciera's face. "We were waiting for the right time to tell you. We didn't want to upset you."

Paige thrust her chin in the direction of the happy couple. Hurt and frustration flanked her already dismal spirit. "Too late."

Ciera squeezed her hand. "I'm so sorry, Paige. I should have told you before tonight, but I honestly thought he wouldn't come. And if he did, I was sure he'd call you first."

Paige watched the happy couple gliding around the floor, and she had an idea of what had been keeping him too busy to pick up the phone. A fresh wave of hurt washed over her. "How long has he been in town?"

"I'm not sure. Georgia told me about it a week ago. I guess his company moved him back to work out of the office here."

"Georgia knows!" Paige shrieked, a little too loud. She glanced around to see if anyone had noticed then lowered her voice. "Am I the last to find out?" Seriously, did any of her friends know how to work a phone? Or drop a text, send a smoke signal, anything? What was wrong with these people?

Ciera took a deep breath. "You're not going to like this next part." She surveyed the room as if looking for help to deliver whatever she was about to say.

"He's one of the groomsmen in Georgia and Lane's wedding.

We were trying to figure out how to tell you."

Paige didn't move as she tried to absorb this news. Georgia, Ciera and Paige had been close friends since they met in college, and the two women were bridesmaids in Georgia's upcoming wedding. The one where they would all be spending the weekend at their favorite beach in the Florida panhandle which just so happened to be the very same beach where she and Brody had first gotten together. She could almost taste the iced white chocolate mocha they would sip as they strolled through the cute town, lost in conversation, letting all the other coffees they'd gone to get for their friends go cold.

Sure, she knew Brody was friends with Lane before they started dating. Lane was the reason they met, but she never even considered him being in the wedding. When he went overseas, Paige had assumed he had abandoned all of them.

She watched the happy couple spin around the dance floor as she let Ciera's words settle over her. So, it really was over. Tears pricked her eyes.

This wasn't how their story was supposed to go. Brody's temporary European assignment was supposed to be a speed bump, something to give their perfect story an interesting twist when they told it at their fiftieth wedding anniversary. But here he was, holding some other girl in his arms.

"Who is she?" Paige whispered, afraid that if she used a full voice her tears would spill over her eyelids. And once they started, she didn't know if she'd be able to stop them.

Ciera didn't bother to turn around to look at the girl Paige asked about. "Some actress who's old summer camp friends with

Lindy Grant. I guess she's about to start a new TV show that will be filmed in Austin, and she's staying with Lindy while she decides if she wants to get a place there or stay here and make the hour commute."

Actress made sense. She held herself with the kind of confidence and grace which begged people to look at her. And she was annoyingly beautiful. She was the complete opposite of Paige, which somehow felt even more discouraging.

"How'd they meet? They look pretty chummy for two people who just arrived in town."

Ciera shifted, stealing a glance at the couple. "According to Georgia, they actually met in Europe a while back. She was on location for some sort of movie near where he was living, and Lindy set it up so he could show her around on her day off. I guess she was charmed by him and they kept in touch."

"And they just so happened to move to the same place at the same time?"

"She's telling everyone it's fate." Ciera rolled her eyes. "They started dating as soon as he got back in town."

"I don't think I like her."

Ciera laughed. "No? If it makes you feel any better, according to Georgia, neither does Lane."

It did make her feel a little better, in a sad, petty sort of way. She propped her chin on her fist and watched the happy couple. "I should get back to work." Or at the very least, she should stop staring at them. Watching Brody with his new girlfriend was a bad idea, but she couldn't make herself look away.

Someone dropped into the chair on the other side of her and startled her. For the first time since the song had started, she tore her gaze away from Brody to see Aiden's cheerful face. And what was even better than seeing a friend was the delicious sweet scent drifting up from the paper baskets he held in each of his hands.

"Food truck's here with the midnight snacks," he said. "Time for some decent desserts."

Paige glanced at her watch. "I didn't realize how late it was. I have to go make sure it's in the right spot."

Aiden and his investment partner owned one of the most popular restaurants in Hilltop. As a wedding gift to his cousin, Aiden had Cedar Break's food truck bring late-night snacks to the wedding partiers. According to her master timeline, she should've been out there five minutes ago to make sure everything was up and running.

"Don't worry, Wedding Boss. I made sure the truck was exactly where you told us it needed to be, and my staff was ready to start pumping out desserts. Your assistant's outside keeping an eye on it." He slid the paper tray holding his famous chocolate lava cake across Paige to his sister. "It's taken care of. And there's already a line." He winked at her and shoveled a forkful of cherry turnover a la mode into his mouth.

Aiden Pierce was more punctual than she was. Tonight was full of surprises. "Thanks." She looked into his eyes, trying to convey how much she appreciated his help.

"My pleasure. Now, what's with the somber mood? What are we talking about?" he asked through a full mouth.

Ciera cut into her cake and the liquid chocolate center oozed out. "Unexpected wedding guests." She nodded her head at the dance floor.

The music had changed to a fast song, but Brody and Sasha were still out there. Even though they weren't touching now, watching them dance to this song was even worse.

Aiden scooped up another forkful of pie and shoveled it into his mouth. "Aww, yes. The European dude." He reached across, snagged Ciera's chocolate cake and slid it to Paige. "Looks like you could use this."

Ciera, whose fork was midway between the cake and her mouth, froze. "Hey. What about me?"

Aiden tipped his chair to look at his sister from behind Paige, held his hand up to block his mouth and pretended to whisper. "Cici, you're not the one whose ex just waltzed back in town with a Hollywood actress on his arm."

"You know I can still hear you." Paige grabbed the fork from Ciera's hand and cut off a hearty-sized bite of her absolute favorite thing on Cedar Break's menu. She hoped the bitter taste of disappointment wouldn't ruin it.

Aiden draped his arm over her shoulder and gave her a gentle squeeze. It had been a crummy night, but the embrace of a good friend brightened her gloomy spirit a bit. Chocolate cake didn't hurt, either.

"If it makes you feel any better, I heard everyone thinks she's not all that," Aiden said.

Paige rolled her eyes. "You've known about her for like five minutes. How do you know what everyone thinks?"

Aiden swallowed the large bite in his mouth. "I've been shooting the breeze with everyone in the room for the past four hours. People talk, and they have a lot of opinions about her."

Ciera took a sip of her drink. "I already told you Lane said she has no personality."

Paige cut off another big bite of the cake and swiped it across the bottom of the bowl to soak up the liquid chocolate. "Is this supposed to make me feel better? Brody's gorgeous new girlfriend is boring?"

"Boring is a big deal," Aiden said. "No one likes boring."

Ciera nodded. "Truth."

It could've been truth to these two, but the fact was, Sasha had Brody and all she had was a growing void where he had once been.

"Maybe being devastatingly beautiful trumps boring."

"Occasionally in the short term, but never in the long term."

The seasoned voice came from behind them. All three turned around to find Aiden and Ciera's grandmother, lovingly known to all as Gram, standing behind them.

Aiden hopped out of his seat and kissed her on the cheek. "Gram, here. Take my seat. How are you enjoying the reception so far?"

"I'd be enjoying it more if I were involved in this beautiful versus boring conversation. Sounds scandalous. I need a little scandal in my life." There was a twinkle in Gram's wise eyes as she sank into the seat Aiden had vacated with her gaze glued to Paige.

Ciera leaned across her to fill Gram in. "Paige's ex-boyfriend is back in town and he brought an actress with him." She snagged the fork from Paige and pulled the cake in front of herself.

Gram nodded as if considering the situation. "And how much of a looker is this new girl?"

Ciera shot Aiden a worried look. Paige appreciated her friend trying to spare her feelings, but it wasn't a secret. Anyone with eyes could see what kind of beauty they were dealing with. Paige looked right at Gram and gave her the most honest answer she could think of. "She could launch a thousand ships."

"She's very pretty," Ciera added. Aiden gave Paige's shoulders an encouraging squeeze.

"I see." Gram twisted her mouth to the side in thought. "This reminds me of the time when Lorissa's ex-husband returned with a supermodel who was as dumb as a box of rocks." Gram often lacked a filter. Whatever thought ran through her head came out of her mouth, which Paige loved. It was always entertaining and so different from anything she'd grown up with.

"Are these real friends or soap opera friends?" Aiden asked. Until Paige met Gram, she was unaware soap operas still existed. Apparently they did. And Gram still watched them with diligence.

Gram gave Aiden a stern look. "Soap opera friends are real friends, dear." She turned to Paige. Her weathered hand wrapped around Paige's. The warm, maternal gesture was like a hug to her broken heart. "Did you love him?"

Visions of their year together paraded through her mind. Happy memories of sweet moments when the word forever sparkled with anticipation.

Paige let out a sigh. "Yeah."

Sympathy flashed across Gram's face. "Do you still love him?" Her voice was a little quieter this time, a little more personal. Which seemed appropriate since the question felt personal.

Sure, her heart had broken when he left, which dampened love's euphoric glow, but hope had managed to keep some of the spark alive. In the back of her mind, even on her loneliest days, she clung to the image of him coming back. Someday they could pick up right where they left off, share life together, grow old together. That was love, right?

"I think so," she said.

Gram squeezed her hand, her voice returning to its normal cheerful tone. "Then do what Lorissa did."

Confusion fluttered through her. Gram's sage advice was coming from a soap opera character? "What did she do?"

"She gave him the ole' one-two." Gram let go of Paige's hand and held her fists in front of her face, jabbing the air in dainty punches. "You have to fight for love."

"Fight for love?" Paige asked.

"It's your life, kiddo. You gotta go after what you want." She punched the air again.

Aiden chuckled from behind her and massaged her shoulders. "Easy there, Sugar Ray."

Gram waved him off. "I do Sit Fit every morning. I'm as healthy as a cow."

Aiden's eyes narrowed. "It's 'as healthy as a horse,' Gram."

"Pshaw. At my age it's ridiculous to think I could run as much as a horse. But a cow who stands around and eats all day? That's more realistic. Now, shoo and get me some of that chocolate oozy cake. I need to talk to Paige."

Paige nodded her head at the door leading to where the food truck was parked. "You heard the lady. She needs some cake."

Aiden shook his head. "I get no respect around here."

Paige considered Gram's wise words. "How am I supposed to win him back when she's Helen-of-Troy beautiful?"

"Be Helen-of-Troy beautifuler."

Aiden stuck his head between Gram and Paige. "Beautifuler' isn't a word, Gram."

Gram wagged a withered finger in his face. "Watch your mouth, young man. And while you're getting my cake, I'd like a glass of milk to go with it." Laughter crinkled her eyes. Aiden shook his head but jogged off in the direction of the door.

"I agree, though." Paige was no stranger to being in the presence of exceptional beauty. Her mother, a supermodel turned fashion designer icon, was known for being a knockout. Paige spent her entire childhood in the middle of the fashion industry among people who turned heads for a living. While Paige considered herself pretty enough, she didn't belong in the same category as they did. "In this case, I'm not sure it's an option."

Paige tilted her head to the side in confusion. "But he's with Sasha now."

Gram's mouth twisted to the side as she studied Paige. Everything got quiet for a second. "Sure it is. Being beautifuler isn't about how you look. It's about who you are. Someone may like a pretty face, but we fall in love with a beautiful soul."

"True. Occasionally people distract themselves with what's around, but when you finally see the one your soul desires, it's impossible to look away." Gram wrapped her warm hand around Paige's. "All you have to do is let the beauty within you shine and the rest will fall into place."

Gram's wisdom swirled around her, breathing life into Paige's deflated spirit. She focused on the memories of their past, the time they had spent together.

"We did have a pretty great thing going." She whispered the words almost to herself.

Ciera wrapped her arm around Paige's shoulders and squeezed. "We simply have to remind him of it."

"Then, go. Fight for love!" Gram cheered.

"But…" A thousand insecurities ran through her mind. *But what if…* Before she could go too far down the rabbit hole, Gram gently rubbed the outside of her arm.

"But nothing. Love is always worth fighting for."

Ciera clapped her hands together, a look of glee spreading over her face. "Operation Get Paige's Man Back commences now."

Gram punched her dainty fists in the air again. "How exciting! I need a little drama in my life." She stopped and looked around. "Also, I need my cake. Where did Aiden go?"

"Operation Get Brody Back. I like the sound of that." Paige watched Brody dance, and her long-lost confidence started to rebloom.

Their life together had been great. He'd be lucky to have it again. Lucky to have *her* again. It was time to get him back. She pushed away from the table, feeling more alive and hopeful than she had all night.

"All right, ladies, back to work. It's time to start gathering everyone for the bouquet toss." She stared out at the group on the dance floor and caught one last sight of Brody and Sasha together. "I know true love has a way of working itself out and all that, but it would make me feel better if we didn't tempt fate any further by letting Sasha catch the bouquet."

Ciera smiled. "Don't worry. I've got your back. I didn't get the award for all-district guard in high school women's basketball for nothing." She clasped her hands and stretched them out in front of her.

Paige laughed and headed off to find the bride. "Fight for love," she whispered to herself. It was a crazy idea, but it just might work.

Chapter Two

The following Friday night, Aiden's restaurant, Cedar Break, was packed and the wait time was over an hour long. It was the exact Friday night scenario he imagined when he first decided to open this place two years ago. Man, he loved it here.

He stopped at the bar to chat with a couple of guys he knew from college.

"Glad y'all made it in tonight. What's happening?"

He did the handshake/one-slap-on-the-back hug thing, then leaned on his elbow to face his friends.

"What's the deal, Aiden? We know the owner and we still can't get a legit table?"

Aiden chuckled and signaled his bartender to bring them another round of drinks on the house. "The action's at the bar anyway. You know you like it here."

The other one held up his drink in a toast. "You've outgrown this place. Is it time to expand?"

The familiar apprehension prickled inside him. His investment partner, Jacob Merrick, had been talking about expansion for some time now. Cedar Break was turning a substantial profit and, according to the money man, it was time to capitalize on it. Normally, Aiden would have thought this was a good thing, that it was time to move on. But for some reason, this time he didn't feel ready.

Beach Wedding Weekend

"You know I don't talk business on a Friday night. I leave that for weekdays or the golf course."

"You only talk about it on the golf course to distract us from your pathetic score." Both buddies chuckled.

Aiden popped some of the bar nuts in his mouth and slapped Ben on the back. "You're on to my tricks, Ben, but I got a new driver. Be prepared to put your money where your mouth is next time we play."

He said his goodbyes and walked to the next table of people he recognized, a group of couples—friends of his older sister. He shook hands, kissed cheeks and made small talk before moving to the next table.

After an hour, he'd worked the whole room and he felt alive. This place had become his favorite hangout. He loved the warmth of the front of house and fast pace and camaraderie of the kitchen. Even though it was his restaurant—well, half of it anyway—it always caught him off guard that he felt like he belonged here more than anywhere else.

Aiden wasn't a trained chef, and before he opened this place he hadn't had any sort of restaurant experience. He was an entrepreneur. He turned great ideas into successful businesses. But this idea, this restaurant, which had been opened on a dare and meant to be a time killer until he came up with his next big idea, had become his favorite project of all time.

Before he could start the rotation again, Jacob, dressed in his signature jeans and blazer, walked through the front entrance. Aiden waved him over to the table where he was talking with a group of men staying at the resort for a golfing weekend.

"I'd love for y'all to meet my investment partner. You want some tips on infamous hole three? He's your guy. Birdie every time."

Jacob shook hands around the table. "It's all in the drive, fellas. You gotta hit it hard if you want any shot at being on the green in two."

27

There was chatter as the men exchanged smack talk about how far each of them could or couldn't drive the ball. Jacob met Aiden's gaze over their heads and nodded to the back offices. An ominous, smoky grey feeling drifted through Aiden, but he kept it off his face.

As soon as the banter wound down, Aiden slapped one of the men on the shoulder. "Enjoy your dinner and let me know how tomorrow's round goes."

He greeted two more tables on his way to his office, as much as a stall technique as to be friendly. As soon as they walked through the door to the back part of the building, the happy buzz of conversation faded away, and Aiden's good mood went along with it. He didn't bother talking on the short walk down the narrow hall to his tiny office. As much as he liked this place, he hated the back offices. They felt cold and empty.

Once in his office, he claimed the chair behind his desk to give himself the upper hand in the conversation. He had no idea what Jacob wanted to discuss, but it always had to do with money. While Aiden liked making it, he didn't love talking about it. Jacob, on the other hand, seemed to live to discuss it.

"I didn't think I'd see you until your son's wedding next week. To what do I owe the pleasure tonight, Jacob?" Aiden leaned back in his chair, crossing one ankle over his knee, and grabbed the football lying next to his computer.

He didn't bother to invite Jacob to sit, but Jacob did anyway.

"This place is a gold mine, kid. It's time to cash in on it."

Aiden glanced around the tiny, plain square of an office, as if this room was what Jacob was referring to. "A gold mine, huh? I thought you told me restaurants never make it."

To be exact, his words were "opening a restaurant would be like flushing good money down the toilet." But Aiden didn't feel the need to bring that up again. In the seven years Jacob had invested in his ideas, Aiden had made millions. His ideas and Jacob's money, it seemed to be a good combination. One he didn't want to sever yet.

"I said most restaurants don't make it. But what you've created is more than a restaurant. It's an experience. A lifestyle. People want this. In fact, people want this to the tune of five million dollars."

The number stunned Aiden. He gripped the football between both hands and leaned forward. "Five mil? Who's saying those numbers?"

Jacob settled into his chair, looking far too comfortable to be on the visiting side of Aiden's office.

"A major investment group out of Dallas. They want to franchise it. Take it national. They've offered a full buyout package. We've thrown around some numbers but haven't agreed on anything yet."

Aiden fell back in this chair, stunned. "Is five mil on the table?"

Jacob had come into the picture when he brokered the deal to sell Aiden's first company, an errand-running business Aiden started in college to earn some extra money. He sold it two years later for just over a hundred thousand dollars. Aiden, who had never known that kind of money, had felt like he'd won the lottery.

Over a celebratory dinner, Aiden mentioned the next idea he was working on. Jacob loved it, and their partnership was born. Aiden came up with the ideas and built the business while Jacob fronted the money and decided when the company was ripe to sell. They split the profits fifty-fifty. The partnership worked because they each had full control over what they did best. Jacob didn't tell him how to manage the business, and Aiden didn't argue when it was time to sell.

Together, they sold the second company for half a million. And the next one sold two years later for just over that. The restaurant was meant to be a pet project, a time killer until he came up with his next great idea. It was never meant as a money maker and Aiden certainly never expected it to be worth more than anything else he had done.

"It's a solid offer, Aiden, but it might need a little persuasion to go through without a hitch. That's where I need you," Jacob said.

Aiden nodded, trying to process everything. This was really happening. They were selling the restaurant for a pile of money. He should have been elated. He should have been digging through his desk drawers to find his lucky pen to sign on the dotted line while dreaming up his next big idea. But he wasn't. Instead, he felt hesitant.

Jacob kept talking. "The head partner is going to be at a wedding tomorrow night at the resort. I heard you would be there as well. I thought you could schmooze him a little. Make this place seem too good to walk away from."

The vibe of the restaurant, the happy hum of the front and the camaraderie in the kitchen, reverberated in his mind. Who wouldn't want to be a part of this? "It is too good to walk away from."

Jacob snapped his fingers and pointed at Aiden. "That kind of passion is why you're the master of closing deals. I knew I could count on you. Anyway, I called the resort and they seemed to think the wedding planner could get you at the same table as the investor and his wife. You have a date?"

"For a wedding tomorrow night where I RSVP'd single?"

Jacob pulled his phone out and typed a text. "No problem. Since they were already going, I'm sure his wife knows people there. How do you know the couple who's getting married?" He waved the question off without looking up from his phone. "Never mind. Doesn't matter. You know the entire town and half of Austin."

"Fraternity brother from college," Aiden answered, because Jacob needed to know that going to this wedding wasn't about making money. His life was about more than business.

Jacob flashed a slick smile. "Fraternity brothers make some of the best business contacts. Which reminds me. I have the whole investment group coming to my son's wedding in Seacrest next week. I figured it would be a great way to wine and dine them and close the deal. I've set up a lunch on Saturday for you to go over all the details with them."

The phone in Jacob's hand buzzed, and his attention went to the screen. He was quiet for the first time since he walked into the office. The silence settled like a brick in the pit of Aiden's stomach.

After a second, he looked up. "So you'll take care of this wedding, and we're good for next week? I'm assuming you'll have a date by then. You know men with commitments come across more trustworthy. I'd hate for them to think we weren't serious."

While his tone might have sounded friendly, Jacob wasn't making a suggestion. Selling the company was his domain, and if he thought it was time and thought that Aiden needed a better half while they were courting the clients, Aiden needed to get on board on both accounts.

"Sure thing. I've got it under control."

Jacob stood and took the one step required to cover the space from his chair to the door. "I knew you would. I'll see you in Florida on Wednesday. I've got you set up in the biggest guestroom at my beach house. We'll talk more then."

He disappeared through the door before Aiden could say anything else, which was just as well, since Aiden had nothing good to say. He gripped the football in both hands and glanced around the room. They had created this place to sell it. This was always the plan. And the price tag was bigger than either of them had imagined.

But he couldn't shake the nagging feeling that this time the bottom line wasn't all that was at stake.

Paige twisted the key in the lock of her townhouse after what could've been the most successful wedding rehearsal she'd ever been a part of. As a chronic planner, she'd always been a big believer in the benefits of running through an event to iron out any unforeseen wrinkles. But this time, the unforeseen wrinkle had to do with Operation Get Brody Back.

She swung the door open, and her cat sat poised on the other side, as if waiting for her.

"Well, hello, Lavender. Miss me?" She bent down to scratch the cat's ears before hanging her keys on the hook by the door and setting her bag in its designated spot on the bottom shelf of the console table.

Lavender purred and rubbed against her legs.

"Yeah. I missed you, too. But tonight, we have work to do. Come on."

Earlier in the evening, as the wedding party drifted into the venue for the ceremony run-through, the mother of the bride had given Paige a seating chart change. Apparently the bride's sister, Lindy Grant, had a house guest, some lifelong summer camp bestie who was in town for a while, and they wanted to include her in the wedding festivities.

"Brody's new fling, Sasha Kane, scored a last-minute invitation to the wedding. And according to the new seating chart, she's bringing a date." Since last week when she'd decided to fight for Brody, Paige had tried to come up with a way to see him again. Perhaps even a time when the element of surprise would be in her favor. And here it was.

"This is our first chance to remind Brody what he's missing." Paige walked straight past the kitchen and up the stairs to the second floor, the cat trotting along after her.

Instead of turning left when she got to the top of the stairs, into the master bedroom, Paige turned right, into the guest room. Lavender ran in ahead of her and jumped on the bed, looking completely relaxed.

"There has to be something in here that will work for such an occasion. Don't you think?"

Of course there was something in the closet that would work. It was crammed full of gorgeous clothes from the latest Gwyneth Blair collection, complete with shoes and accessories. Most of her friends called it the dream closet, and the ones who wore the same size as Paige often came "shopping" in it for their own special occasions. But as far as Paige was concerned, the only thing the closet held was a reminder of a life she didn't want.

"But they're just clothes, Lavender. Clothes that Mom designed. And they'll probably look great on me." Paige clutched the cold, hard knobs of the closet's double doors and drew in a long, deep breath. "You ready for this?"

She swung open the doors. Before she had time to talk herself out of it, she scooped up an armful of the newest additions and dumped them onto the bed, kicking one of the doors closed with her foot.

She stood with her hands on her hips and stared at the pile of her mom's latest creations. It wasn't that the outfits weren't cute. To be honest, most of them were stunning. Although, every now and again, she would get some bizarre frock that looked like something from a sci-fi movie gone wrong, which was always good for a giggle.

No, Paige didn't like the clothes because they reminded her of the life she'd left behind. As the only daughter of a single mother, Paige grew up going where her mom's job took them. And building a fashion empire took them all over the world. Los Angeles, New York, Paris, Madrid. They had flats, apartments and lofts all over the world, but they never had a place that felt like a home. For as long as she could remember, Paige used to tell people that when she grew up she wanted a house with a two-car garage and a swing set in the backyard.

She decided to go to college in Texas because she thought it sounded friendly and it was so different from everything she knew. Gwyneth approved the idea because she thought the small college town in the middle of the country would make Paige miss city life. But she was wrong. Paige had finally found where she belonged.

Leaving the fashion world behind wasn't hard, since Paige never felt like she belonged there anyway. Leaving her mom, on the other hand, was more difficult. But living the lives they were both meant to live meant they had to be in different places, which they made work the best they could. Gwyneth still cleared her schedule a couple of times a year to visit her daughter, and Paige never missed spending Fashion Week in New York with her mom. In between, Gwyneth Blair made sure her daughter had everything she needed to be well dressed in a small town, which Paige promptly stored in her guest room closet, never bothering to take the tags off.

"But tomorrow, Lavender, we're going to fight for love. And we're going to look amazing while we do it."

She lifted the first outfit and held it at arm's length to examine it. It was a black one-piece romper with long, flowing pants and a plunging neckline. She'd seen a picture of her mother wearing something similar to a benefit recently.

She stepped into the outfit. So what if it didn't look like anything she would normally wear and the neckline plunged down to her ribcage? At which point, was it still considered a neckline? Well, tomorrow wasn't about hanging out in her comfort zone. It was about looking stunning.

Her mouth twisted to the side as she examined her reflection in the mirror. "What keeps you from falling out of this?" She pressed the fabric against her chest, hoping it would magically stick to her skin. "Maybe if I don't move much, everything will stay in place?" Lavender cocked her head to the side. Even her cat didn't think it was realistic.

Paige peeled it off and grabbed the next outfit. This one was a pencil skirt and white silk blouse. She remembered the note attached had deemed the outfit "work attire." While characters in television shows often wore these kinds of things to their places of employment, Paige had never seen anyone at the resort wearing anything like this. Probably because it was impossible to take a full stride in the tight skirt, much less try to sit down.

The one thing the outfit did have going for it was that it fit well. At least her mom knew what size she wore.

Paige ran her hands over her curvy hips. She could stand to lose a few pounds. The trouble was she really liked to eat good food.

"What do you think?" she asked the cat. Lavender yawned and sprawled out on her side.

"I agree. Not exciting enough." Plus, she found being able to sit very important. She stripped it off and tossed it into the *no* pile.

She plucked up the next outfit, a dress that didn't seem exciting on the hanger. She slid it over her head and turned to the mirror. The rich amethyst color was brighter than anything she would ever choose. It had three-quarter-length bell sleeves and it wasn't exactly tight, but the fitted silhouette clung closer to her than anything she normally wore.

On the other hand, the color brought out the golden flecks in her hazel eyes while the knee-length dress showed off her shapely legs. Honestly, the dress made her look good.

"It's not the most practical wedding coordinator dress, but tomorrow's not about being practical, right?"

The cat licked her paw and rubbed her face, looking unconvinced. Paige sighed. "At least pretend to be supportive." It didn't matter what her cat thought. She liked it. And choosing this dress meant she didn't have to try on any more. She opened the closet again and flipped on the light. "Let's see, I think there are shoes in here somewhere."

She stood on her toes and looked through the boxes on the shelf until she found the one she remembered arriving with the dress. Pulling off the top, she stared at the strappy high-heeled sandals inside.

"I mean, people wear these kinds of shoes all the time." She slipped her finger through one of the straps and pulled it out to examine the four-inch stiletto heel. "We can manage it for one evening, right?"

The shoe dangled from her finger as she rotated it. She could've sworn the heel grew as she did. Lavender sat up on alert, her full attention on the shoe.

"You're right. They're tall. But maybe they're not as bad as they look once they're on."

Paige sat on the edge of the bed and slid her foot through the straps, fastening the tiny buckle. Then she held her foot out to admire it. "You have to admit, Lavender, they are amazing. They're the kind of shoes people notice." She expected nothing less from her mom's choice of footwear.

She slid the other one on and fastened the buckle. "Okay, let's see how this goes." Pushing off the bed, she straightened her legs and tried to stand. It was like trying to balance on toothpicks, and she wobbled, almost turning her ankle. Her arms flew out to the side to steady herself. She bent her knees and thrust her bottom out to lower her center of gravity. The reflection in the mirror looked like she had to stop off on her way to a cocktail party to catch for the Texas Rangers. All she was missing was her mitt.

So, she needed a little practice.

Holding on to the edge of the bed, she attempted to straighten again. This time, she widened her stance and held her arms out.

"I can do this. It's just going to take a little getting used to."

She couldn't say for sure, but she swore the cat rolled her eyes.

"Come on now, Lavender. You're on my side, remember?"

Arms still out to the sides for balance, she took two clunky steps across the room. When she reached the wall, she paused, smoothed out her dress, and turned. Arms held slightly lower this time, she took three smaller steps to her bed. "Not a problem at all. I can own the stilettos. Now, time to accessorize."

She pulled out the jewelry that had been tucked inside the shoe box. The intricate silver and jeweled earrings were several inches long and had to weigh close to half a pound.

She looked at the cat. "Surely these were safety tested before they made it into production, right? I don't need some sort of extra support so they don't rip through my ear?"

Lavender dropped her head down to her paws, which Paige didn't take as a good sign. She hooked one through the hole in her ear.

"How do people wear this stuff on a daily basis?" Gently, she let go. The bottom of the earring hovered right above her shoulder. She slipped in the other one and rotated her head to examine how they looked in the mirror.

"As long as I don't turn my head too fast, I think we'll be okay."

She pulled the heavy necklace out of the box and fastened it around her neck. It looked as if it were made to go with the dress. In fact, it seemed as if the entire outfit was made to go together. Each piece on its own was impressive, but together it was in a whole different league. The kind of league her mother's fashion circle belonged to. The league Sasha Kane played in.

She pulled her hair up with one hand to show off her long neck and collarbone. "What do you think?"

Paige admired her reflection in the mirror, and the cat's ears perked up. It was like looking at a different, more glamorous version of herself. Her legs looked longer, her waist slimmer; her overall appearance sparkled.

Nothing about what she had on was in her comfort zone, but it was stunning. She felt like one of her mother's models gliding down the runway. Sure, she would have to work on the gliding part, but it could be done. Plenty of people wore heels this tall all the time. She could do it for one night.

It was the kind of look that demanded attention. The kind that would force Brody to see her, to remember her, to show him she was willing to fight for love.

She turned to her cat, trying to strike one of the red-carpet poses her mother had forced her to practice for pictures. "What do you think? Will this remind Brody of what he walked away from?"

The cat purred.

"Right? I look good. Operation Get Brody Back is in full swing. He won't even know what hit him." Paige punched the air in front of her. Her pose combined with the tall heels sent her off balance. She stepped forward, almost falling onto the bed and the cat. Luckily, she caught herself with her hand before she landed flat on her face.

She reached out and scratched the cat's head before she pushed herself up to standing and turned to the mirror. "The shoes might take a little more work, but other than that, we're a force to be reckoned with."

The cat let out a little meow, which Paige took as confirmation. Her plan was perfect. This was totally going to work. Brody was one day away from being hers again. She was almost sure of it.

Chapter Three

WHOEVER DECIDED HAIR SHOULD FALL in soft curls had never stepped foot into humid Texas Hill Country. Paige had spent forty-five minutes in her bathroom slathering her hair with whatever product her mom had insisted she buy and wrapping it around a curling wand that got so hot it recommended wearing a heatshield glove so she didn't melt her skin off. The whole ritual was absurdly time-consuming, but she did it anyway.

The endeavor earned her the privilege of being ten minutes late to the resort. She pulled into the employee parking lot, settled into the lowest part of the property, and stepped out of her car into the sweltering June heat. As if on cue, every curl drooped around her face.

"Just this once, couldn't we pretend all that product made a difference?" She twirled a strand of hair around her finger in hopes to re-inspire the curl as she clunked across the parking lot to the stairs carved into the side of the hill. Five grueling flights loomed before her. She'd fallen in love with this resort and its breathtaking views the moment she saw it, but getting to live in the beauty of the hill country came with a few compromises. One of them was always trudging to the top of a hill, but the views made it worth the effort. Normally, this climb from the lowest parking lot to the ground floor of the five-star resort was annoying. But today, with four-inch toothpicks attached to the ends of her feet, the never-ending concrete steps seemed foreboding. And to make matters worse, she needed to hurry.

One step at a time, she reminded herself. They were only stairs. She took them almost every day. With a deep breath, she starred, clutching the railing and trying not to let her toe slip off each step as she left her heel hanging over the side.

Her hair wasn't made for the humidity, and her shoes weren't made for the stairs. This whole beauty thing was a lot more complicated than it looked.

Lucy, her assistant, was standing at the top of the stairs with a clipboard and a frown.

"The mother of the bride wants to change the seating chart and the bride hated all the bouquets. Says they're not what she asked for."

Paige climbed the last two steps, breathing harder than she normally did. "Good morning to you, too."

Lucy looked like she was about to burst into tears. "It's eleven-fifteen. Morning started three hours ago when the mother of the bride showed up at the concierge desk demanding my presence." In the middle of her rant, she paused and examined Paige. "Nice dress. What's the occasion?"

Paige waved off the question. "It's a gift from my mom. Thought I'd try it out." She wiped the sweat starting to bead on her forehead. "Now, what's wrong with the flowers? I spent almost an hour with the mom last night as she examined each one of the bouquets individually and approved them."

Lucy shrugged. "She said she changed her mind. It wasn't what she envisioned and the more she thought about it last night, the more she thought her daughter deserved what she wants." Lucy rolled her eyes. "Which, by the way, the bride has been causing havoc in the salon and giving room service grief."

"Did you call the florist?" The florist who did all the flowers for the resort was amazingly talented. Paige could vouch that every one of the bouquets looked exactly like the inspiration picture she'd been given.

Lucy nodded. "She's in the cooler working on them. And the mother is in her suite and wants to see you the second you arrive."

Paige glanced to her right and left, trying to decide where she should start. Hilltop Resort was a massive structure with over 1,200 guest rooms, a conference center, wedding and events venues, four award-winning restaurants and two top-rated golf courses. Not to mention a state-of-the-art water park. It was the ultimate vacation destination. However, all the amenities made it very large. The sprawling grounds spread out in front of her started to spin a little. Of all the days she picked to wear the most impractical shoes, it had to be the one where she would be running all over the place.

She held onto the rail and circled one of her ankles to relieve some of the achiness. So today wasn't an ideal day to wear these shoes. What was it her mother always said? "Beauty doesn't have to be practical, darling. It has to be inspiring."

Paige let out a sigh. This was going to be a long night. "I'll go talk to the mom. You check on the flowers. This bride is going to walk down that aisle at five o'clock one way or another."

For the next four hours, Paige ran all over the resort in her four-inch stilettos and her impractical dress redoing almost everything they had spent months putting in place because the nervous bride and her mother had "changed their minds." She'd never realized that one major reason she pulled her long hair up was because of how hot it made her neck. Also, she felt like she needed to write the designer of ballet flats a thank-you note.

By five minutes before five, everything seemed to be in place. The flowers were fixed, the changes in the seating arrangements taken care of, the string quartet settled into their third location, and they finally found the right combination of food for the bridal suite to agree with the bride's tastes of the day.

Paige stood in the grand foyer of The Chateau and cherished

the momentary silence. Her feet were killing her and her earlobes ached. It was time to get the processional started, but she needed one second to rest.

She balanced her tablet on the banister at the bottom of the grand staircase and reached down to massage her aching foot. Whoever had designed these shoes hadn't meant for people to actually walk in them. But it was worth it, right? Fighting for love and all of that?

She switched to the other foot, closing her eyes for a brief second in attempt to harness the relaxation of the moment.

"The resort must keep you busy." The smooth, low voice in the otherwise empty room startled her, making her pulse race. Once it registered who the voice belonged to, her heart thumped even faster.

She glanced up. Brody strode down the steps, his bright eyes dancing against his tan skin. Geez, he was handsome. He was the kind of good-looking that made even the most elegant women lose their thoughts for a second or two, which annoyed her. How was she ever supposed to deliver one of the witty lines that'd make him swoon if her thoughts scattered every time he smiled at her?

The fact that he'd caught her doing something not-so-poised in the outfit she clearly wasn't used to wearing made a flame of embarrassment sear her cheeks. She lowered her foot to the ground and smoothed her dress as she stood up, forcing herself to not tug on the hemline.

"It's wedding season, soooo, you know." It wasn't witty, but at least it was a coherent thought, which was more than she managed to get out last time they met. She fiddled with her necklace as she tried to shift her focus from her aching feet and crazy day to reminding Brody she was the best thing that ever happened to him.

"Summer was always a busy time at the resort," he said.

"Not much around here has changed." So maybe she wasn't going to win him back with her clever conversation, at least until she could get this brain-scatter thing under control. Hopefully her new look was enough to make up for it. She ran her hand through her hair, wondering how many of the curls had survived. Surely some, right?

A slight grin tugged at the corner of his mouth. "No, I guess not. It's good to see you, though. I think I forgot to say that last time."

The familiar words sent a warmth swirling through her. "You, too. Welcome home."

The air between them had a slight sizzle, almost as if trying to remember what used to burn between them. Or perhaps it was a hope of what could burn between them again. Either way, it sent a shot of confidence through her. Maybe her throbbing feet were worth it after all.

"Might I remind you, that while you're over there gallivanting with the guests, I have a wedding which needs attending to?" The mother of the bride's voice boomed through the room, dampening the mood.

Paige sucked in a deep breath and tried to summon her inner peace-keeper. "Sir, the ceremony is about to begin, but if you make your way out the side door, I think you can still find a seat on time." Paige used a voice loud enough for the mom to hear, hoping the excuse would be enough to defuse her quick temper. With her back still to the mother of the bride, she shot Brody a stare that pleaded with him to cooperate.

Brody nodded, looking amused, and lowered his voice so only Paige could hear him. "Ahh, Lindy's mom. Sasha said she was a piece of work."

Paige smiled, but didn't comment. The connection between them sizzled again, a bit stronger this time. She held her arm out to gesture to the door in question, just for show.

Brody stepped off the last step and turned for the door. "Maybe I'll catch up with you later."

Another burst of warmth swirled through her. Yep, even the earrings were worth it. She watched him for another moment, cherishing the glow of success before she turned to the mom.

"I think he was the last guest. Now, let's get your beautiful daughter married. Such a lovely day for a wedding, isn't it?" And for the first time that day, she meant it.

The mom's perma-scowl melted into a more neutral expression. It wasn't a smile, per se, but it was the most pleasant expression Paige had witnessed from her so far. Paige's optimism soared. She'd had a rough start, but things were looking up. She was getting this day under control.

Hopefully.

Aiden pulled into the parking lot two minutes before the wedding was supposed to start. He knew he was late, but he didn't care. Coming to this particular wedding had the same draw as a trip to the DMV. It had nothing to do with his college buddy getting married or even the wedding in general. Normally, he loved celebrating with his friends at a party with good food, great conversation and dancing. He was dragging his feet to this particular event because he'd have to spend the evening sucking up to an investor he'd never met in order to sell his restaurant.

It was a task that shouldn't have been a problem. Selling his startup companies for big bucks was what he did. It was the business he was in. A deal offering a crazy profit should have made him elated. Instead, he felt heavy, like he was trudging through mud.

He climbed out of his car and shrugged on his suit jacket. On the bright side, his tardiness meant he wouldn't have to sit outside as long in the sweltering June heat. The heavy air hung around him like a wool blanket while cicadas serenaded him from the trees with their hypnotic buzz. Summer was here in full force.

Despite the humidity, this was the season he loved best. He

loved the long days and the excuse to take a break from normal hectic schedules. It was the season people flocked to his restaurant. Every night from June through August was packed with the happy hum of summer vacation. By far, this was when the restaurant had its highest sales. Last summer was more profitable than the year before, and this summer was shaping up to follow suit.

Although, as he walked around the building to sneak in the side door of The Chateau, Aiden decided he might keep the summer talk centered around the awful humidity when he was with his new investor friend tonight.

"I'm starting to think I need to permanently reserve a latecomer's chair for you." The hint of laughter in her familiar voice coaxed out a smile. He should've known he wouldn't have been able to sneak past her. There wasn't a detail small enough to slide by Paige Westmoreland.

She stood next to the doors in the center of the wall of windows overlooking the gardens where the bride was already marching down the aisle. She hugged her ever-present tablet against her chest, a sarcastic smirk pulling at the corners of her mouth. Just the sight of her seemed to lighten whatever it was about this evening that was weighing him down. Her presence always had that effect on him. Maybe this wedding wasn't going to be as painful as he'd feared.

"The problem is not that I'm late. It's that you jumped the gun. According to my watch, I still have a solid thirty seconds until five o'clock and yet your bride is already halfway down the aisle." He tapped his watch and strolled across the wide-open marble floor to where she was standing as "The Wedding March" drifted in through the closed doors.

Paige tucked a lock of her long chestnut hair behind her ear, highlighting her face. It dawned on him that he didn't usually see her with her hair down. It was pretty. For a second, he was distracted by it.

"Today I'm not apologizing for straying from the schedule. If I could've gotten away with sending this bride down the aisle fifteen minutes early so she would stop terrorizing the entire staff, I would have."

"Bad day at the office?"

She chuckled. "You have no idea."

There was a pause as her attention returned to the action outside. The bride made it to the end of the aisle and the music stopped. In a second everyone would sit down, and his discreet late arrival would become much more noticeable.

"I guess I should grab a seat while I still can." He nodded at the far door he intended to use, but he made no move toward it. He liked the company in here.

"There are a few empty chairs over there on the aisle."

"Thanks." Aiden took two steps toward the door, then stopped.

"You look nice today, by the way."

Looking nice was an understatement. The way her dress skimmed her curves and the sassy smile that brought out the sparkle in her eyes made her downright gorgeous.

A look he couldn't quite interpret washed over her face. She stared down at the dress, as if considering something, and ran her hand across the front of the skirt to smooth it out. Then she met his gaze with a look of sincerity. "Thanks. That means a lot."

Something was troubling her, he could tell, but before he could ask her about it something outside caught her attention. She stared out the window with a look of confusion that shifted into concern.

"Oh my. That's not good." She tossed her tablet onto a nearby cocktail table then skittered across the floor to the side door, the click of her heels echoing through the room. Since the ceremony seemed to be going on uninterrupted, Aiden wasn't sure what the emergency was, but he followed her anyway.

She pressed the button on the headset she wore. "Lucy, call the medical team. One of the bridesmaids collapsed." As soon as she finished speaking, she pushed through the door to the garden.

From this angle, for the first time, Aiden could see what must have captured Paige's attention. The bridesmaid on the end lay in a crumpled pile on the ground. He was impressed Paige had caught it from inside because most of the guests, even the ones standing close to where the incident happened, were still focused on the happy couple.

Paige scurried down the aisle, taking quick little steps his own long strides struggled to keep up with. She had just reached the bridesmaid when a gasp from the front row alerted the rest of the guests to what had happened.

The bride's head whipped around, a look of dismay distorting her face. "This is supposed to be my big moment!"

If this was any indication of how she'd been all day, Aiden now understood why Paige wanted to get her down the aisle early. Paige didn't pay the huffing bride any attention. Instead, she pressed the bottom of her skirt against the back of her legs and squatted down next to the fallen bridesmaid.

"Are you okay?" she asked in a voice so gentle even Aiden could feel its calming effect.

"I'm so sorry, I don't know what happened. My heart started racing, then everything just went black." The bridesmaid's voice was weak, but she threw a hesitant glance in the direction of where the bride was still throwing her fit.

Paige rubbed her arm. "These things happen, especially when it's this hot out. Did you hit your head when you fell?"

The bridesmaid gingerly touched the back of her professionally styled hair. "I don't think so."

Paige placed her other hand behind the girl's shoulder and helped her sit up. "Why don't we move you into the air conditioning and get you some water. Do you think you can stand?"

The bridesmaid nodded, but the lingering cloudiness in her eyes made Aiden doubt her answer.

"Here, let me help you." He slid his arm around her waist

and, supporting most of her weight, pulled her to her feet. As he expected, the bridesmaid's legs wobbled underneath her. Paige snagged the bouquet she had dropped and flashed a sweet smile at the crowd.

"Sorry for the disruption. Bria is in good hands. Please, continue. Nothing is going to stop these two from getting married."

The officiant took the cue, making a joke and pulling most the attention back to the wedding couple.

Supporting the majority of her weight so her feet barely skimmed the ground, Aiden started walking toward The Chateau with the fallen bridesmaid. Paige stepped up on the other side, allowing the girl to drape her arm over Paige's shoulder. Together, they made their way to the side door rather quickly, but Aiden could tell Paige was struggling to keep up. The heels of her shoes sunk into the grass with every step she took. Aiden didn't know how girls could wear stuff like that.

The resort's medical team met them at the door and took over, carrying the girl to a nearby chair. One person put an icepack on her head while the other took her pulse and asked her questions. Paige's assistant appeared from the direction of the kitchen holding a bottle of water.

Paige stepped away from the patient and checked on the action outside. Everything seemed to be back on track, to Aiden at least, but worry lines crinkled her forehead. She chewed on her lip and her breathing was still labored from the exertion of supporting the bridesmaid.

Aiden stepped up next to her. "The grounds crew owes you a favor, since you aerated the wedding lawn for them." He pointed at her shoes.

An amused grin pulled at the corner of her mouth, and she lifted her foot to touch the mud caked to the spikey heel. "I'll remind them of that next time I make them replant flowers for a high-profile wedding."

"You weren't kidding about this wedding being a challenge."

She glanced over her shoulder at the medical exam and then looked at him. "Today has kept me on my toes, for sure." The movement outside distracted her again, and she turned her attention to the scene beyond the wall of glass. The guests were taking their seats as the bride and groom turned to each other, holding hands in anticipation of the coming vows. A warm smile softened Paige's face. "But usually, watching couples get their happily-ever-after makes it all worth it."

Paige was a stunning person and seeing her in action at what she did best reminded him of some of the qualities he admired about her, like her strength and positive attitude. "The bride and groom are lucky to have you on their side."

She waved the compliment off. "It's all in a day's work. But thank you for your help out there. I wouldn't have been able to carry the bridesmaid out by myself."

"It's what I'm here for. To rescue damsels in distress." He jerked his thumb toward the door. "I'm going to head out and catch the rest of the I-do's, but call me if anything else goes wrong and you need another hand."

Paige chuckled. "That's one offer I really hope I won't have to take you up on."

Chapter Four

PAIGE DIDN'T WANT TO JINX it, but in the four hours since the fainting bridesmaid incident, there hadn't been any other issues at the wedding. Not even a single petty complaint from the bride or her mother. In fact, the bride seemed to be enjoying herself for the first time since Paige had met her. Maybe marriage agreed with her. With less than thirty minutes before their grand exit, Paige was cautiously optimistic that this wedding might have a happy ending after all. Knock on wood.

But the recent run of good fortune wasn't enough to keep the over-stressed muscles in Paige's shoulders from tensing when she spotted the mother of the bride walking toward her. She hoped the knots weren't evident, promising herself she would schedule a massage, and refreshed her smile.

Mom-of-the-bride held her arms out and grasped both of Paige's hands. "Dearest Paige. How can we ever thank you for all your hard work? You have gone above and beyond to make this day truly special for all of us." It took Paige a second to process the compliment, as this particular mother of the bride did not have a history of handing them out. It seemed watching her daughter get married might've eased some of the stress she'd been carrying around since Paige met her.

"It has been my pleasure," Paige said, letting the kind words resonate within her. It was nice to know all her sweat, tears and blisters had been noticed.

"If you don't mind, I'd like to ask one more favor. The bride's father and I would like to offer one last toast to the happy couple before they're off. Could you get champagne for the four of us and bring it to the DJ stand?" She gave both of Paige's hands a gentle squeeze before she released them and gestured to the dance floor.

"Absolutely. What a great way to end the night." Paige headed for the kitchen. After the long, rather stressful day, she was ready for this event to be over. One more task. One more happy toast, and then they could send everyone on their way and finally have a chance to relax.

Lucy was standing next to the kitchen entrance when Paige walked up. "Final task of the night," she said to her assistant. "Four glasses of bubbly for one last toast."

Lucy followed her into the kitchen. "That's it? She didn't ask for the same crystal used at the royal wedding or a brand of champagne not sold in the U.S.?"

Paige giggled. "Nope. And let's get it out to her before she changes her mind." She grabbed one of the last bottles of champagne chilling in the cooler and popped the top. Lucy set four flutes on the stainless steel counter in front of her, then propped her chin on her fists.

"Since this wedding's under control, tell me what's going on with your handsome European businessman."

Paige poured the first glass, trying to push away the frustration rising up in her. Other than the brief conversation when he arrived, which still sent tingles running through her, Brody hadn't so much as glanced in her direction the entire night.

"He's not European. He was just living there for a while."

Lucy waved the difference off. "Did he say anything about your dress? I want your mom to get one for me."

Paige tugged on the bottom of the frock in question. "You can have this one, but I have to warn you. It might not have the effect you want."

Lucy gave her a knowing look. "I think it had more of an effect than you think."

Before Paige could question her assistant about what she meant, Lucy stood up and popped one of the cherries from the bar service into her mouth. "While you're delivering that, I'll start getting the sparklers out for the exit. Let's put this wedding to bed."

"Sounds like a plan." Paige hoisted the tray to shoulder level and followed Lucy out the door of the kitchen, still replaying what she'd said in her mind. Had Lucy seen something Paige had missed?

Lucy took off to the left toward the storage closet while Paige paused in front of the kitchen door to adjust the tray. She needed to be balanced if she planned on walking across the slick marble floors from one end of the massive room to the other in her ridiculous-yet-unnoticeable shoes. At this point, she had walked so much that the balls of her feet were going numb, and she was pretty sure the blister from the strap had spread across her entire baby toe. But, with any luck at all, this would be her last mission. She took a deep breath and stepped out of the kitchen.

"Great wedding." The strong voice caught her by surprise, but it was a good surprise.

She turned to Brody, who was leaning against the wall next to the kitchen doorway. Had he been waiting for her? The thought sent a jolt of exhilaration darting through her. She could feel the wide, silly smile spread across her face, but she didn't bother trying to fix it into something more alluring. Brody Paxton was here, waiting to talk to her. Maybe Lucy was right. Maybe the dress had worked after all.

"All in a day's work." Perhaps it had required a little—or a lot—more effort than that, but what could she say? Seeing Brody here made her glow with optimism.

He crossed his arms in front of his toned chest and gazed at her with a smoldering look. "You had just started this job when I left. It suits you."

His low, seductive voice left her feeling like someone had turned up the heat in the room. "Thanks. It's easy to come to work when you're doing something you love. I always was a sucker for a happy ending."

This conversation right here was what she'd waited for all night. This was the reason she'd endured all the pain.

"What about you? You haven't told me why you're back in town."

Brody stood and slid his hand into his pocket. "Promotion. I'm running my old department."

"So they finally got rid of Janis, huh?"

The mention of his old, awful boss brought out a grin more personal and intimate than anything she'd seen since his return.

"I was beginning to think it would never happen, but wishes do come true."

Something sparkled in his eyes. A memory, perhaps? She took it as a positive sign, and a golden ray of confidence shot through her. Her plan was coming together!

"And I hear we'll be seeing more of each other soon." The thought filled her with giddy excitement. "You're going to be at Georgia and Lane's wedding next week?" The two of them would be at the very same beach where they first fell in love. It had certain poetic justice to it.

"I will." There was a pause and something in the air between them shifted. "And I'm bringing Sasha with me."

Paige's soaring spirit plummeted to the ground like a balloon that had popped. Her focus slipped off his face, which caused her to wobble. Or was it the news he'd shared that knocked her off balance? Of course Sasha would be going. She was his girlfriend, and the beach was a romantic place to go. Especially this beach.

"Seacrest is amazing. It'll make a great getaway." Defeat was thick in her voice, but she didn't bother trying to fix it.

"I absolutely can't wait. I've never been to the Florida panhandle before, and I'm hoping it's as picturesque as I imagine," a voice said from behind her.

Paige whipped her head around to look at Sasha walking toward them. The quick movement sent her heavy earring swinging wildly and caused a sharp pain in her left earlobe. Her hand flew up to see if it was bleeding.

"It's a special place. I'm sure you'll enjoy it." Someone should. The emerald waters and snow-white beaches shouldn't be lost on the lonely and heartbroken.

Sasha stepped closer to Brody, "I bought two new bikinis for the occasion."

Brody's gaze transferred to Sasha and whatever not-so-sweet thought was running through his mind while Paige's disappointment grew. She starred to walk away, but Gram's words rang in her ears. *When you finally see the one your soul desires, it's impossible to look away.*

So Paige wasn't expecting Sasha to come on their walk down memory lane, but life often didn't line up with what she was expecting. If what Paige and Brody had shared was the real deal, he would see it whether the new girl was there or not. And if Brody really had fallen for Sasha, in such a short time...well then, nothing Paige said or did would make a difference, anyway.

"The forecast looks great, so we should have plenty of beach time." She shifted her gaze to Brody. "Remember that one time when we stayed out on the beach from sunrise to sunset? That was a great day."

Brody's gaze met hers and the memory lit his eyes. "It was."

Excitement shot through her. Maybe all wasn't lost after all. She gestured at the champagne on her shoulder. "Duty calls. But we can catch up this weekend. Maybe we can all find time to grab a frozen mocha at that cute little café we used to love. You can tell me everything you've been up to, and Sasha and I can get to know each other."

Beach Wedding Weekend

Brody smiled. "I'd like that." Sasha looked lost but nodded enthusiastically anyway.

With one last lingering glance at Brody, Paige started across the marble floor in her best attempt at a saunter. True, she hadn't practiced this particular walk in these heels, but she'd been around it enough to know the basics of what to do. She added a slight arch to her back, the way her mother had always instructed her models. She glanced over her shoulder to make sure both of them were noticing and added a bit more swing to her hips. She wasn't one to brag, but she was owning the moment.

Then her tractionless shoe hit a wet spot on the slick marble floor, sending her foot sliding out from under her. The momentum from her quick pace sent her flying forward. Perhaps if she had been facing forward she could've done something to regain her balance, but she wasn't.

The drinks were the first to go, tumbling off the tray and shattering across the floor. The tray hit the ground next, followed by Paige who barely got her hands out in time to keep her nose from breaking her fall.

It didn't matter if pain shot through her ankle where she twisted it, or if her knees throbbed from the impact. What mattered was that there was nothing attractive about a wet mess sprawled out on the floor. And Brody and Sasha had witnessed every humiliating second of it.

Aiden was sitting at the table with the investor and his masters-of-the-universe friends, listening to yet another story about how they had the world on a string, when Paige landed face-down on the floor right at his feet.

It just so happened that the piercing shatter of glass was perfectly timed with the silence at the end of a loud dance song. The entire room went quiet and every single eye focused on Paige sprawled out

55

on the floor in the middle of the mess. A wave of concern rolled through him, bringing with it a prickle of fear. He dropped onto his knee next to her and laid a gentle hand on her back.

"Paige, are you okay?"

"Is everyone looking at me?" Her muffled voice was thick with defeat, but she didn't sound like she was in pain. Aiden's concern simmered into sympathy.

"That was freakin' hilarious! Tell me someone caught that on their phone," some jerk yelled from the dance floor. The whole room erupted into laughter. Paige, still face down, let out a weary sigh.

"Maybe one or two people," Aiden tried to joke. He signaled for the DJ to start the next song. The thumping bass from the loud, upbeat music filled the air, along with the announcement that this would be the final dance of the night. Most of the guests drifted toward the dance floor.

Paige's assistant appeared and hovered over Paige, who remained face down on the floor, lying perfectly still. With wide eyes, she looked over at Aiden. "Is she okay?" she whispered.

"Besides the big ol' bruise on my ego?" Paige's muffled voice said. "Yeah, I'm fine."

Aiden and Lucy exchanged a look. "Do you think you can handle the reception from here on out by yourself? I'll take her to the back and make sure she's not hurt."

Lucy nodded. "I'm on it." She disappeared, and Aiden and Paige were left alone on the floor between two of the tables.

"So, you wanna try to get up, or should we hang out here for the rest of the night?"

"Is turning invisible an option?" she muttered from her face-down position.

"We can try." Aiden pulled his legs into the most cross-legged position his tight muscles would allow, ready to sit next to her for as long as she needed. "But I gotta tell ya, it would've helped if your dress was the color of the floor instead of purple."

Her shoulders shook, which he took as laughter.

She reached around and pulled down the bottom of her dress as she rolled to her side and sat up. "How many people saw my underwear?"

"Not nearly as many as who wanted to." It elicited another half grin. She was going to be okay, which filled him with relief. "Are you hurt?"

Paige circled her wrists and rubbed her knees. With a sigh, she ran her hands through her hair and focused her attention on her feet. "I think I twisted my ankle."

She pointed to her left ankle, which was already beginning to swell. That wasn't a good sign. "Come on, let's get you to the back."

Aiden helped her to her feet as housekeeping arrived.

"I'm so sorry about this mess, guys." She laid her hand on the uniformed maid closest to her and looked in her eyes. "Thank you so much."

"It is no problem, Ms. Paige," she said.

Even in the midst of her personal drama, Paige went out of her way to be kind. It was another thing Aiden had always liked about her. The world could use more people like Paige Westmoreland. He remembered thinking that the very first time Ciera brought her new best friend home from college.

With the rest of the guests focused on the final toast being given on the dance floor, Aiden slid his arm around Paige's waist and supported her as she limped in the opposite direction to one of the conversation areas hidden in an alcove in the back corner. He stopped in front of a plush armchair.

She sank into the large chair and propped her arms on the high armrests. "I'm over today."

"That good, huh?"

"I mean, there have been some highlights, but this ankle thing kinda tipped the scale on the overall rating of the day."

"How's it feeling?"

Paige winced as she rotated it in a slow, timid circle. "I don't think it's broken, but I'm going to feel it tomorrow."

"May I take a look?" She nodded and he took a knee on the floor next to her, cradling her foot in his hand. The touch, along with the close proximity, filled him with an odd combination of calm highlighted with a faint buzz of excitement. It was as if being near her was both the most natural thing in the world and the best part of his evening. But they were friends, so being around her should feel natural, right?

His large fingers fumbled with the tiny buckle as he attempted to loosen the thin leather strap that was already cutting into her ankle. But as hard as he tried to be gentle, it was nearly impossible for him to free her foot without moving her ankle. "Are these shoes or torture devices?"

Paige chuckled. She closed her eyes and she massaged her temple with one hand. Everything about her look tired and defeated. "They weren't made for comfort."

He finally got the first strap undone and slid her shoe off. Deep red lines crisscrossed down her foot from where the straps had been, and there was a pretty good-sized blister forming on her toe. The sight of her physical pain made him ache with sympathy from a place deep inside his chest, and he looked up into her warm eyes. "You okay if I move it? Let me know if I hurt you."

She nodded and watched the ankle in his hand.

With a growing desire to protect her from any more pain, he slid his hand up to her calf to be able to fully support her leg. With his other hand, he gently moved her ankle in a slow circular motion. He wasn't a doctor, but he'd been involved in enough sports injuries to know the basic signs of what to look for.

"It doesn't appear to be broken, but you probably should get it checked out." Aiden placed her foot back on the floor. "I can take you to the ER if you want."

Paige shook her head and leaned down to touch her swollen ankle. "I'll make an appointment with my doctor tomorrow."

With his examination done, he stood and sank into the armchair next to hers.

She gave her ankle one last rub before she switched to taking the shoe off her other foot. "Let's hope it's nothing serious. I don't want to have to hobble down the aisle in some sort of splint at Georgia's wedding." Once the shoe was off, Paige lifted both sandals up by the ankle straps with the long, spikey heels dangling right in front of her face. "Keep 'em or burn 'em?"

"Burn 'em," Aiden said. "They don't even look like you. What made you want to try out stilt shoes when you'd be on your feet all day?"

"It's too embarrassing to talk about."

"With me? We're practically family. We don't judge."

"Families do plenty of judging." Her expression looked as discouraged as her voice sounded. Aiden ached for her, but in an effort to make this increasingly somber mood a little lighter, he stuck with his attempt at sarcastic humor.

"You're right. I'm judging your choice of hanging those bowling balls from your ears. Were the five-pound weights already spoken for?" His dumb joke managed to coax out a smile, as intended.

Paige pulled the giant, dangly earrings from her ears. The tiny red specks of dried blood clustered around one of her piercings confirmed that the earrings were too big for her delicate ears.

She closed her fingers around them and stared at her fist, as if considering something. "It was part of Operation Get Brody Back, remember?"

The familiar pang of unease that had plagued him all night hit him square in the gut. All during the reception, he'd pretended to be interested in conversations he cared nothing about while cozying up to people he didn't care to be friends with to nurture his multimillion-dollar sale. Yeah, he understood playing the part to close the deal.

"I get that."

"I thought maybe if I caught his attention, got him to notice me, he'd remember what we had."

That shocked Aiden. He'd always thought Paige was stunning. She was the kind of pretty that made you not want to look away. How could she question that?

He clasped his hand over hers. "You, Paige Westmoreland, are beautiful without boulders hanging from your ears. And you don't need to wear ridiculous shoes to remind him of what you had."

She kept her gaze on his hand covering hers and silence hung over them. He was starting to think she didn't believe him when he caught a hint of her confidence returning and her lips curled up in a slight grin. "Thanks." She massaged her earlobe with her free hand. "I don't think I was made to wear these kinds of clothes."

"I said the boulder earrings and the shoes with weapon-heels were ridiculous. But you were made for that dress. You look terrific."

Pink tinged her cheeks and she glanced down at her dress, looking unconvinced. Was it possible she didn't realize she was a knockout?

He added, "I mean, if you were trying to turn heads, you succeeded."

The pink in her cheeks deepened to scarlet. "Thanks."

She glanced up at him from under her lashes and something soared inside him, which was weird. They didn't have that kind of relationship. She was his kid sister's best friend.

Aiden cleared his throat and tried to return the conversation to a more neutral topic. "We should probably get you some ice for that ankle."

He started to stand up, but she caught his arm. "Not yet. Let's give it a few minutes until everyone clears out. I'm not up for questions."

He nodded and sank back into his seat. She rested her head against the back of her chair and closed her eyes. "What was so important that I had to rework the entire seating chart today so you could sit with the old people at table eight instead of your buddies at table four?"

It was Aiden's turn to sigh. "Business. He's a key decisionmaker in a pretty big deal."

"Big enough to make my blisters worth it?"

Her eyes were still closed and her face relaxed, which indicated that he should take her casual, joking tone for what it was: giving him a hard time. Joking and friendly razzing was the kind of relationship they had. But there was enough truth in her words that they stung.

"Yeah, sorry about that. If it goes through, I'll buy you some orthopedic shoes perfect for the demands of a wedding planner."

She chuckled. "That would get me noticed, for sure. Too bad I won't have them in time to turn Brody's head at Georgia's wedding."

Aiden snapped his fingers. "Which reminds me, I could use your help."

She cracked one eyelid to look at him. "Sure. What do you need?"

"The investor and his partners are going to be at the beach all weekend, and I have to do some sort of lunch presentation thing on Friday to finalize the sale of Cedar Break. Jacob wants me to put together something that will wow them. Grilling burgers on the beach wows me, but I don't think that's what he had in mind."

Paige opened both eyes and arched an eyebrow. "You own the most successful restaurant in Hilltop and you can't come up with a lunch menu?"

Aiden didn't know how to explain it. It wasn't just the menu or the lunch or the presentation. There was something about this deal that made him hesitant. Maybe it was the fact that the price tag was staggering or that after three years of wasting time, he still didn't

61

have his next great business idea. Whatever the reason, it left him uninspired when it came to the sales end. Maybe if he had some help planning it, he could pull off the sales pitch with the same gusto he was known for.

"Food I understand, but it's combining the lunch menu and the presentation and the atmosphere where I need some help. I need, maybe, an event planner to help me make it go from a bunch of dudes eating lunch in a plain room to whatever it was you did out there."

Quiet settled over them. Paige twisted her mouth to the side in the cutest expression that showed she was considering it. "Do I get two pairs of orthopedic shoes?"

"I'll get you a pair in white and in black."

She chuckled, and for the first time all night he thought she looked like her normal relaxed self. "You have yourself a deal."

At the same moment, Brody peeked his head around the corner. "Hey, Paige. Thought I'd check on you before I took off. You okay?"

Paige whipped her head around to look at him. The confident expression she'd just recaptured fell away, and her whole body tensed. She blinked a few times, as if considering what to say. Then she motioned to her leg, her forced smile attempting to cover up the strain on her face. "Probably a minor twist. Nothing to worry about."

Brody glanced at Aiden before looking back at her. "Great. Good." He stood there for a moment, looking somewhat awkward.

Aiden had never liked this guy. There was something about Brody that made Aiden think he wasn't sincere—or good enough for Paige. But since Paige seemed to be convinced Brody was the one she wanted, Aiden was willing to put his own hesitations aside.

Finally, Brody jerked his thumb in the direction of the main room. "I gotta run because Sasha's waiting for me." He looked right at Paige. "But I'll see you this weekend."

"Yep. I'll see you then."

"See ya," Aiden added. He couldn't help himself.

Brody's gaze jumped from Paige to Aiden, and his expression went from shocked to possessive. Aiden probably should have let him walk away, but then again, he was the reason Paige had such an awful day. Well, one of the reasons, at least. He didn't get to pop around the corner and make everything better with one comment. So Aiden matched Brody's gaze with his own look of authority.

After about a second Brody looked away, casting one last weak smile at Paige before he disappeared around the corner.

"He's jealous," Aiden said.

"Jealous?" Paige's gaze lingered on the spot where he'd been long after he'd gone.

"You got carried off by another guy. His territory has been threatened."

Paige turned to him. "First of all, I'm not his territory. Secondly, it was you that helped me over here. Our relationship isn't like that."

"I know that, and you know that, but Brody doesn't know that."

Her face twisted in concentration. "He knew you when we were dating."

"That was before he left. A lot can change in a year."

Her eyes focused on something in the distance as she seemed to be working through the situation in her mind. "You really think he's jealous?"

"Positive."

"Huh." They were both quiet for a moment, then she shook her head as if to clear her thoughts. "Sorry, back to your lunch dilemma. Tell me what you need and let me see how I can help."

"I need food, a place, something to make it look impressive. Normal stuff. And if you're up for playing matchmaker, I need a date. Jacob's convinced the investors will take me more seriously if I'm committed instead of some party-throwing bachelor out for a good time." Aiden paused and studied Paige. "Actually, do you want to be my date?"

"Me? Be your date? And here everyone was worried I was the one who hit my head." Paige rolled her eyes and reached down to massage her ankle.

But this could work. The more he thought about it, the more brilliant this plan was. For both of them. He leaned forward and launched into his best persuasive mode. "I need a date, but I don't want the hassle of anything romantic. And you need to get Brody back. So, be my date and help me put together this investors' lunch, and I'll pretend we're together in front of Brody to make him jealous. At the end of the weekend, my investors will be ready to write me an insane check and you'll have your boyfriend back. Win-win."

Paige's eyes narrowed. "We're going to one of my best friend's wedding. Your sister will be there. Everyone knows we aren't together."

Aiden waved her concerns off. "We'll get Ciera to play along and everyone else won't take much convincing. Jacob will be happy I'm committed, and Brody already thinks something's up with us." Maybe this was the piece that was making him feel hesitant about the whole deal. "It's the perfect plan. Operation Wedding Weekend."

Paige nibbled on her lower lip. "You really think making him jealous will work?"

"Nothing reminds you of what you used to have like seeing someone else have it."

"Operation Wedding Weekend," Paige repeated, seeming to consider the idea. "Do we have to use pet names for each other?" Aiden relaxed in his chair. "Only if you want to sell it, Sugar Lips."

Paige shot him a look. "Try again."

"Cupcake?"

Her warning look intensified, creating a cute line between her eyebrows. This was going to be fun. If he had to pick a fake girlfriend, Paige was the perfect co-conspirator.

Aiden's confidence surged. "Thing is, Smoochems, you don't get to choose your pet name. It sort of chooses you."

Paige chuckled. "That's how we're going to play it? Just be ready for the name that chooses you."

"I'm looking forward to it."

Chapter Five

IT WAS STILL DARK WHEN Ciera and Aiden picked Paige up outside of her townhouse. There was a ten-hour drive ahead of them to the picturesque beach town of Seacrest, and they needed to get there before the barbecue dinner that would launch the wedding weekend.

Paige hobbled out and tossed her luggage into the trunk of Aiden's SUV before she climbed into the backseat.

"How's the ankle feeling?" Ciera asked.

Paige fastened her seatbelt, then twisted to the side so she could stretch her leg out across the rest of the empty backseat. Even in the predawn darkness, the massive black walking boot demanded attention. "Who knew a sprain could cause so much trouble? But the swelling is finally better, and the doctor said as long as I wear the boot most of the weekend, I can downgrade to a small brace for the wedding." She wiggled in the seat to find the most comfortable position while keeping her ankle propped to relieve the pressure from the swelling. "But no high heels for a while. Or maybe ever."

Aiden laughed. Ciera punched his arm. "Be nice to Paige. She's had a rough week."

"It has been a hard week, but we're on our way to the beach, and the ocean has magical healing powers." It was the combination of the salt air and the sound of the waves rolling into the shore. The beach had always been her happy place.

Ciera pulled her phone from the center console and tapped on the screen. "Right? Georgia texted me a picture last night from the condos where we'll be staying. It looks amazing."

She handed the phone to Paige. Snow-white sand fading into sparkling water filled the screen. Eagerness to sink her feet into the powdery sand seized her, making her toes wiggle.

"I can't wait." Only ten more hours. She reached for her e-reader to help kill some of the time, mentally deciding which of the recently downloaded beach reads she should start with. "After last week, I'm in desperate need of some relaxation."

"You can't be too serene, Westmoreland. You still have plans to make." Aiden eyed her in the rearview mirror.

Paige's mind flipped back into full speed, recalling all the details of the business lunch she was helping Aiden plan. "Shoot, my laptop's in the trunk with my bag. I'll pull it out at our first stop, but it won't take too long to go over. The major things are set. I just have a few questions about minor details to go over with you."

"Not the lunch," Aiden said. "The other half of Operation Wedding Weekend. Getting your man back."

Heat burned her cheeks. "Oh, right. I almost forgot about that."

Ciera twisted around in her seat and stared at her. "Forgot about it? Brody has been at the top of our conversation topics since he left town a year ago."

So, maybe "avoiding that" would've been a more accurate statement. It was a lot easier to talk about winning Brody back when every part of her masterful plan would theoretically work the way it was supposed to. It was a different story when real limitations, like slick marble floors and gorgeous new girlfriends, made all of those plans backfire. Paige let out a weary sigh. "Fight for love, yada yada. The thing is, he's going to be there with *her*. The last time I was around them I fell flat on my face and almost broke my ankle. I'm not eager to have a repeat performance."

Ciera put her hand on Paige's knee. The friendly gesture wrapped around her wounded ego like a warm hug.

"You missed the point the other night. You don't have to dress like someone you're not to remind him of how great you are. You're amazing just the way you are."

Paige was starting to consider the truth in her friend's words when Aiden jumped in.

"That purple dress was nice, though. You should keep the dress."

Ciera glared at him.

"What?" he said, looking innocent. "She looked good in it."

Ciera rolled her eyes and flipped down the sun visor mirror to reapply her lip gloss. "You're hopeless. I'm not even sure why we let you tag along."

"Umm, because I offered to drive you. And Paige needs me."

Ciera glanced at Paige in the tiny lighted mirror. "I can't believe you agreed to pretend that this knucklehead is your boyfriend."

Since Paige was an only child, she found the sibling banter between Ciera and Aiden to be fascinating. Watching it never got old. "He was already going, so it was more of a relationship of convenience."

Ciera shook her head before she returned the sun visor to its stowed position. "Just so we're all on the same page, how long have you two been together?"

"One month," Aiden said.

"Two months," Paige said at the same time. He looked at her in the rearview mirror.

"Two months is hard to believe. I haven't dated anyone for that long in…" He paused, and Paige wondered if he was trying to remember the last time he'd been in a serious relationship. In the seven years she'd known him, no girl had gotten past the third date. After a second, he shrugged. "Well, it's long enough that no one would believe it."

"I thought a lot could change in a year," Paige tossed back.

"I have to agree with Aiden on this one," Ciera said. "There are too many people there who can disprove a long-term thing. But something new? I can support that."

Aiden's knowing eyes met Paige's in the rearview mirror again and he nodded.

The faint tingling that pulsed through her caught Paige off guard. He was Aiden. Behind this fake relationship, they were just friends. Nothing more. She shook off the feeling and focused on the planning. "The official word is that it's still fairly new. We'll leave it ambiguous."

Ciera nodded her head once. "It's new. Got it." She held up one finger. "So step one is to make Brody jealous with your new boyfriend."

Aiden glanced at Ciera. "He's already jealous. You should've seen the way he looked at her at the wedding."

"Then we should be ready to move on to step two rather quickly."

"How many steps are in this plan?" Paige asked, equally feeling left out of a conversation about her and disappointed that she didn't come up with a multi-step plan of her own. Planning was what she did best.

"Three. One is to make him jealous, and step two is point out the flaws in his current relationship."

A small pang hit Paige somewhere deep in her stomach. It took her a second to register what the feeling was. Guilt, maybe?

"Do you really think I need to sabotage Sasha?"

"Not sabotage." Ciera shook her head and her tight blonde curls swished back and forth. "Simply bring to light some of the ways they aren't right for each other. Which, from what Georgia tells me, won't be hard. She's got the personality of a wet blanket."

From what Paige had witnessed, that assessment wasn't far off. She giggled. "That's not nice."

A smile spread across Ciera's face. "No, but it's true. You won't have to point out her flaws. Four days with her standing next to you will do that all on its own."

Paige pictured Sasha with her perfect body in her brand-new bikini standing next to Paige on the beach. Her spirit starred to fall. "I'm not sure standing next to her will help."

Ciera twisted her mouth to the side in her best schoolmarm way. "Don't make me go back to my pre-plan pep talk. She held up three fingers. "Let's move on to step number three."

"You've put a lot of thought into this plan," Paige said, a little impressed. Ciera was an artist and, generally speaking, more of an improvisor than a planner.

"I have. Because what is it you always say? Nothing great happens without a plan?"

"You're right. Planning is imperative. So what's step three?"

"Remind him of what you had when you were together."

As soon as Ciera uttered the words, Paige's mind flipped through snapshots of their happy memories. Laughing so hard their sides ached, intimate moments that still left her heart racing. The question in her mind wasn't if what they had was great or not, it was how could he walk away from it? A fresh wave of sadness washed over her, along with the familiar ache of missing him. What they had was special. There was no debating it.

"How exactly am I supposed to remind him?"

Ciera looked confident. "Simple. After we get him primed with steps one and two, you find a time when you're alone and bring up one of your happy memories."

The thought of being alone with Brody on a moonlit beach sent shivers of excitement racing through her. He had been gone a little over a year, but she felt like it would be easy to pick up right where they left off. The hurt of being left behind, of seeing him with some other woman, would all melt away with one kiss. They were meant to be together. She was sure of it.

Paige mulled over the plan, figuring out the details of how to best implement it. "Three steps to get him back, huh? Sounds simple enough. What happens if it doesn't work?"

"Trust me." Aiden's warm blue eyes met hers in the mirror. "He'll never know what hit him."

Nine hours and thirty-three minutes after they left Hilltop, Aiden pulled in to the beachfront condos where the girls were staying. Considering someone had to stop at least every two hours for a bathroom break, Aiden thought it was a travel-time worth bragging about.

But now that they were here, it was time to slow down and drink in the scenery. As usual, the picturesque town of Seacrest, Florida, welcomed them with a sparkling ocean, plenty of sunshine and a heap of traffic. Even the tiny parking lot in front of the condo building was already full. To be fair, Aiden wasn't sure there were even enough parking spots for each unit to have one, but that was par for the course down here where parking was at a premium. He pulled into the handicap spot to help them unload, hoping he wouldn't be blocking it too long.

"I was going to ask if you were sure you'd be okay without a car, but it would appear that having one would be more of a hassle." Aiden shifted the car into park before he climbed out and walked around to the trunk.

"With all the traffic and parking problems around here, bikes are much more practical." Ciera motioned to the fleet of brightly colored beach cruisers chained to the wooden fence. Signs with her name and Paige's hung from two of the baskets. "And looks like the rental company already dropped ours off. We're all set."

"As long as I can pedal in my boot." Paige held on to the side of the car and hoisted her leg up in the air to show off her hard, molded plastic boot.

Aiden eyed it, trying to decide if it was safe for her to ride a bike without any flex in her ankle, but if anyone could do it, it would be Paige. She didn't seem to know the phrase "give up." "If it doesn't work out, I'm sure we can get one of those carts for kids to ride in and attach it to the back of Cici's bike," Aiden said as he pulled their suitcases out of the trunk.

Paige giggled, a happy tinkling sound that always filled the air with joy. "Now there's an idea. Why didn't I think of that?" She grabbed one of two matching garment bags with the dress designer logo emblazed on the front and threw it over her shoulder, then pulled up the handle on the small rolling suitcase he had set on the ground. Aiden watched as she arranged all her luggage so she could carry it up the four flights of stairs on her bum ankle by herself. Her determination was impressive.

He might not be able to help her out with the bike situation, but as long as he was around, she didn't have to conquer the stairs by herself. Before she took more than a couple of steps, he stopped her. "Please, let me carry that up."

Paige looked relieved. "That would actually be very helpful. Thanks."

He snagged her suitcase in one hand and grabbed his sister's in the other, then followed them up the steps.

"Will you be back for the barbecue tonight?" Ciera asked.

They stopped in front of a door on the fourth floor and Ciera typed a code into the keypad on the door. Aiden put the suitcases down while he was waiting and wiped the sweat off his forehead. They talked about the Hill Country being humid, but it had nothing on the Florida panhandle.

"Of course. I wouldn't want Smoochems to have to brave it all on her own." He slung one arm around her shoulders.

Paige gazed up at him and exaggerated batting her eyes. "I'll miss you while you're gone, Honey Bear."

Ciera pushed the door open. "Seriously, this is the kind of

relationship I'm pretending I knew about but haven't thought to mention to anyone?"

"You're just so thrilled we're happy." Aiden set the suitcases in the small hallway inside the door and gave his sister a quick squeeze. "I gotta run, but I'll see you ladies in a couple hours."

He backed out of the narrow hallway and trotted down to his car to drive to where he, along with all of the groomsmen, would be staying. Jacob Merrick's beach house.

Back on the main road, he rolled down the windows letting the sea air blow through his car. Even in bumper to bumper traffic on the two-lane road, there was something about being on 30A that brought peace to his soul.

Most people said they loved this particular stretch of beach, which had been nicknamed after the two-lane highway that ran through a series of small towns, because of the powder-white sand and the crystal-clear ocean. Admittedly, those were two of the main reasons he loved it. But what he loved most were the memories.

This was where his family had always vacationed, long before the manufactured perfection of storybook beach towns starting popping up. Back when sea oats and weathered clapboard houses were native, not novelty.

He wasn't complaining about the development, as long as the building codes continued to prevent mega-resorts from taking over the entire coastline and the tourist dollars supported the conservation of the beach instead of destroying it. Plus, the ever-growing list of places to eat was a benefit. It sure beat the single seafood shack with the greasy floors he remembered from when he was a kid.

Jacob's house was a little less than a half a mile down 30A from where the girls were staying. It was a new community nestled in between two of the other small towns. As recently as two years ago, this space was nothing more than a wide lot holding some sea oats and two unpretentious beach houses. Somehow in that space they had managed to lay out a community that held fifteen houses and a central clubhouse/pool area. The houses were in rows, three deep, with the ones closest to the beach being the biggest and having the most room in between them.

Naturally, Jacob had an oceanfront house.

Aiden wound through the narrow streets lined with palm trees and old-fashioned street lamps to the Merrick's house on the far end. He pulled into the spacious three-car driveway and, grabbing his bag from the back, mounted the stairs to the elevated main level.

The beauty of the sparkling Gulf of Mexico made him pause on the huge wraparound porch. He stood there for a second and marveled at the grandness of the emerald waters that stretched all the way to the horizon. The combination of its breathtaking beauty and raw power made it magnificent. How could one stand on the edge of the ocean and not be acutely aware of how small he was? He hoped he never got to the point where wonder wasn't attached to this view.

"Aiden! Glad you made it," Jacob strolled out the front door wearing the kind of expensive shorts and designer flip-flops that Aiden had started calling "preppy beach bum."

"Glad to be here," Aiden wiggled his toes in his own favorite, broken-in leather flip-flops. He couldn't wait to get his feet in the sand. He adjusted the duffel bag hanging from his shoulder and nodded out at the ocean. "You've got quite the view."

Jacob took a sip from the lowball glass in his hand and looked out at the water as if noticing it for the first time. "A million-dollar view. Or, if we want to get technical, a three-point-seven-million-dollar view. The wife had a hard time reining it in with the decorator. Do you know the Brazilian blue marble in the master bathroom has a semiprecious stone rating and had to be purchased through a specialized dealer in Japan? Because the composition of marbles that could be purchased through North American import companies didn't match her color scheme."

Aiden didn't know how to respond to that, so he made some generic humming sound and nodded.

"Well, no need to melt out here all day. Let's get into some air conditioning." He threw open the door and motioned for Aiden to enter first.

Aiden took one last look at the beach. He could stay out here all day, heat, humidity and all, but he headed inside with his host. "Thanks for the invite. Last time I was here this place was still under construction. I'm excited to see the finished product."

Jacob led him through the great room to the open-concept kitchen behind it. "Glad we got it finished on time. Watching your son get married is a crazy thing. It's a good weekend." He pulled a glass out of the cabinet and fixed Aiden a drink before he topped off his own. Aiden took this to mean they were going to chat a while, so he dropped his bag on the floor next to him and leaned against one of the bar stools at the massive granite island. He briefly wondered from which continent this piece of stone was imported.

"Your son's marrying a great girl. Georgia has been one of my sister's good friends for a long time."

"Indeed. We have a lot to celebrate. Cheers." He slid the drink across the counter to Aiden, then held up his own drink in a toast. There was a pause as they both took a sip before Jacob continued.

"Unfortunately, this weekend isn't only about the wedding festivities. We have a deal to close." Jacob's expression turned more serious. "There are four partners in the investment firm, and they all have to agree on the purchase. Which means we have four different people to convince that Cedar Break deserves top dollar."

Aiden didn't hesitate. "Cedar Break is worth every penny of what they're offering." Five million was a staggering number, even for Aiden, but there was something about the restaurant that resonated with him.

Sure, he'd been attached to the last three companies he sold. Watching them get purchased and developed into megacompanies was like watching a baby bird find its wings and learn to fly. There was a sense of pride at the end of those deals.

But this sale felt different. There was something about the restaurant that made him protective. It made him want to have the investment firm prove they were worthy of buying it instead of the other way around.

It was just a building, he reminded himself. Selling big ideas was what he did, and this should be no different.

Jacob slapped him on the shoulder. "That's the kind of attitude I'm talking about. Having total confidence in your product. Anyway, they all have their wives here. You said you'd have a date with you this weekend? Someone to help entertain the ladies?"

Aiden was still lost in thought about the sale when the last question registered. "Yes. My, um, girlfriend is here." Nothing about those words came out naturally. Aiden hadn't had a girlfriend in a very long time, and even then it wasn't serious.

Jacob gave him a questioning stare before his eyes darted around the room, in search of the missing date.

"She's actually in the wedding party. One of Georgia's bridesmaids."

Jacob nodded, looking impressed. "A bridesmaid? Nice. Sometimes I forget how much younger you are than the rest of us. It's been a long time since I've gotten to date one of the bridesmaids."

The way he made Paige sound like a prize instead of a person made Aiden want to defend her.

"Paige is an amazing woman. Everyone who meets her loves her."

"Sounds like she'll be a great asset. I look forward to meeting her." He took one last swig from his drink, then plunked the glass down on the counter with a loud clank. "But we can't sit around here chatting all day. We have a barbecue to get to. Let me show you to your room before we need to take off."

Aiden picked up his bag and followed Jacob up the flight of stairs, thankful for the break in the conversation.

Chapter Six

"I CAN'T BELIEVE YOU'RE GETTING MARRIED!" Paige flopped down on the bed next to Georgia, who was dressed in a worn button-down shirt and her favorite pair of shorts, and stared at the white dress hanging from the top of the closet door.

"I know! Isn't this so exciting?" Ciera lifted the veil from the box on the chair and tucked the comb into her hair. She stood in front of the mirror to admire her reflection before she turned to Georgia. "Lane is one lucky man."

Georgia beamed, her bright blue eyes sparkling, and she pulled her long blond hair up into a ponytail. "I'm so glad you guys are here with me. Thanks for making the drive." She squeezed Paige's hand.

"We wouldn't have missed it," Ciera said.

"Not a chance," Paige added. "But I have to admit, your choice of venue is pretty amazing. Does it get any better than a condo on the beach with your best friends?"

"Seacrest has always been the place where perfect memories were made. And now everyone I love is gathered here." Georgia clapped her hands together and sighed, looking blissful and romantic. Seeing her best friend in love was uplifting to Paige's soul. But then Georgia's face fell as she clasped her hand around Paige's.

"I'm so sorry about Brody. Are you sure you're okay with him being here?"

Just hearing his name made her pulse quicken, but she tried to keep her expression nonchalant. "Of course. He's one of Lane's friends. He deserves to be here."

"The better question is, are you okay that he brought *her* with him?" Hadley, the final member of their best-friend quartet and the third bridesmaid in Georgia's wedding, appeared in the doorway. She leaned against the doorframe, still dressed in her business suit from work with her long brown hair pulled back into a neat knot. A garment bag identical to Ciera and Paige's was slung over one shoulder, and she had a small rolling suitcase behind her.

"You made it!" Ciera, who was closest to the door, hugged her.

Hadley played with the tulle veil that was flowing down over Ciera's shoulders and gave her a questioning look.

Ciera grinned. "Just trying it out."

Hadley left her luggage at the door and walked over to embrace Georgia first. "Happy wedding weekend!" Then she hugged Paige. "I heard about the ankle. Sorry."

Paige waved it off. "It feels better already. This new accessory is to remind me not to wear shoes I have no business wearing."

Hadley sank down on the bed and grasped Paige's hand. Her eyes were filled with concern, which was unusual for Hadley, who always kept her emotions in check. "But, seriously, I don't know what he sees in her. She's not you."

A lump formed in Paige's throat, but she refused to let herself cry over him. Okay, sure, she'd shed a few tears after that horrid night when she discovered he was back, looking better than ever, and had some new girl with him. But that was to be expected. She was past that now.

"For the record, she was not invited. I had to rearrange the entire rooming situation to accommodate her." Georgia had a guilty look, and glanced both ways before leaning in, as if she were sharing a secret. "She's sharing a room with my cousin who snores like a dragon. Ever since her days at summer camp as a kid, Elle's had a hard time finding a roommate."

It wasn't much, but it did make Paige feel a little better. "She'll look good with bags under her eyes," Hadley declared. The whole room giggled.

"Honestly, I'm fine." Paige tried to say the phrase with as much confidence as she could muster. She should be fine, after all.

Apparently, it wasn't confident enough for the three people who knew her best in the world. Georgia's head cocked to the side with a worried expression, Hadley crossed her arms and glared like an investigator trying to rattle a witness, and Ciera looked amused.

"She has a plan to win him back," Ciera reported to the other two.

"A plan? Do tell." Georgia sat up on her knees and focused all her attention on Paige.

A nervous energy buzzed through her, making her jittery. She stood up to keep herself from bouncing on the bed. "I don't know that you would classify it as a plan." Since the details were still vague and it was far from being foolproof, Paige considered it more of an idea than a plan. The thought made the nervous buzzing intensify.

She could feel the heat of three pairs of eyes burning into her, but she tried not to let it rattle her. She walked over to the dresser and busied her hands with straightening all of Georgia's jewelry that was lying on top of it.

"It has three steps." Ciera held up three fingers. Paige could feel the warmth from her cheeks work its way down to flush her neck. She was a firm believer in planning. Her life motto was that nothing important happened without a plan. Reclaiming her soulmate and the life she'd imagined for herself was important. After Gram's pep talk, Paige was convinced that fighting for love was noble. But now, when she heard it reported from someone else, coming up with a plan to get Brody back sounded a little juvenile.

"A three-step plan? This we have to hear." With all her patient attention focused on Paige, Georgia crawled to the end of the bed and sat cross-legged like she was one of the kindergarteners she taught.

"I just thought, you know…" Paige fingered the string of pearls she knew belonged to Georgia's grandmother. "Maybe he needed to remember what we had."

The only sound in the room was the hum of the air conditioner. Paige moved her attention to lining up the bracelets that had been dumped in a pile. Several of them sparkled as the overhead light hit them, and then there was one plain bracelet that seemed like it didn't belong. A tarnished silver circle that looked unimpressive, out of style and dull.

"How are you planning on sparking his memory?" Hadley asked.

Paige took a deep breath and turned to her friends. "You're going to think this is ridiculous."

Georgia's eyes got wide, but she shook her head. "Honey, we'd never think your plan was ridiculous."

The nervous buzzing ramped up again, so high this time that she wondered if she was visibly vibrating. "Well, I'm going to…" She paused and took a deep breath, trying to calm her nerves. "We're acting like Aiden and I are together to make Brody jealous." She blurted out the words as if spitting out something that didn't taste good. She nibbled her lip and studied her friends' faces to gauge their reaction. Georgia and Hadley exchanged a look she couldn't quite read. Instead of waiting for them to comment, she launched into a further explanation.

"He needed some help putting together a business thing, and Brody has already seen us together several times. With how much he's been around and how much time I'll be spending with him this weekend, it seemed like it made sense."

She stopped and held her breath, bracing herself for the ridicule that was sure to follow.

For a second the room was completely silent. Finally, Georgia nodded in her typical, understanding way. "Sounds like a perfect plan."

Hadley looked a little more smug, as if she knew a secret that Paige wasn't privy to. "A relationship with Aiden? I think it's brilliant."

"Fake relationship," Paige reiterated.

"Right. Fake relationship," Hadley nodded.

Her three friends smiled confidently at her, but Paige couldn't help the feeling that this "plan" had a lot of contingencies she couldn't control. "I don't know. I guess we'll see."

Georgia squeezed her hand. "Don't worry, sweetie. I have a feeling everything is going to work out just the way it's supposed to."

The sun was dropping toward the horizon as the luau was starting to heat up. The wedding guests who'd spent the day traveling were gathered on the beach in front of the condos dressed in shorts and leis. Tiki torches flickered against the dusk sky and reggae music drifted through the air, mingling with the happy hum of conversation.

Paige had just stepped up to the plates in the buffet line when Aiden sidled up next to her. "Did you miss me, Smoochems?"

"More and more with every tick of my watch." Her voice had the same flirtatious note that his did, but her words matched his sarcasm.

He waggled his eyebrows and his eyes twinkled in the dusk light. "Absence makes the heart grow fonder."

He leaned closer to the lineup of smoked meats, closed his eyes, and drew in a deep breath. The look on his face echoed the way the rich, spicy scents of Texas barbecue made her feel. Comfortable and nostalgic. The way Hilltop had begun to feel. Like home.

Except tonight the delicious smoky scent mixed with the fresh salt breeze, elevating it to a whole new level. Everything about the scene, from the sound of the waves to the friends that were around her, made exhilaration bubble up inside her and she felt almost buoyant.

"This smells amazing." Aiden opened his eyes and reached for a plate. As he did, his arm grazed hers, which intensified her euphoric feeling. Strange. Since when did Aiden have the same effect on her as all of her favorite things?

Aiden grabbed the serving tongs next to the first tray of barbecue. "Makes me think we need to add some new barbecue dishes to the menu at Cedar Break." He scooped a couple of pieces of beef from the first tray and held them over Paige's plate. "Brisket?"

Paige glanced over her shoulder at the long line of hungry guests stretched out behind them. "Seriously, you're going to cut in front of all these people like that?" She tried to give him her sternest look, but his charming grin made it impossible to do anything but smile at him.

"You're right. How rude of me." He placed the two slices on her plate and scooped up two more. Turning to the lady behind him, he flashed another one of his charming looks. "May I serve you some brisket?"

He instantly won over the woman Paige knew to be Georgia's aunt. Paige shook her head but couldn't manage to hide her amused smile. "You're incorrigible."

"If that's your fancy way of saying adorably sensitive, then thank you."

Paige laughed and stepped up to the next station. "Are your—what did you call them? Money men?—here tonight?"

Aiden spooned some sauce over his brisket. "Nope. All four couples arrive tomorrow. Tonight is all about fun."

"Lucky boy. Whatever do you plan to do with all your free time?" Paige grabbed a silverware roll from the end of the line and turned to wait for him to finish filling every inch of his plate.

"Eat this, get seconds and flirt with you." He winked.

"Solid start to your vacation." She motioned to the mountain of food on his plate. "Although I think you could've gone bigger with your first helping. Your plate could've held at least one or two more ribs before it buckled under the weight."

"Good to know." Aiden reached over and took the only rib on her plate and moved it to his. "Thanks for the tip."

"Hey, I was going to eat that."

"Don't worry. I'll share my coleslaw with you." He shot her a playful grin as they walked over to the table where Ciera and Hadley were already sitting.

"Well, if it isn't the happy couple," Hadley said as Paige and Aiden set their plates at the two places across from her.

"Hadley, lovely to see you as always." He sat and forked a giant bite of food into his mouth. "Hey, sis," he managed through his mouthful.

"Did you get enough to eat?" Ciera joked.

"He stole my rib," Paige reported, sliding into the chair next to him.

The whole table was laughing at their back-and-forth banter when Paige was distracted by another sight.

Brody strode down the wooden steps that led from the condo down the bluff to the beach. He wore blue cotton shorts and a V-neck t-shirt. His casual outfit matched his casual confidence. Sasha walked next to him, her flirty sundress fluttering in the

Ciera shook her head. "It's as if he was raised with no manners. Watch your desserts. He has a tendency to come after those, too."

"Sample," Aiden said, cutting a piece of brisket. "I just like to sample everything that's available, so I can confirm you made the very best choice."

sea breeze. She looked like she was on some photo shoot for a dream vacation destination.

Why did she always see them walking down from the top of the steps? It was ridiculous, like they thought they were some royal couple gracing the crowd with their presence. For the first time since he'd returned, Paige found Brody's presence slightly annoying. She'd been enjoying the light-hearted conversation with her friends, and then he showed up and disrupted it. Still, she couldn't make herself look away.

"Paige." Hadley's voice pulled her out of her daze. Three pairs of eyes stared at her.

"Sorry, did I miss something?" She tried to focus on them, but it was impossible with the royal couple still floating down the stairs behind them.

"We were asking you about the plans for the bachelorette party," Ciera said.

Hadley's eyes narrowed on her before she turned to look over her shoulder in the same direction that was distracting Paige.

"Ahhh. He's arrived." Everyone at their table turned and watched the couple walk down the final short flight of steps and onto the powdery sand. Sasha paused at the bottom and grabbed Brody's arm for balance as she slipped out of her sandals. The flickering torches highlighted the definition of his toned forearms. The sight scattered every logical thought in Paige's mind, and she had the irrational desire to swat Sasha's hand away from him.

Hadley turned back to the table. "Showtime, kids."

Paige ignored her snicker and tried to focus on anything other than Brody walking up to them. What did Hadley say they were talking about?

"So, the bachelorette party. It's tomorrow night." True, it was stating the obvious, but at least it was on the right topic and had nothing to do with Brody and how he was hijacking their conversation.

Ciera threw a sidelong glance in the direction of Brody and used the patient voice Paige had heard her use with kids in her art class. "Did you make the reservation?"

She turned back to Ciera and Hadley with a renewed focus. "Yep, it's all set. Cocktails at Skippers, then the escape room, then I've arranged for a table in front of the live entertainment at the Courtyard." She could feel the presence of the power couple standing at the end of the table, but she refused to let them distract her from chatting with her friends. Well, in theory, anyway. "There are eight of us going, but I made the reservations for ten in case anyone else wanted to join."

"Guess we'll see if we end up with any tag-alongs," Hadley said, a knowing smirk tugging at the side of her mouth.

Aiden was the first to acknowledge the couple at the end of the table. With his arm still draped over Paige's chair, he leaned back and transferred his attention to them.

"Brody. Third weekend in a row to see you at one of these shindigs. Looks like you're working the wedding circuit."

Brody might have maintained his friendly smile, but his stare meant business. "It's been a busy few weeks of being back in town, but celebrating with friends is always worth it. What's your excuse?"

Aiden shrugged. "I'm in it for the food." He speared a giant bite of brisket and shoved it into his mouth, his wide grin still in place while he chewed.

The joke lifted the heaviness that had descended over the table. Or at least over Paige's mood. She'd forgotten how being around Aiden made her feel light and free.

Brody turned to Sasha to explain the joke. "He and Lane's dad own that restaurant you told me you wanted to try."

For a second she looked confused, but then her face lit up like a light bulb. "Oh, right! So he doesn't need free food." She giggled. "That's funny."

Hadley shot Paige a knowing look.

Paige tried to ignore it as Brody shifted his attention to her. "We stopped by to check on your ankle. I heard you were in a cast."

His first stop at the welcome dinner was to check on her? The realization made everything seem a bit brighter. She leaned back into Aiden's embrace and lifted her foot up for display.

"Not a cast. Just a walking boot. It should be back to normal in another week or two."

Aiden casually rubbed the outside of her arm with the hand that was draped around her shoulder in the sort of familiar gesture that confirmed a relationship to any onlooker. In fact, the gesture looked so authentic that the warm touch even flowed through Paige, sending tingles pulsing through her. Brody's gaze went from Aiden's hand, to Aiden, and then back to Paige.

Oh, Aiden was good at this. She'd chosen a fake boyfriend well. Confidence tugged at the corners of her lips, pulling them ever so slightly upwards.

"It looked like a bad tumble. I was hoping you were okay," Brody said.

Paige returned her foot to the ground and gazed into Brody's eyes. "I've been in good hands, but thanks for the concern. It means a lot."

Brody's gaze met hers in a look laced with intimacy. It only lasted a millisecond, probably not even long enough for anyone else to notice, but she noticed. She waited for the air between them to be electrified like it used to be, but the sizzle never came. Maybe she was doing a better job of blocking out his distraction than she thought she was.

The pause was starting to become awkward and Brody reached for Sasha's hand, intertwining his fingers with hers. "Well, glad you're on the mend. We're going to get some food."

They wandered off and Paige turned her attention back to the table, still giddy from the attention from Brody.

"So, the bachelorette party. Seems like we're all set," she said and took a bite of her baked beans.

Both Ciera and Hadley had silly grins on their faces. Hadley jerked her head toward where Brody had just been standing. "We aren't going to talk about that?"

Paige tried to act nonchalant about it, praying she didn't have her own silly grin plastered all over her face. "What's there to talk about? He was checking on my injury. Manners dictate it's the polite thing to do."

"Manners? Or male ego?" Ciera said.

Aiden rubbed the side of her arm again, sending another jolt of confidence through her. Then he pulled it away to take another bite of his meat. "Looks to me, Smoochems, like step one of your plan is complete."

"He's jealous, all right. Did you see the way he glared at Aiden?" Ciera giggled.

"What's step two, again?" Hadley asked.

"Point out what's missing in his relationship." The words ran through Paige's mind even as Ciera said them.

Hadley chuckled. "That shouldn't be hard. From what I've heard, Sasha will be able to do that all on her own."

Chapter Seven

FRIDAY MORNING, PAIGE STEPPED OFF the final step onto the powder-white sand and paused to draw in a long, deep breath.

"Walking down four flights of stairs on a bum ankle is no joke." She sat down and rested her sore leg while she surveyed the pristine beach in front of them. This view would never get old. "But this makes it all worth it."

Georgia, who had been wrestling a pop-up canopy down the wooden staircase, paused to catch her breath. "It's a perfect day. Let's hope my wedding day looks like this."

Ciera dumped the four chairs she'd been carrying in the sand next to the canopy and squeezed Georgia's shoulders. "It will. The whole weekend will be perfect."

"It will be perfect as soon as we get it all set up. Let's go, ladies. The sooner we get done, the sooner we can relax." Hadley reached the bottom step with her large cooler and breezed right past them.

"She is so bossy." Ciera's blond curls were a little frizzier than normal, and she tried to tuck them behind her ear before she reclaimed her stack of chairs.

Paige pushed herself up and held onto the railing for balance as she slung the beach bag full of towels over her shoulder. "Does Hadley relax? I'm not sure I've ever seen it."

"I heard that," Hadley called over her shoulder. She dropped the cooler in a prime spot in the middle of the beach and turned to face her three friends. "I do plenty of relaxing. As long as there aren't other things that need to be done."

Paige and Ciera exchanged a knowing look. Hadley's take-charge, get-'er-done attitude served her well as a construction project manager in a male-dominated industry, but she rarely sat still—even on the beach on a perfect day.

She jogged back to help Georgia, who was now attempting to drag the canopy through the sand. It took ten more minutes of work to get the tent up and everything arranged, but as soon as it was, all four girls fell into the low beach chairs.

Paige wiped the sweat from her forehead and propped her throbbing ankle on a stack of towels. The sound of the waves washed over her and relaxation seeped into her body. "Life should be lived on the beach."

Hadley took a big swig from the water bottle in her hand. "Agreed. This beach always seems especially calming." She paused and looked at her watch. "But at the moment it's a little too calm. Where is everyone? It's already ten-thirty."

"Lane texted me a little bit ago and said he and the guys were headed in this direction." She leaned forward and craned her neck to look in the direction of Lane's parents' beach house. "Maybe the half-mile walk is taking them longer than they thought it would."

"Which gives us some extra time to hear how Paige is going to implement phase two of her plan." Ciera glanced over her sunglasses at Paige.

Paige groaned. "It is far too pretty outside to waste on planning. Today should be about having fun."

"Exactly." Hadley maneuvered her chair into the sun and stretched out. "Having fun is a great way to show him what he's missing."

Ciera slipped on a sun visor. "What kind of fun are we talking? Does it include chillaxing in this chair?"

"I am at my favorite beach with all of my favorite people.

How can we not have fun?" Georgia grinned at the rest of them. "Speaking of which, there's Lane." A group was rounding the curve in the beach about two hundred yards down. The cartoon hearts shooting out of her eyes were almost visible. She jumped up and ran to meet them.

"I can't decide if their love is sweet or going to throw us into sugar shock," Hadley said.

Paige watched as Georgia reached the group. She threw her arms around Lane and he picked her up and swung her around. It was a picture of pure, innocent love. The fact that her friend had found it caused joy to blossom inside her. "I think it's sweet. Georgia deserves someone who loves her like that. We all do." Her gaze drifted to Brody, who was in the middle of the group of guys, tossing a volleyball up in the air and catching it. Their relationship had been different from Lane and Georgia's. It had a slower transition, almost as if they were wading in, instead of cannonballing the way Georgia and Lane had. It didn't mean they weren't as in love, they just hadn't had all the time they needed to get to that same level. But they were destined for that same sort of all-in, no-holds-barred kind of love that Lane and Georgia had. She was almost sure of it.

As if feeling the connection between them, Brody broke away from the group and jogged over to the tent where they were sitting. "Morning, ladies. Perfect day for the beach, huh?"

"There's nothing like Florida's Emerald Coast." Paige squinted up at him.

"I had forgotten how beautiful it is." He glanced over his shoulder at the water to take in the view. He tossed his volleyball in the air. "Who's up for a volleyball game? We were thinking groomsmen verses bridesmaids?"

"Don't you think that's a little unfair?" Hadley didn't bother to open her eyes. "We'll annihilate you."

"How about a friendly wager to back up your big words?" Lane walked up on the conversation.

Georgia snaked her arm around his waist. "Guys win, we serve you breakfast on the beach tomorrow morning. We win, you do the same for us." She patted his chest. "And just so you know, I usually like fresh squeezed orange juice and omelets at eight-thirty sharp."

"Then you better eat before you come serve us at nine." He kissed her forehead and turned to the groomsman behind him. "Let's get the court set up."

"I better oversee your work. To make sure you're keeping it fair." Hadley jumped out of her seat and followed them over to an empty patch of sand.

Ciera and Paige were left alone in the shade of the tent. "Do you think we should help them?" Paige asked.

Ciera shook her head. "Too many people will only get in the way. Besides, someone needs to enjoy these chairs. It took a lot of effort to get this set up."

"Well, in that case, I better take our job more seriously." Paige slid her legs out into the morning sun to drink in its warmth.

As she was angling her chair in the right direction, she caught sight of Aiden jogging down the beach coming from the other direction. Other than his phone strapped to his arm, the only thing he wore was swim trunks. It had been a long time since Paige had seen him shirtless. Something inside her stirred.

He spotted her and Ciera, waved and slowed to walk through the loose sand toward them.

"You're staring," Ciera said. "At my brother."

A warmth flushed her cheeks. "Am I?" She put on the most nonchalant expression she could manage. "Just trying to make our relationship look legit."

Ciera rolled her eyes, but thankfully let it go.

Aiden pulled his earbuds out as he got close to them. "Morning,

Cici. Morning, Smoochems." He dropped into the abandoned chair next to Paige.

"How was your run?" Paige asked.

Aiden's breathing was still more rapid than normal, but he smiled a contented grin. "Nothing feels as good as running on the beach." He pressed a button on his phone and unstrapped it from his arm.

Paige stared down the beach, her legs longing to stretch out, to feel the burn in her lungs as she breathed in the salt air. Dumb ankle injury. "I love a morning jog."

Aiden twisted around in his chair to look at the action behind them. "What's going on here?"

"Volleyball game," Ciera said. "Bridesmaids verses groomsmen. There's breakfast on the line."

"The most important meal of the day, huh? Those are some serious stakes." He glanced at Paige's ankle before he leaned in to Ciera and pretended to whisper. "What are you going to do about this one and her bum ankle?"

"I can still move. I've been walking all week."

"Hobbling. You've been hobbling all week." Ciera said.

Aiden patted her knee. "You're doing the best you can, Smoochems."

The beach around them continued to fill up as more of the wedding party made their way down. The volleyball net was in place and Hadley volleyed with one of the groomsmen.

"All right, girls. We're ready. Time to show those boys how to play volleyball," Georgia called. "Elle and Tara, you want to play?" She waved to her cousins who had just settled into chairs under the canopy.

"Afraid you can't win on your own?" Lane taunted.

"Just trying to be friendly, babe."

"Plus, we have Paige who can't walk." Hadley pointed to her boot as Paige limped over to the court.

Going up and down all of the stairs had made her ankle start to swell again, and she could feel the sand stuck inside the boot starting to rub a blister.

"I'll admit, I'm not in my prime, but I can hop." Paige demonstrated by hopping the last two steps onto the court, which left her more out of breath than she had anticipated. She stopped to catch her breath and heard Aiden chuckle behind her. "Well, I still have my awesome serve, anyway."

"Since Paige only has one good leg, I'll be her human crutch." Aiden appeared next to her and slid his strong arm around her waist. "Come on, Smoochems, I'll get you where you need to go, and you can take care of the rest."

Paige giggled. "This is going to be interesting." She leaned on him and hopped on her good leg, only using her toes for support. Having Aiden at her side touched her in ways she hadn't anticipated. Sure, his physical support allowed her to take her weight off her ankle, which was a welcome relief. But there was something else about having him at her side, something that filled her with encouragement. It was as if together they could do anything, even maneuver a sandy volleyball court with a hurt ankle.

As they hopped onto the court, Sasha finally made her way down the wooden steps to the beach. She paused on the bottom step.

"Morning, babe. Come play with us," Brody called from the other side of the court.

"No, thanks. I'm not dressed for volleyball."

"I don't think there's a dress code," Brody said. "Come on. It'll be fun."

Sasha slid off her sandals and examined the court. "It's not really my thing." She wrinkled her nose. "I think I'm going to do some lounging."

Brody's gaze followed her as she walked through the sand to one of the beach chairs in the sun. Paige could tell he was frustrated

Rachel Magee

94

by his strained smile, but he didn't say anything else. He spun the ball between his hands. Everything got uncomfortably quiet for a second before Hadley broke the tension.

"So, are we going to stand around all day, or are we going to play some volleyball?"

Brody shook his head and tossed the ball over the net to Paige, who was standing in the service spot. "Just giving you guys a few extra minutes of peace before you lose."

"How noble of you," Paige said. "Serving."

She hit the ball with all her might, and it sailed over the net. Lane dove for it but missed. It landed, untouched, in the middle of the court.

The girls cheered. Aiden high-fived her, the proud look in his eyes filling her with confidence. Lane dusted the sand off of himself.

Brody picked up the ball and rolled it under the net to her.

"Lucky shot," he said, looking equally taunting and impressed.

Paige could feel her smile radiate all the way through her body.

"I'm just getting warmed up."

"Atta girl. Show 'em how it's done." Aiden retrieved the ball and tossed it to her.

Paige winked at him and got ready to serve again. Step two of her plan was well underway.

It was a close match, but after winning a game each and keeping the tie-breaking game neck-and-neck, Paige served her final ace for the win. The girls bounced and cheered in a big huddle-hug, and the guys offered their humble congratulations before they decided to go for a swim to cool off. Everyone jogged down to the beach and dove into the water. Everyone, that was, except Paige.

Even with Aiden there to help her hop around the court, the game had taken a toll on her ankle. She walked slowly down to the shore and paused at the water's edge to take off her boot.

The rest of the party had made it through the deep part to the sandbar fifteen yards out, oblivious that she wasn't with them.

Laughter rang out over the splashing and the whole scene made Paige happy. She loved it here, in this place, with these people. She paused to watch the scene for a second and caught Aiden's gaze. He smiled and left the group on the sandbar to swim back for her.

She had gotten her foot out of the boot and was massaging her ankle when he walked out of the water and plopped down on the sand next to her. "You're going to need to ice that." He pointed to her ankle.

"You don't think one-footed sand volleyball was what the doctor had in mind when he said to take it easy at the beach?"

He chuckled and ran his hand through his wet hair. "Probably not. But then again, if he'd known the girls didn't stand a chance without your ace serve, I'm sure he would've approved."

"Georgia had us training for such occasions. We take breakfast-making very seriously."

"Apparently." He stood up and offered her a hand to pull her up. She kept all of her weight on her good ankle, and he helped her hop down until they were standing ankle deep in the water. "Hey, I gotta head back to the house to welcome the investors, but as soon as I get them settled, I'll be back."

"Always working an angle, aren't you?" she joked.

"No rest for the wicked." He leaned over and brushed a quick kiss across her cheek, causing her pulse to quicken. It was the kind of instinctive move a doting boyfriend would have done before he walked away. In fact, Paige had seen him do it before to the handful of girls he'd had very brief relationships with. But he'd never done it to her.

She wanted to be proud that he thought to do such an intimate gesture so naturally, a tiny display of affection that would sell their fake relationship to any onlooker. But the truth was the only thing she could think about was how the kiss still lingered on her cheek and how the sensation seemed to shimmer through her.

She hopped deeper into the ocean as she watched him jog down the beach in the direction of Lane's parents' beach house, dipping her hands into the cool water to keep from reaching up to touch the place where his lips had grazed her cheek. Clearly, it had been far too long since she'd been kissed.

As soon as Aiden got far enough around the bend that she couldn't see him anymore, she dove into the water to swim the rest of the way to the sandbar. If all went well, her dry spell would be a thing of the past soon enough. Until then, she needed to shake off whatever was making her thoughts scatter anytime she saw attractive men like Aiden Pierce.

By two o'clock that afternoon, Aiden was more than happy to take a break from the business side of things to drive an ATV down the beach to deliver an array of water toys to the wedding party. Jacob Merrick had become more demanding than usual this weekend, and it was starting to annoy him. Ever since they started working together five years ago, their partnership had been equal. Sure, they both had their strengths. Jacob had money and influence that came in handy when making big deals, but Aiden had the ideas. One did not work well without the other. That was why, as far as sales and everything else, their partnership had always been fifty-fifty.

But this weekend, something had shifted. Maybe it was the fact that they were staying at Jacob's house. Or perhaps it was because he was the father of the groom, hosting a huge destination wedding for his only son. Or maybe it was the staggering amount of money this single sale was going to make them. Whatever the reason, Jacob seemed to see Aiden as an employee this weekend. Someone he could order around.

Well, tomorrow, as soon as he was in charge of the meeting and selling all the investors the beauty of his grand creation, Aiden would be back in the driver's seat. Until then, his plan was to stay out of Jacob's way. At the moment, the best way to do that was to volunteer to drive the ATV to deliver the pile of beach toys Jacob had purchased for the "kids" to play with.

Aiden didn't even bother to remind him that the "kids" were the same age he was.

The area in front of the condos had gotten more crowded since he'd left earlier that morning. It seemed like every one of the wedding guests in town was there. Well, everyone except for the investors and their wives. They were hanging out in rented cabanas with a full wait staff at the private beach near Jacob's house.

He pulled the ATV up to the dunes next to the staircase and waved Lane over to meet him.

"A gift from your dad. He thought y'all might enjoy playing with these."

Several members of the wedding party including his sister came over to help unload the six standup paddle boards and oars and carried them down to the water. Paige, however, wasn't one of them. She sat under the pop-up canopy, her ankle still free from the walking boot and propped on the cooler in front of her.

"I brought you something." He pointed to the bright yellow tandem kayak that had been at the bottom of the pile. "I thought you could use a beach toy that took the pressure off your ankle."

A huge smile lit her face as she pushed herself up from her chair and hobbled over to him. "You're a godsend."

He loved the way her smile didn't stop at her lips. It reflected in her eyes, shone off her face, lit her entire body. Her smile had always had the power to brighten a dark room, but this weekend in particular, it seemed to have a different effect on him. Seeing her awe-inspiring smile made him feel like he had the ability to conquer the world, much less wow the four moneymen staying at the rented house a half mile down.

He drank in the feeling, selfishly hoping to harness some of its confidence during their time together. "If you carry these, I'll carry this." He handed her the double oars.

Beach Wedding Weekend

"Deal." She grabbed the paddles and used them as a sort of crutch as she waited for him to heft the massive boat off the cart. The sea kayak wasn't too heavy for him to carry, but it was large and unwieldy and took some concentration to haul it through the soft sand to the water's edge.

"You sure you got it?" Paige lifted a questioning eyebrow as she watched him struggle.

"Nothing to it." He readjusted it halfway down the beach, his breathing more rapid than it had been after his three-mile jog this morning.

"If you say so."

He struggled a few more yards. *Had the beach gotten wider?* He didn't remember covering this much sand when he drove the four-wheeler up it. Sweat poured off his forehead.

"Knowing when to ask for help is a sign of strength, not a sign of weakness." Paige pressed her lips together in a way that looked like she was trying to stifle a laugh.

"I'm not sure asking an injured person to carry something applies."

Paige shook her head. "I only have a sprained ankle. Check this out." She tossed the paddles into the boat and picked up the back part. "If I balance the back for you, you can carry most of the weight from the front."

He shifted around to the front. He still wasn't convinced he carried most of the weight, but the last fifty yards were easier.

"Thanks," he said as he set the boat in the shallow water. The waves lapped at the front and he stood to admire the gulf sparkling before them.

She stepped into the ankle-deep water next to him. "We couldn't have asked for a more perfect beach day."

He motioned to the front seat of the kayak. "Get in. Let's put all that hard work and perfect weather to good use."

She eased herself in and started paddling as he pushed them off.

99

They stayed in the deep water in front of the sandbar and headed in the direction where the sandbar faded away. Several of the paddle boarders had gone past the sandbar and were exploring the deeper water on the other side. Many of the other wedding guests were gathered in the ankle-deep water of the sandbar about twenty-five yards off the shore to watch.

"We'll be back." Paige waved as they paddled by, picking up speed as they went. Aiden didn't miss the way Brody looked at Paige as they passed, or the way he glared at him.

"Seems like phase two of your little plan is working," he said.

"Today's success has less to do with me and more to do with a certain someone who refuses to do anything too beachy." He noticed that she didn't even turn to look at Brody. "He tried to get her into the water earlier and she told him she didn't swim in the ocean. There are too many sea creatures in it." She looked back at him and giggled. "To be fair, though, I'm not sure her bikini was made to get wet. My mom sent me a similar one once with a warning label that said 'do not fully submerge in water.'"

"At that point, is it even considered swimwear?"

He heard a chuckle. "Par for the course when it comes to Gwyneth Blair." At the mention of her mother's name her back straightened and some of the pep seeped out of her voice. In the eight years he'd known Paige he'd never met the woman, but her physical reaction to her mother's name made him curious. *What was she like?*

He was about to ask when Paige changed the subject. "So where are we headed?"

"As far toward the horizon as you want to go," he said. "In full disclosure, I do have a selfish motive for our little boat ride. I wanted to go over some of the details about tomorrow."

She twisted around in her seat and raised an eyebrow. "You hijacked my boat to get my undivided attention?"

"I whisked you away on an adventure that would ignite your

imagination and thought we might find a few minutes to chat about business stuff." Plus, he needed to get away, and being around her always made him happy. Which was a completely normal reaction to a friend, wasn't it?

She balanced her paddle on her lap and looked around. "At least it's a scenic business meeting."

He took in the beauty surrounding them. Their paddles moved through the water in a slow rhythm, alternating from side to side. A warm breeze blew and the sun danced on the soft waves. It was the most relaxed Aiden had felt since he arrived at Jacob's house.

"Maybe I should hold all business meetings in a kayak."

Paige nodded. "Not a bad idea. I think the paddling could help some of my brides work out their wedding planning aggression." She flashed a smile over her shoulder. "But back to your thing, I confirmed the cabana this morning. It should be set up and ready by eleven. I spoke with the caterer yesterday after we got here. They'll arrive at eleven-thirty and will set up in the clubhouse kitchen. They're bringing a staff of two. One will do most of the food and plate prep and one will serve."

She rested her paddle across the boat and spun around in her seat to face him. "I didn't even think to ask if anyone had any dietary restrictions."

Aiden scanned his memory of their short meeting together. "None that I know about. Should I ask?"

"That's up to you. The caterer is going to make the recipes from Cedar Break that you requested. But just to give you a heads-up, he loved the brisket taco. He asked if it would be okay if he added it to his own menu. I told them they'd have to talk to you about it."

It always caught him off guard when people raved about his recipes. They weren't anything special, just something he thought sounded good. In fact, the barbecue brisket tacos, the most popular item on his menu, were something he threw together in the kitchen one afternoon because he was hungry. He brought some out for a few of his buddies to try and the table next to them tried to order it. It was such an off-the-cuff invention that he had trouble telling his head chef the correct measurements to recreate it.

"It's just a recipe." And if he did his job well tomorrow, he wouldn't need it much longer. The thought settled on him like a gray cloud. He dug his oar into the water, trying to push the feeling behind him.

"Still, be prepared at some point to speak with them. And Hadley and Ciera are going to help me put the centerpieces together. I brought some of the things we use at the resort that will give it the same vibe as Cedar Break with a coastal twist."

"I have no idea what that means but it sounds good."

"There's a TV screen that you can sync your computer to if you need it for a presentation. The manager said he could help us with that when we get there. So, looks like we're all set on my end. How about your end?"

The grey cloud got darker, dimming his mood along with it. "I need to finish up the presentation tonight, but selling them on what makes Cedar Break special shouldn't be hard."

Paige nodded. "It's a great place. It'll be weird not seeing you in it."

"Time to move on." It's what he did. Develop a great idea, sell it to the highest bidder, then move on to the next adventure. He never stayed anywhere long enough to get bored. Usually the sale of his business came with a light and airy sensation. Usually it was freeing. But right now he couldn't shake the strangled feeling that arrived every time he thought of dealing with the investors, which had to be because he didn't feel ready for the presentation. Right?

"Time for something bigger and better," Paige said, but he couldn't tell if her voice was serious or sarcastic.

"Yep. Bigger and better." Except...

"Oh, Aiden! Look!" Paige's excited voice interrupted his thoughts. She pointed her paddle at the water ten yards away to their right side. A pod of five or six dolphins swam near the surface, their heads popping up then disappearing below the water in what looked like a playful dance.

She rested her paddle across her lap and sat very still, watching the wildlife. Her face softened and every part of her from her eyes down to her fingertips looked like it was smiling.

Aiden glanced back at the beach to see if anyone else had spotted the beloved sea mammal, but they were farther away from the shore than he'd realized and the stretch of beach they were near was mostly vacant. As far as he could see, they were the only two people around.

The dolphins swam closer until the entire pod was no more than seven or eight feet away from them. One jumped out of the water in a perfect arc, cutting back into the water so smoothly that it hardly made a ripple.

"Aren't they magnificent?" Paige's face was filled with wonder and Aiden had to agree. He'd only seen dolphins in an aquarium, never in the wild. Here, swimming freely in the ocean, they seemed bigger, grander, more relaxed and more playful all at the same time. It was unlike anything he'd ever experienced before.

Several of the dolphins raised their heads above the water to look at them and Aiden could have sworn they were smiling. Their kind, dark eyes looked directly at them, and they made a clicking noise as if they were introducing themselves.

"Well, hello, darlings. It's lovely to meet you, too," Paige's voice purred in a calm, soothing tone which seemed to coax them a little closer. Another one jumped, and this time he was so close, Aiden could see the soft pink of his belly.

Two dolphins broke away from the rest of the pod and swam right up to them. One positioned himself only inches away from their kayak. He'd looked big when he was several feet away, but right next to them he seemed massive. His long, sleek body was slightly longer than the kayak. The other dolphin swam under them and popped out right in front of them, staring at them over the bow.

"Aren't you some handsome boys." Paige sat perfectly still, with her hands clasped in her lap, but looked completely at ease. Completely comfortable.

Aiden had felt more comfortable when there was a nice six-foot barrier between them. Now, they had the big, burly club bouncers of the dolphin pod flanking their boat. Everything was copacetic at the moment, but he wasn't sure what would happen if the bouncers decided they needed to enforce a rule. They could easily flip the kayak with one nudge and they probably weighed north of six hundred pounds.

The thought caused Aiden's pulse to pick up and he eyed the big guy swimming next to him. "We're all friends here, right?"

Paige laughed, a tinkling sound that rippled over the water. It caused the one in front of them to lift his head and smile at her. Aiden didn't blame him. Paige's laugh made him want to smile, too.

"Of course, we're all friends. Aren't we?" she said to the sweet, smiling face in front of her. The big guy next to them glared at Aiden.

"But they're protecting something." Her expression turned more serious and she looked out to study the rest of the pod. "Do you have a baby with you?"

Aiden scanned the group as well. What he'd thought was a pod of six had now grown, and he counted at least ten. And that's when he saw it. It was so precious it could have softened the hardest heart. "Yep. A tiny one, right there next to its mom."

The tiny dolphin stayed just below the surface. He was hard to spot because he hovered close to the front flipper of the larger dolphin Aiden assumed was his mother.

Both of Paige's hands went to her heart and she made a muffled cooing sound. "Oh, Aiden, have you ever seen anything so adorable in your whole life?"

As if the mother had heard her, she swam a little closer, showing off the calf. The baby couldn't have been more than three feet long and had a sort of clumsy newness about him. Aiden wouldn't have been surprised if he was only a few days old.

"What a treat," Paige whispered. The mistiness in her eyes glistened and joy glowed around her. Aiden agreed. This moment was a treat. And what was even more surprising was the realization that there wasn't anyone else he would've wanted to share it with.

They sat there like that for at least ten minutes with the waves gently rocking them, encompassed in a bubble of wonder, escorted by a pair of large dolphins while they watched the rest of the pod play in the water next to them.

Finally, Paige turned her attention to their escorts. "What a precious little baby. Thank you for sharing him with us."

The one in front popped up, smiling right at them as if to acknowledge the compliment, and then both escorts joined the others and the whole pod disappeared into the darker waters.

She reached back and covered his hand with hers. The warmth of her touch flowed through him, which caught him off guard. He stared at her hand in amazement for a moment before looking up at her. The peaceful expression on her face washed over him, too.

"Dolphins are my favorite animal, and I've never been this close to them in the wild. Weren't they spectacular?"

Aiden shrugged and tried to look humble. "I arranged for them to be here as a thank you for helping me."

She playfully pushed his hand away and turned her full attention back to where the dolphins had been, breathing out a contented sigh. "It doesn't get much better than this, does it?"

No. No it didn't.

Aiden finally lowered his paddle into the water and started to turn the kayak around.

"I guess we should start heading back before people think we got lost at sea."

"If we have to." She waited until they were facing the correct direction before helping him paddle. "Don't tell Georgia, but this was the highlight of my weekend."

"Mine too, so your secret's safe with me."

True, seeing the beautiful creatures so close was inspiring, but there was something else about this boat ride that resonated deep inside him. Something that had a whole lot to do with the girl sitting in front of him.

Chapter Eight

SO FAR, TODAY HAD BEEN pretty perfect. Spending the day on the beach with her friends was always a recipe for a good time, but her kayaking adventure with Aiden had elevated it to a whole new level. Paige found herself humming as she got ready for the bachelorette party and her rosy glow continued all through their happy hour.

She couldn't help but think life was good as they walked into the escape room. In theory this portion of the bachelorette party was supposed to a fun, bonding time. When Georgia mentioned it to Paige, they both agreed that being locked in a room searching for clues with some of their favorite people would produce moments they would remember forever. It had set off an afternoon of storytelling and giggling over old college stories.

In reality when the game host pulled the door shut the rosy glow from Paige's perfect day started to dull before the lock even clicked into place. It had less to do with being trapped in a sinking submarine with only an hour's worth of oxygen and the riddle of a madman to help them get out, and more to do with who else was locked in the room.

"Do you have any idea how many people have been in here touching things? It probably has more bacterial growth than a bargain motel room. I'm not touching one single thing until we wipe it down. Who has the antibacterial wipes?" Elle glanced around the room with a look of disgust. Paige knew Georgia often lacked patience for her opinionated cousin, but she hadn't realized how thin that patience had gotten until she saw the annoyed look on Georgia's face. In an attempt to ease Georgia's tension, Paige jumped in.

"I don't have wipes, but I did bring hand sanitizer." She pulled it out of her small crossbody purse and squirted some of the Midnight Passion scented gel onto Elle's hand. She had purchased this particular scent because she was curious as to what midnight passion would smell like. Now, the scent would forever be associated with a musty room and a germ-conscious cousin.

"So now what?" Georgia asked. She stood in the center of the room and rotated slowly.

"I guess we look for clues?" Ciera wandered over to a control panel with lots of flashing lights. "The trouble is, I've never been in a submarine so I don't know what looks normal and what's out of place."

"We need to attack this in a logical order. I say the first thing we do is figure out the madman's message," Hadley announced.

Elle, who was still rubbing sanitizer into her hands, glared at Hadley. "This is Georgia's party. I think Georgia should tell us what to do."

Before any more hostile words could be exchanged, an ear-piercing alarm blasted through the room, causing Paige to jump.

"What's that?" Ciera yelled over the high-pitched shriek.

The noise was so loud it made it hard to think. Several of the girls, including Georgia and her cousin, stood looking dazed, pressing their hands over their ears. Ciera and Hadley examined the control panel, hitting buttons next to all of the flashing lights. Paige started to help them when, from the corner of her eye, she caught sight of a guilty-looking Sasha standing on the far side of the room.

Paige made her way through the chaos over to her. "Do you know what happened?"

Sasha chewed on her lip and pointed to a large, round, red button on the wall. In bold block letters it said "DO NOT TOUCH."

"That was the button that got pressed? The one button that says don't touch."

Sasha gazed at the floor, looking like a kid who had been caught getting in trouble. "I wanted to see what happened."

Hadley, who had heard the conversation, huffed. "Great. So now what?" She glared at Sasha, as if she were hiding the answer.

"I tried pushing it again, but I think it only made the sound louder."

Paige examined the button and discovered tiny letters all the way around it. She leaned in closer. "Wait, I think it says something here, but it's hard to read."

"To counteract your oversight, turn your attention to the light," Sasha mumbled. "But I don't know what it means."

Georgia pointed to the large light switch on the wall next to the hatch. "Maybe there? Try flipping that."

Elle turned her nose up in the air. "Can you imagine how many people's hands have been on that switch? I'm not touching it."

One of the other girls in the room flipped it down. The noise stopped at once and the lights flickered. A message scrolled across the screen at the top of the room.

"Your foolishness has cost you ten precious minutes of oxygen. Pay attention so you are not so careless in the future," Georgia read. The giant digital timer on the wall went from 58:03 to 48:03.

"Sorry," Sasha mumbled and hung her head.

"It happens. We just have to figure out the puzzle a little faster," Paige said, then turned to Hadley. "Read us the riddle again."

"If you want to get out alive,

It's crucial to stop the dive.

To achieve that, you'll need to know

To what depths you're Willing to go." Hadley looked up from the card in her hand. "Is there a dive meter anywhere?"

Ciera pointed to a gauge next to her. "There's a meter here. It's spinning around backwards and there's a stop button right next to it."

Sasha squinted at the gauge. "Well, it says to stop the dive, so push the button." She went for the button.

Georgia, Paige and Hadley all lunged for her. "No!"

Even Ciera's sweet smile looked strained when she turned to Sasha. "I think we should try to figure out the clue before we press anything else."

Sasha didn't look like she had any idea why, but she wasn't willing to cross Hadley. She backed away from the control panel and leaned against the wall.

Then a voice came from above. "Can I help you?"

"Yes, can we get some appetizers in here? Or maybe a bottle of champagne. What do you have out there?" Georgia's other cousin asked.

"Tara? What are you doing?"

"I thought we could use some snacks, so I pressed the help button."

"That's not really what the help button is for," the voice from the ceiling said. "You have two helps remaining."

The intercom clicked off and the electric board lit up that read "hints requested: 1."

"So that's a no to the snacks?" Tara asked.

Hadley massaged her temples. Georgia looked like she might start yelling. Paige made a mental note that kayaking on the surface was far superior to being trapped in a submarine in the ocean's depths.

"New rule. No one touches a button until we all agree on it," Hadley said. "Since Georgia is the bride, she's the only one who gets to press things."

Tara crossed her arms in front of her chest and sat down on the floor. "Whatever. This game is stupid."

Elle shrugged. "I wasn't planning on touching anything anyway."

Hadley went back to reading the clue. Paige leaned over the control panel next to Ciera. "I guess we need to figure out what level we're willing to dive to. There has to be something around here that tells us."

"How about a hundred," Sasha said. Everyone stopped what they were doing to look at her.

"Why a hundred, sweetie?" Ciera's voice had the faint strained sound that was her telltale sign of being annoyed.

"Isn't that where you need to get out? Like at the surface? And we are trying to get out, right?"

"Surface level is zero," Georgia said. Hadley rolled her eyes and turned her attention back to what she was reading.

"Zero? That seems like a funny place to start. Everyone knows one hundred is a perfect score. Nobody wants to get a zero."

"The number measures how many feet below the surface you are, so surface level is zero," Ciera explained.

Sasha looked thoughtful. "Oh. They should probably explain that before they locked us in here."

"I think I found something." Georgia diverted the attention back to the game as she pointed to a note pinned on a board.

"It's a memo about someone named Will. The word 'Willing' is capitalized in the riddle, maybe it means something."

"Is there a depth next to it?" Paige asked.

Georgia shook her head. "Only a date. March 21. What do you think that means?"

"Maybe transfer it into numbers? 321?" Paige suggested.

"Worth a shot. Does everyone agree?" Everyone nodded their approval. Everyone except Sasha, who still looked to be working through something in her mind.

Georgia turned the dial and hit the button. The flashing lights stopped and a hidden drawer popped open, revealing a small box locked with a tiny padlock.

"Guess we need a key." Hadley examined the box. "It must be hidden somewhere in this room."

Everyone scattered throughout the small room, searching every nook and cranny for the next clue.

As the time ticked down, the clues got harder to figure out. With about thirty minutes remaining, Tara sat down on the floor and pulled out her phone, saying she had enough. Georgia used one of the helps to see if someone would come let one person out of their room. Paige wasn't sure if saying yes was standard policy or if Georgia's voice sounded so frustrated they didn't dare say no.

With ten minutes remaining, Sasha accidentally bumped into the 3D puzzle they were putting together and knocked it over, making them have to start over. She said she'd help by finding all the straight pieces for the edge.

"It's a sphere," Ciera told her. Sasha nodded and searched through the pieces on the floor.

Paige couldn't help but compare all the ways she and Sasha were different. For the first time since meeting Sasha, she wondered why Brody was attracted to someone who seemed to be the complete opposite of her. What did that say about the relationship they'd shared? But that was a topic she would have to consider at a different time. Right now her goal was to figure out these clues so they could get out of this room before what was left of her rosy glow got swallowed up by its darkness.

There were two minutes and twenty-seven seconds left on the clock and they were down to their final clue. All they had to do was figure out the correct order to put the eight digits into the security keypad to open the door into the override room.

"Why can't we try putting them all in different orders?" Sasha asked again.

"It takes off twenty seconds every time we're wrong. We have to get it right in less than six attempts." Even Ciera's normal saintly patience was starting to sound a little strained.

"Come on, girls. We can do this." Paige tried to keep her voice peppy. "Hadley, read the riddle one more time." The four friends kneeled on the floor around the clue and the paper numbers.

"If you start out From Here to Eternity you won't have much more. Then remembering from where you came will get you out the door."

They each gave ideas about how to arrange the numbers that might make sense with what was written. They tried two of their attempts with no luck. Paige was starting to get frustrated, and if the look on her friends' faces was any indication, they were feeling the same way.

"Well, the first four numbers are 1953." Sasha said from the wall behind them. They all turned to look at her.

"Why do you say that?" Ciera asked.

"It says to start with From Here to Eternity. That movie came out in 1953, so those have to be the first four numbers."

Well. Paige couldn't help but be impressed. Georgia arranged the paper numbers on the floor so those four were first. "That leaves us two, four, six and seven."

"Wait." Paige rearranged them. "That's the number over the door where we walked in."

There were only fifteen seconds left on the clock. Hadley shrugged. "It's worth a try. At this point we have nothing to lose."

Georgia typed in the numbers. Even though they really weren't sinking and regardless of what happened the exit door was about to spring open to a balmy Florida night, everyone held their breath. Georgia pushed *enter.*

Lights flashed and the word "Congratulations" scrolled across the screen. "We beat the clock!" Ciera threw her hands in the air to cheer.

"Barely." Georgia breathed out a sigh of relief. Ciera flung her arms around her.

"Doesn't matter. We still won!"

They all spilled out into the courtyard to take pictures declaring they had beat the clock and that they were, in fact, geniuses, before climbing on their bikes and heading down the path to their dinner destination five blocks away.

As Aiden had warned her the first day, riding a bike in a walking boot was not easy. She'd never thought about how much ankle flexion went into pushing a pedal.

Earlier, she'd been able to find a rhythm, but as the night wore on and she got more tired, she struggled to keep her balance long enough to move forward at any sort of obtainable speed. And now her friends were so far in front of her that she couldn't see them anymore. She pulled over to the side of the path to catch her breath and wipe the sweat from her forehead.

"Do you need help?" Sasha pulled up next to her and stopped, which caught Paige off guard. She thought everyone was in front of her. Where had she come from?

As if Sasha could read her mind, she answered, "I had to make a phone call, so I stayed behind. How's your ankle?"

Paige shook her foot to try to get rid of some of the tension, but it didn't help. Between the pain in her ankle and the added weight from the boot, her entire leg throbbed. "We're almost there. I can make it, then I can prop my leg up for a while." She pushed off, moving slowly and wobbly, kind of like a new baby giraffe learning how to walk. She imagined all the people in the passing cars pointing and laughing. But Sasha didn't point or laugh. Instead, she rode slowly, right next to Paige, without any sort of judgment in her eyes.

"It's amazing how much pain one little ankle can cause. I got a minor sprain last year during filming. It hurt so bad I could barely walk on it, but I had to push through because of the production schedule. When we were done filming I stayed in bed for two whole days so I wouldn't have to feel the pain."

"That must have been tough. Right now, I can't imagine trying to walk normally."

Sasha tucked a strand of her perfect hair behind her ear. "It put my acting abilities to the test, that's for sure."

Were she and Sasha really bonding over ankle injuries? This night was not going at all how she'd imagined.

"Thanks for your help in there. We wouldn't have made it out in time if you hadn't figured out the clue."

Sasha's mouth pulled to the side in thought as she steered around a pothole in the bike path. "That was an easy one. Movies I know. Submarines, on the other hand? They didn't teach us that in cosmetology school."

"I don't think any of us know a whole lot about them." Paige offered a sympathetic smile. Maybe Sasha wasn't as bad as they had made her out to be. "You went to cosmetology school?"

"Yeah. After high school my dad said he wouldn't pay for any more acting classes unless I had training in a career that actually paid money. Since I was still doing small stage productions and budget photoshoots at the time, I was doing all my own hair and makeup. I thought it wouldn't hurt to know more about it."

"Makes sense." It also explained why her hair always looked so good.

The path got more crowded as they neared the beachside food complex where they were having dinner. It was one of the major hangouts for this little beach town, featuring six different counter service restaurants around a central courtyard. The faint sounds of the band playing on the main stage mingled with the talking and laughter of the crowds on the trail. The bike traffic brought them to a stop and they had to get off their bikes.

"I guess we should walk it from here," Paige said.

"Can you push yours on your ankle? I'm pretty good at handling two bikes. My older sister used to make me push hers up the hill to our house when we were kids."

Paige shook her head. "Thanks for the offer, but I think I can make it. Walking is a lot easier than riding," Also, all the concentration it required to push her bike while hobbling on one leg took her mind off thinking about how Brody's new girlfriend might not be so bad after all.

Aiden had just handed over his credit card to pay for the appetizers when he spotted Paige limping up the crushed shell pathway to The Courtyard with Sasha by her side. He held his hand up to wave. Paige's whole face brightened when she saw him, and he had a strange suspicion that his own face did the same thing. Being around her made life feel easier, sunnier. The more time he spent with her, the more he liked it.

She turned to Sasha. "You can go ahead. I need to talk to him for a few minutes."

"Nice to see you, Aiden," Sasha said before heading off to the reserved table right in front of the stage.

"I know we're trying to sell the whole relationship thing, but crashing the bachelorette party? Seems a little much, Pierce, don't you think?" Her playful grin was contagious.

"Go big or go home is what I always say. But look at you, making friends with enemy number one." He moved down to the window to wait for his order with her in tow.

"That was all her. I was struggling riding with my ankle and she stopped to help me."

"Still hurting?" He noticed she was standing on her left foot with only the toe of her right foot barely touching the ground.

"Too much activity today."

"I thought you said you were going to stay off it."

"I thought you told me you were going to get me one of those carts to put behind Ciera's bike."

The thought of Paige sitting in the back of a kid's cart looking like Cleopatra made him smile. "I'll call tomorrow."

"So what are you doing here?" Paige asked again.

Aiden nodded his head at the round table on the far edge of the courtyard hosting some of the investor couples. "Thought I'd take them out to enjoy the nightlife. Any chance I could talk you into coming by to say hi? They'd love to meet you. And to know you're a real person and not a figment of my imagination."

"I'd love to, Honey Bear."

He picked up the two paper plates holding the steaming fried seafood laid out on a portion of a brown paper bag. The rich smells made his mouth water and he had to force himself not to snag the piece of calamari hanging off one side and pop it into his mouth for the walk to the table. Instead, he looked at Paige and gestured to his shoulder.

"If you want, I'll give you a piggyback ride so you can rest your ankle."

Laughter crinkled her eyes. "Tempting, but I think I can make it to the table."

"Just checking. You know, I'm chivalrous like that."

"That's what I like about you, Honey Bear. You're such a giver."

He knew they were meant as jokes, but for some reason her words swirled through him, and by the time they had reached the table every inch of him felt vibrant and alive. "Look who I found lurking around. I'd love for y'all to meet my delightful other half, Paige Westmoreland."

Everyone offered their hellos and Paige made her way around the table personally greeting all of them.

"Aiden tells us you are in the wedding this weekend. A bridesmaid?" one of the ladies asked.

Paige nodded and slid into the empty seat next to her. "I am. The bride is one of my best friends. Former college roommate."

"College roommates are the best kind of friends, aren't they?" the lady on her other side said. Paige shifted until her full attention was on her. "I still try to get away with my college girlfriends every year."

"If your college roommates are anything like mine, I bet you make great memories. Where do you usually go?" Paige leaned in, the way she always did when she was listening. She was a great listener. The kind that made you feel important and validated. It appeared that the investor's wife felt the same way.

"Of course we all love a beach, but our favorite destination is a spa resort."

Paige's face lit up and she turned to the wife sitting on the other side, pulling her into the conversation with the same flattering attention. "There's nothing like a great spa, huh?"

Wife number two nodded enthusiastically.

"Our absolute favorite is one we go to in Scottsdale. You've never seen a spa as fabulous as this one. Aromatherapy pool, personal chefs, every spa treatment you can imagine. It's amazing."

Paige's eyes sparkled. "Wow. Sounds wonderful." Aiden knew Paige. She was not the type who hung out in spas. She was more of an adventure girl. They kind who considered the highlight of her day kayaking in the middle of a pod of dolphins. But right now, she looked enthralled in the spa conversation. Her attention, in turn, had caused the wives to look like they were enjoying themselves for the first time since Aiden had met them.

The first wife launched into details about what made the Scottsdale resort "fabulous," and the other lady added her own recommendations for other spas. Paige nodded and listened and validated until they looked like three best friends swapping stories.

"I'd love to stay and talk to you all night, but I have to get back to the bachelorette party. Before I go, though, I have to tell you that

118

the spa at Hilltop Resort is one of the best I've been to in the world. Even better than that one in Palm Springs you always hear about."

"I've heard that. We should have a girls' weekend and try it out."

"Plus, you'll just love the town of Hilltop. It's absolutely charming. There's no place like it." She tossed a charming grin at Aiden. The warmth of her glance resonated somewhere deep in his chest, deeper than he thought normal. It was a spot he kept guarded, off limits, almost as if he were afraid of the power it could have. And now, completely without his permission, one smile had broken the barrier.

He walked around the table to her, trying to ignore this new feeling. He needed to lighten the mood, keep it casual. "Thanks for stopping by, Smoochems."

Out of instinct, he slid his arm around her waist and brushed a kissed on her cheek, which was a mistake. He felt like his arms were made to wrap around her waist and he had the sudden urge to pull her into him, to hold her close and press his lips against hers. And he wanted to be able to do that from now until a very long time into the future.

It ignited a string of strong emotions. They were the sort of emotions that were uncontrollable. Big and loud and unexpected. The kind that promised to bring unimaginable joy but also threatened unrecoverable destruction.

The thought made him pull his arm away, as if touching her was making him think those crazy thoughts. Aiden didn't do big, messy emotions. He did fun and easy and avoided the rest. Life, in his experience, was less complicated that way.

His sudden movement left her off balance and she swayed. He caught her elbow to steady her.

"You okay? I think it's time to get off that ankle."

Paige's face flushed and her eyes met his. The warmth deep in his chest intensified.

"Will do." She looked flustered at first, as flustered as he felt, but then she turned to the others at the table. "It was so nice to meet all of you. I'll see you tomorrow."

She limped over to her table, and Aiden returned to his seat.

"She is just great. I adore her," the first wife said.

"Thanks. I happen to agree." Except this time, he wasn't feeding them some line to sell the fake relationship. That answer came straight from his heart.

Chapter Nine

DESPITE NOT GETTING IN UNTIL late the night before, Paige woke up early. No matter how hard she tried to sleep in, it was an impossible task. She'd been that way for as long as she remembered. She tiptoed to the to the kitchen to make coffee, then she took it out to their balcony.

The balcony was her favorite part of this condo. It made the four flights of stairs worth it, even on a hurt ankle. From here, the white sand blended into the aqua waves, which stretched out until they touched the horizon. It was an unobstructed visual display of tranquility.

Her mom's job had taken her to beaches all over the world, yet this stretch of coastline touched her in ways none of the others did. Maybe it was because this particular water was her favorite shade of blue-green, or maybe it was because the sand gleamed so bright white it looked fake. Or maybe it was because all of her trips to this particular area had been with her favorite people in the world, the people she was here with this weekend, and friendship was really the most beautiful scenery.

Whatever the reason, the picturesque scene in front of her sparkled all the way through her. It was good to be here. She pulled her knees into her chest and clutched the warm coffee mug between her hands as she watched the ocean.

The water was so clear that from her angle she could see below the surface. A couple of giant rays about a hundred yards off the shore dipped and glided in what looked like a choreographed dance. A pelican soaring over the waves dove into the water and returned to the air with a fish in its bill. She could sit out here and watch the wildlife all day.

Besides an older man walking with a metal detector at one end and a guy out for a morning jog at the other end, there was no one on the beach. All of Paige's attention could be on the playful wildlife and the peacefulness of the ocean.

A dark form appeared in the water as far out as she could see. As it swam closer, the form started to look more like a group of smaller forms swimming together. Then one form jumped out of the waves.

Her dolphin pod! Excitement rolled through her. She walked to the rail, straining to get a better look and wishing she'd remembered to bring binoculars with her. They were swimming closer to the shore, but they were still pretty far out, beyond the sandbar where the water turned darker.

It was hard to tell exactly how many there were because they moved so quickly, swimming between each other, diving deeper and coming up for air. Yesterday she had counted ten including the baby, which seemed about the same as what she saw now. Most likely, it was the same pod who made these warm waters their home. She leaned against the rail, still clutching her coffee for warmth on the cool summer morning and watched as the dolphins played in the waters directly in front of her. She wished someone was here to share this with her.

Another one jumped, closer to the shore this time. The splash must have caught the jogger's attention. He slowed to a walk and focused on the ocean. That was when she recognized the lazy gait. Aiden.

She wanted to call to him, but he was so far away she would've had to use a voice loud enough to wake the entire condo building for him to be able to hear her. She considered texting him, but her phone was still inside, and she didn't want to leave the balcony while the dolphins were still visiting. So she settled for silently watching him.

He stopped at the water's edge directly in front of where she was standing and scanned the ocean. The pod was still playing, but they were under the surface now. Paige knew from his vantage point he wouldn't be able to see them at all, but he stood there, the muscles of his strong bare back highlighted in the morning sunlight.

They were friends. Since the first time Ciera introduced them, she and Aiden had connected. He made her laugh with some dumb joke when they were introduced, and their playful relationship had been born. For years, things between them had been friendly and casual. He was fun and she enjoyed being around him, but she'd never considered anything more. He was just Aiden. So why did she feel a burst of sunlight shimmer through her every time she saw him this weekend?

With no more splashing going on in the water, he rotated until he was looking at the tall condo building. When he saw her, his face lit up in a bright smile and he lifted his hand to wave. She waved back.

He used his arm to pantomime fish swimming in the water and pointed out to the ocean. He was showing her the dolphins. She nodded and used her hands to form a heart that she put over her chest to tell him that she loved watching them. She especially loved watching them with him, but she kept that tidbit to herself mostly because she was still trying to figure out what it meant.

They both stood there watching for a few more minutes. Two of the dolphins stuck their heads up to look at the shore and one more jumped in the waves before the pod turned and swam out to the darker waters.

That scene right there was why she loved this balcony, why she loved this beach. And she felt like maybe Aiden's presence added to it. When the water was quiet again, he turned back to her and gave her a quick salute before he continued to jog down the beach.

The sound of the sliding glass door opening behind her made Paige jump. Ciera stepped onto the patio holding her own steaming mug.

"What a beautiful morning." She joined Paige, draping her arms over the rail.

"Gorgeous." She was talking about the view of the ocean, wasn't she? Suddenly she felt fidgety, like she'd been caught doing something she shouldn't. She quickly took a sip of her coffee to cover it up. What did she have to feel guilty about? She was only enjoying a moment with a friend.

"This view will never get old." Ciera's voice had a dreamy quality to it. She wasn't paying any attention at all to Paige, and Paige wanted to keep it that way.

She struggled to keep her own voice as carefree as Ciera's. "Nope. It's pretty perfect."

"Hey, is that my brother?" Ciera pointed in his direction.

"Yeah, he just ran by. Morning jog, I guess."

Ciera seemed to dismiss it. She sank into one of the cushioned chairs, blowing on the top of her coffee. "Today are we on step two or step three?"

Step two or three? It took Paige a second to shift gears before she realized what Ciera was talking about. "Oh, right. With Brody." She cast one last glance at Aiden before moving on to the new topic. "I don't know about step two. Maybe she's not as bad as we think."

Ciera screwed her face up to show Paige that was being crazy. "She called the beach too sandy and she thought surface level was at a hundred feet because that's a perfect score."

True, but she had also stopped to help Paige when she was struggling and was perfectly nice to everyone at dinner. "I'm just saying maybe we should be done with step two."

"Fair enough. Then on to step three."

"Remind him what we had." She sipped her coffee, letting her mind drift back to the days when she and Brody were together. They were happy then, she was sure of it. It was just that at the moment, she couldn't recall any specific examples.

Clearly she was operating on too little sleep. They had tons of good memories. Eleven solid months of them. She just needed more coffee to think of some.

"You outdid yourself." Aiden looked around the Grand Cabana and admired his lunch meeting spot. It certainly looked worthy of entertaining four self-absorbed money men. The luxury wooden deck raised twenty feet off the ground offered breathtaking views of the ocean while guests lounged in plush furniture in the shade. He could get used to this being his office, although he would rather be taking Paige out in the kayak again than setting up for a boring meeting.

"Tell me your agenda for the meeting. I want to make sure I have all the bases covered." Paige's businesslike voice broke into his thoughts.

He let out a heavy breath and turned away from the water to face her.

"Agenda? I'm more of a fly-by-the-seat-of-my-pants kind of guy."

She pulled glossy folders emblazoned with the Cedar Break logo and heavy silver pens out of the tote she'd brought with her and set them on the side table. "You still need some sort of game plan. Successful meetings don't happen on accident."

She was meticulous, lining up the supplies in neat rows, arranging items on the table in a way that made it look inviting. But she did it cheerfully, with the same calm, peaceful attitude that relaxed him. The one that he was drawn to every time he was around her.

"Did you get that motto off a cat poster?"

Her smile radiated through her body and danced in her eyes. Looking at her was more distracting than admiring the ocean.

"Slogans from cat posters come in handy. How else would the world be inspired to 'hang in there'?"

"Our game plan is to shoot the breeze, eat lunch, have a business meeting."

Paige made a note in a manila file folder. "Business meeting before or after dessert?"

"We're men. We don't eat dessert."

She shot him a look that said she didn't agree. "The only line longer than the women's bathroom last year at the PGA tournament was the one of grown men waiting for an ice cream cone."

Aiden remembered that line. The ice cream was worth it. "Then business meeting during dessert."

"I can work with that." She held up the logoed folders. "Do you want these on the table now, or want me to pass them out during dessert?"

Aiden practiced his golf swing, trying not to think about how all of the details of the one place that felt more like home than any actual house he'd ever owned could be summed up in black and white on the pages inside those glossy folders.

"You ask a lot of questions."

"Be glad you're not one of my brides." Her lips turned up in the playful grin that lately had made him want to do dumb things. Like kiss her. He swung his imaginary golf club again to distract himself.

"Pass them out later."

She stacked the folders into a neat pile and placed them on the back corner of the table. "Good plan."

She fiddled with the computer and checked the wireless connection to the flatscreen TV mounted to one of the posts. The ruffled sleeves of her white silk blouse fluttered in the sea breeze. It was the first time he noticed how she was dressed. Her black pencil skirt and silk blouse looked professional, but the ruffles and her wedge sandals looked beach-appropriate. She and the space were the perfect visual representation of the image he wanted his restaurants to project. The only thing missing, he realized, was her big black walking boot.

Aiden motioned to her ankle. "Where's the boot?"

She lifted up her foot and wiggled her toes. "Ahh, yes. As of today, I am officially free of the black beast. I now get to downgrade to this less obtrusive flesh-colored brace." She returned her foot to the floor and leaned down to adjust it. "I'm not sure if it actually supports my ankle or is meant to act as a reminder of what happens when I try to walk across marble floors in big girl shoes."

She had thought of everything. The same strong emotion from last night swelled in his chest.

He watched her for a second. "Thanks again for doing this. I would've been lost without you."

She leaned against the table and casually crossed her arms in front of her chest.

"My pleasure. Hopefully all our hard work will pay off and we both get what we want at the end of the weekend."

If everything worked out the way it was supposed to, was he getting what he wanted? His restaurant would go to a group of investors with deep pockets, and his fake girlfriend would be kayaking among a pod of dolphins with someone else. He'd be alone.

No, not alone. He'd be free, which was what he liked. That was his goal. Ready to conquer the world with nothing holding him back. There were places to go and adventures to be had. The only reason it felt off at the moment had to be because he didn't have it yet.

"So what step of your plan are you on now?"

Paige turned and straightened the already-straight rows of folders. If he didn't know any better, he'd think she was trying to distract herself, only she did it with organization and not golf swings. "Step three. Remind him what we had."

This was going faster than he thought. "And what you had was great?"

It was a personal question, but if he had to give up everything he cared about, he needed to know that at least she was going to be with a good person.

She stopped what she was doing and looked out at the ocean, chewing on her bottom lip. Everything got so quiet that the only noise around them was the sea breeze rustling the long drapes hanging in the corners of the cabana and the soft waves off in the distance.

He wasn't sure how to read her expression as she stood there thinking. Were they good memories? Sad memories?

After a long moment, her face softened into a sort of glowing joy. It was a look that made him both happy for her and a little jealous.

"Yeah, it was pretty great."

He wanted to press her on it, to know exactly why it was great. What did this guy do that made him worthy of her love—the guy who had dropped her the second he flew out of town? But they were interrupted by the caterer, who came up with the appetizers and to ask a couple of final questions. And, if he was being honest, it wasn't his business anyway.

As the food was finished being set up, he saw Jacob pull up in a golf cart with the investors.

"It's showtime." She clasped her hands in front of her and straightened her posture. Pride swept through him. Fake girlfriend or not, at that moment he realized there was no one he would rather have by his side. The feeling was exhilarating and terrifying all at the same time, but he didn't have time to think about it right now.

The look on his face must have shown her that he was thinking about something. She arched an eyebrow. "You okay?"

"I'm great."

"Ready to dazzle them?"

He pushed back whatever apprehension was making him want to say no. "It's what I do best."

It was a truth that normally inspired him. Perfect pitches, closing deals, making things happen. It was what made him successful. Yet today, for some reason, those skills didn't sound inspiring.

They sounded like the prelude to his death march.

Chapter Ten

PAIGE STOOD AT THE BACK of the cabana and watched Aiden finish up his meeting. Over the years, she'd seen Aiden at his places of business tons of times. In fact, the very first time she met him was when she and Ciera were freshmen living in the college dorms. He would start off his errand delivery runs, his first company, by bringing them fast food bean burritos. But seeing him at work then, or even now when she saw him at the restaurant, he was always charming the customers and building up loyalty. Today it dawned on her that she'd never seen Aiden acting as the boss.

As a leader, he was impressive, a true master of the boardroom. He had this way of establishing control and leading while still being attentive and affirming to everyone at the table. And he did it all with the laid-back charm she loved.

"And what do you think made Cedar Break so successful?" one of the investors asked.

"Besides the amazing brisket tacos and me?" Jokingly, Aiden posed and swept his hands down his body in a playful attempt to show off his physique. He held the pose just long enough for the men at the table to laugh, then straightened and slid his hands into his pocket.

"As ya'll are well aware with your own business, success doesn't happen by accident. It takes a solid business plan fueled by market research and a lot of hard work. Our business plan has proven to be successful and we stay up to date on market research, which we've shared with you."

Another one of the investors studied one of the handouts in the folder. "And you think these results can be duplicated?"

Aiden nodded his head once, his entire stance exuding confidence. "Absolutely." He paused as if considering it then shrugged. "I mean, you won't have me, but ya'll aren't a bad-looking group of fellas." The table laughed again.

Aiden knocked his knuckles on the table. "All right, gentlemen, enough business talk. We're on vacation, after all, aren't we?"

The men closed their folders and pushed their chairs back from the table, transitioning into casual conversation. As Aiden shook hands and said his goodbyes, Paige started to gather up the business materials from the side table. When he walked the group down to their waiting golf carts, she cleared the center pieces and decorations. She'd almost returned all of their supplies to the boxes she brought them in when Aiden reappeared at the top of the stairs.

"Finally. I thought they'd never leave." His joking tone made her smile.

"It looked to me like the presentation was a success." She put the last of the centerpieces in an open bin on the table. "Well done."

"Thanks." Aiden slipped his hands into the pockets of his slacks, looking humble. "I think it went okay." She thought she detected a hint of concern creep across his face, but it disappeared as quickly as it had appeared. *Was something troubling him?*

"Do you need to follow up with them? I can finish in here." She snapped the lid on the bin and picked it up to move it to the side table where she had stacked the others.

He shook his head, his easy grin returning. "Giving them some space to mull things over is part of the plan. By the time we get to the rehearsal tonight, they'll be begging to sign on the dotted line."

She pushed the bin against his chest. "In that case, you can help me carry these down."

"With pleasure." He took it and she stacked another box on top before she grabbed the last box for herself. With one last glance to make sure they weren't leaving anything, she followed him down the stairs to his golf cart.

"You got someplace to be right now?" he asked as they loaded the boxes onto the floor of the golf cart's backseat.

Paige glanced at her watch and sank into the passenger seat, running through the to-do list in her mind. "Let's see. I have just over two hours until the rehearsal. I need to help Georgia gather everything she needs, work on my toast, change clothes…"

"Perfect. Sounds like you have plenty of time to stop for ice cream." He released the brake on the golf cart and eased forward.

Paige paused mid-sentence and looked at him. "Where in that list did you hear plenty of time?"

Aiden maneuvered through the twisting streets of the small neighborhood toward the front gate. "Mostly I heard ice cream, and there's always time for that."

"I didn't say ice cream."

Aiden grinned. "No, but I did. Come on. Sunny days like this were made for frozen treats. Plus, I owe you for all the work you put in up there."

Ice cream on a hot day like today did sound appealing. Plus, she enjoyed the company. Paige let go of her mental list and relaxed into the seat of the golf cart. "I guess I have a little time to spare."

"That's what I like to hear." He turned right onto the bike/cart path that ran along the main road, headed the opposite direction from her condo. They drove a few long blocks down to a small shopping center she hadn't ever spent much time in. Most of the space was taken up by two restaurants boasting ocean views. She'd heard they were good, but more formal than anything she and her friends ever wanted to try on their relaxed beach weekends. Most of the other retail spaces were home to high-end fashion boutiques and a couple of art galleries. The combination of those things meant Paige had never had a good reason to come to this shopping center before.

Aiden pulled into a cart parking spot and pushed down the break. Paige scanned the row of shops again, still not seeing anything that looked like the ice cream she'd been promised. "Are you sure we're in the right place?"

"I'm sure. The best ice cream in Seacrest is hidden back here."

She stepped out of the cart and followed him around the side to a tiny shop stuck in the corner. Aiden opened the door for her and she walked into an adorable old-fashioned ice cream parlor. White iron stools with pink-and-white striped cushions stood in front of the long white marble counter. Behind it, different sized glass dishes sat in neat rows on the shelves. Small round tables with chairs matched the bar stools and filled what was left of the floor space.

They made their way over to two empty spots at the counter and Aiden slid a menu in front of her. "Have you ever made your own ice cream before?"

Paige glanced around, realizing for the first time there was a modern twist to this classic shop. Instead of cases holding premade ice cream, there was a long bar of ingredients, stacks of stainless steel bowls and a single freezer with a swirl of frosty fog escaping every time it was opened.

"Like using liquid nitrogen to freeze it?"

"Yep. You get to pick everything down to what kind of milk you want to create your own personal perfect bowl of ice cream."

"Craft the perfect ice cream, huh? That seems like a lot of pressure." She scanned the list of available ingredients.

"Not pressure. Freedom. Let your tastes guide you." He shot her a dazzling smile that sparked confidence in her.

"And if my tastes guide me in the wrong direction?"

He leaned in, as if sharing a secret. "It's ice cream," he whispered. "How wrong can you go?"

She couldn't help her smile. Being with him was fun. "Let's try the fresh summer berries and cheesecake sweetened with honey," she told the server.

Aiden gave her an impressed look. "Solid choice. But you should add some basil. It'll elevate the flavors."

She wrinkled her nose. "Basil? I'm ordering ice cream not pesto."

"Trust me."

She shrugged. "Okay. Add some basil," she told the server. "I'll have the same." Aiden pushed his menu across the counter and turned to Paige. "And should we get it to go? No need to sit in here when we could be enjoying the beach view."

Paige nodded. "Agreed."

Less than five minutes later, Aiden paid and they both walked out holding a paper cup containing their custom-made, nitrogen-frozen, berry and basil ice cream. They walked down the sidewalk to the wooden boardwalk running across the ocean side of the complex. Paige waited until she stepped into the warm sun to take her first bite.

As soon as the creamy creation hit her tongue she had to stop to savor it. The sweetness of the berries blended perfectly with the richness of the cheesecake, and the brightness of the basil seemed to bring it all to life. "This is fantastic," Paige said, spooning another large bite into her mouth.

"Would you even be willing to call it perfect?" There was a teasing glint in his eye.

She scooped up another spoonful. "That kind of classification is going to require more research, but initial reports are looking positive."

He chuckled. They stopped and leaned against the railing, looking out at the ocean.

"This is my favorite stretch of beach in this town," Aiden said as he took another bite.

"I don't think I've ever come down this far," Paige admitted.

For the most part, it looked similar to the beach they were staying on. It had the same white sand and water that was the exact shade as a blue-green crayon. But there was one distinguishing feature that made it stand out. A low rock formation started at the bluff and stretched out into the water. It wasn't tall, maybe only two feet above the sand, but it added character to the beach, and she could only assume it created a natural habitat for sea life. In fact, there were two young boys in matching seersucker swim trunks hunched down and staring at what she guessed was a tide pool.

Aiden used his empty spoon to motion to an area down the beach. "When I was a kid, the only public beach access was a staircase over there. Every summer we use to rent an old beach house with our cousins up that way." He turned and waved his spoon at an area behind them. "Long before any of this was here."

"You have a lot of history in this place."

He nodded, thoughtfully. "Lots of memories." He spooned another bite of ice cream into his mouth, staring at the beach below them. "I got stung by my first jellyfish right over there."

Paige raised an eyebrow. "Your first jellyfish? You've been stung more than once?"

Aiden gave her a sheepish grin. "The first one was due to some misguided curiosity. That was on me."

Paige chuckled, imagining a young Aiden exploring the brightly colored sea creature. "And the other one?"

"The other two," Aiden corrected. He shook his head, as if contemplating the tragedy. "They were deliberate hostile attacks on a peaceful, unexpecting target. I was minding my own business, trying to get out of their way and…Pow!" Aiden's animated reenactment of his jellyfish encounter made Paige laugh harder.

He took a deep breath and another bite of his ice cream. "Me and the jellies have had a rocky co-existence ever since."

"Awww. Poor Aiden." She rubbed his arm. "And yet, you still come back year after year."

He nodded. "I'm not gonna lie. It took a lot of soul searching and contemplation, but eventually the joy of body surfing beat out the fear of the jelly sting." He smiled. "Also, I never make the trip without packing a new bottle of meat tenderizer. It takes the sting out, you know." He paused, as if considering that for a second. "At least that's what they told me. It still hurt like crazy. Those boogers pack a punch."

Paige giggled. "Confidence and an emergency back-up plan. That's what I like about you."

He gave a humble shrug, shoveling a spoonful of ice cream into his mouth.

Actually, there were a lot of things she liked about him. For starters, she liked the way it felt to stand out here with him, listening to old stories, laughing and eating ice cream. It was what trips to the beach and lazy summer afternoons should feel like.

The noise of a loud group walking down the boardwalk to the restaurant behind them distracted her. She scooted closer to the railing to give them more room on the crowded walkway.

"This place has grown so much since I first came here. It must look so different from when you were a kid."

He turned to study the buildings behind them. "It has changed a lot. Sometimes it's hard to remember what it used to look like."

"Is that ever sad?"

He looked at her and smiled. "Naw. Change is a good thing. If everything had stayed the same, we wouldn't have experienced this." He held his ice cream up to display what he was talking about, but his eyes met hers in an intimate way that pulsed through. "And missing out on this would be a true tragedy."

"Agreed," she said. She took another small taste, letting his words settle over her. They were talking about ice cream, but part of her couldn't help thinking about them. It might have taken a rocky road for her to get here, but she wouldn't change any of that if it meant giving up the time she'd spent with Aiden this weekend.

Chapter Eleven

AIDEN WAS SITTING ON THE bottom step of the staircase to the beach when Paige and the girls came down to walk to the rehearsal. Even though she had left him only an hour and a half ago, seeing him again made Paige's already cheery mood brighten a bit.

"What are you doing here?" Ciera asked.

"I thought you lovely ladies might want an escort to the rehearsal site."

Ciera's eyes narrowed. "You mean, the one that's directly in front of the house where you're staying?"

Aiden stood and offered a lazy crooked grin. "I was in the area."

Georgia patted his shoulder as she stepped around him and off the final wooden step into the sand. "I, for one, am happy to see you here. Want to give us a hand with some of this stuff?" She held out the bag containing things she needed for the rehearsal like a bow bouquet she was going to use and the veil she wanted to test out in the sea breeze.

Aiden slung it over his shoulder just in time for Ciera to hand him a large plastic storage bin full of decorating items. Hadley stacked a tote bag on top of it.

Aiden fumbled to organize everything to make it manageable to carry half a mile up the beach. "You realize there are easier ways of getting things to the Merricks' house. In a car, for example. Or even one of the handy golf carts parked in front of their house."

Ciera shrugged and slipped off of her sandals, heading down the soft sand. "None of us have a car at the condo and everyone else already left. But lucky for us, my dependable brother is here to help out."

They all walked through the powdery sand in the direction of Lane's parents' house. Georgia chatted nonstop about everything from the setup for the ceremony to what she hoped the weather would be like tomorrow. She was radiant. Paige had never seen her so happy, and it filled her with joy.

They were about halfway between the condo and the beach house when Paige realized Aiden wasn't with them anymore. She turned to look for him. There, about fifteen yards behind them, he was slowly trudging through the sand with all their stuff like some sort of handsome pack mule. Sweat was beading up on his forehead, but his signature crooked grin was still in place. She stopped and waited for him to catch up.

"What's in this box?" He motioned to the large plastic bin balanced on one shoulder.

There was a lightness to his voice that added to her joy. "Glass lanterns and shells, I think. It was supposed to go in the car with Georgia's parents, but they forgot it."

Aiden paused to wipe at his brow. "And Cici thought she could carry this all the way?"

"No way. We struggled carrying it down the steps. There was a wagon under the stairs we were going to use."

Aiden stopped and stared at her. "What? Why didn't you tell me about the wagon?"

"Well, a big, strong guy offered to help us." She playfully squeezed the bicep that was holding the box on his shoulder. "Plus, now we don't have to worry about bringing the wagon home with us. Win-win."

"For you maybe." Aiden shifted the box from one shoulder to

the other, with a flowered tote still hanging off each arm. "The things I do for my little sister and her friends."

"We are forever in your debt." They walked a few feet in silence. "You're avoiding the investors again, aren't you?" Paige questioned.

"Not at all. I'm just actively choosing to be places they aren't."

He was trying to joke, but she could tell that something was bothering him. It was the way his normally relaxed expression tensed a little every time the investors were mentioned. She first saw it at the last wedding when she had asked about who he was sitting with. His brows furrowed and his jaw tightened, his telltale sign that something was concerning him.

She'd thought it was odd then, but with everything else going on, she'd dismissed it. However, there was no denying it now. The tension seemed to be growing with each day this trip went on.

"I thought your pitch was pretty perfect. Did you get a chance to talk to any of them about it this afternoon, after you got back to the house?"

There was a pause before he spoke again. "They loved it. From what I can tell, they're more interested than ever."

She thought that was good news, but the tone of his voice was anything but cheery. "Which is what you want, right?"

Aiden sucked in a deep breath. Despite his grin, she could see the muscles around his jaw tighten. "Yep, this is the dream."

They walked for a few seconds in silence before he spoke again, and this time his tone was softer, more sincere. "Thanks again for your help today."

His words—or was it the way he looked at her?—did something to her. It danced inside her like sunlight shimmering on the turquoise waves. Strange.

"My pleasure. Anything for a friend." She ignored the crazy feeling. Right now, on her way to her best friend's wedding rehearsal with the plan to get her relationship with Brody back to where she wanted it to be, she didn't have time to try to figure out why she felt giddy when her *friend* smiled at her.

"Also," Aiden continued, "I have some good news and bad news."

"This is the real reason you came down to walk with us, isn't it?"

"Questioning my chivalrous intentions? You insult me." He put his free hand over his heart to feign his insult. "But giving you this heads-up is an added benefit."

"Give me the good news first."

"You and your dashing date will absolutely be sitting with the wedding party at the wedding reception."

A big wave rolled onto the shore and Paige darted around it.

"Fantastic, since I am, in fact, one of the three bridesmaids."

"You mock me, but I happen to know from experience that getting a wedding planner to reassign the seating chart the weekend of the wedding is no easy task. In fact, I still owe one planner a pair of orthopedic shoes for just such a favor."

"True. My mistake for RSVP'ing single. So what's the bad news?"

"It's not bad news as much as a favor. Will you, my delightful date, do me the honor of joining me at the investors' table this evening at the rehearsal dinner?"

Paige stared at the waves, taking in what he was asking her. She wouldn't be sitting next to her best friend at her rehearsal dinner. But she'd promised to help Aiden with his project, too. It was unfair of her to assume she wouldn't have to give up anything.

"This is really important to you, isn't it?"

"It's the biggest deal we've ever entertained."

Paige ran through the timeline of the evening in her mind. The seated dinner on the beach was only one small part of the festivities planned for the evening.

"But only dinner, right? The rest of the night I can be with my friends?"

Aiden nodded. "Absolutely, as it should be. You're here as Georgia's bridesmaid first."

She watched the waves roll into the shore, leaving their jagged print before rolling back out. He was her friend and he needed her. "I guess I should come up with good dinner party conversation. I think we exhausted the spa topic last night."

He visibly relaxed and a playfulness returned to his tone. "Too bad. It was an invigorating discussion. Almost as good as the conversation about cigars we had at lunch today."

"Apparently the wedding coordinator isn't the only one working at this wedding."

He readjusted the box on his shoulder. "Everyone has an angle."

She chuckled and they continued walking in silence. Before this weekend, she knew Aiden was good at what he did, but he'd always made it look so effortless. She'd never realized how much thought, planning, and work went into it. Now that she was aware of his effort, it made her see him in a different light. In fact, this whole weekend had made her look at him differently, as if she was seeing him for the first time.

"Seriously, thanks for doing this. I owe you one," he said.

"We'll be even as long as they keep your sinful chocolate cake on the menu. I've drowned a lot of bad days in that dessert."

"I'll make sure we add a clause to the contract. Now, what stays down here and what do I need to take up to the house?" He stopped just before they reached the crowd that had started to gather on the beach were the ceremony would be held.

"I'll take this." She pulled Georgia's flowered bag off his shoulder. "Everything else goes up. Thanks." She watched him walk across the sand and up the private wooden staircase that led directly to the Merricks' house. It looked newer and sturdier than the one by their condos, but somehow it lacked the charm that made their weathered staircase so picturesque. What was it about history and familiarity that made her feel extra warm and fuzzy this weekend?

She walked over to where her friends were standing and pulled the bouquet made out of bows from the bag. "You ready for this?"

Georgia beamed as she took the bouquet. "I know it's just practice, but I've been waiting for this since the day I met Lane."

All three girls gave her a questioning look. Georgia and Lane's relationship had started off a little rocky. In fact, Paige remembered a lot of slamming doors and huffing the night Georgia came home and told them she'd met Lane. Or, to be more accurate, she told them she had met the most infuriating man on the planet.

Georgia shrugged. "So maybe not the first day we met."

Ciera pulled the veil out of the bag and tucked the comb into Georgia's hair. "He's one lucky man."

Before they could spend any more time getting caught up in the moment, the wedding coordinator clapped her hands together. "Listen, people, if we want to get through all of this in the hour we have, I'm going to need everyone's cooperation."

Ciera leaned into Paige and whispered. "You don't ever clap your hands at people, do you?"

"I don't think so," Paige whispered back. "But if I ever have, I'm never doing it again."

The wedding drill sergeant snapped her fingers in their direction. "Ladies, your attention, please."

Paige straightened her posture and turned to the lady, pressing her lips together to show she was finished talking. Ciera covered her mouth to hide her giggles and Hadley crossed her arms in front of her chest, looking defiant.

"I'm going to start with just the bride and groom to make sure we have all the important details in line. Attendants, we'll add you in next. Stay close but not in our way. Like over there." She waved her hand as if shooing a bug away from her.

The girls and the three groomsmen turned and walked several

yards in the other direction. "Who does she think she is?" Hadley looked offended. "She knows we've all been to a wedding before, right?"

"I think she's trying to get through all the details in the most efficient manner possible." Paige tried to make her voice cheerful when defending a fellow wedding coordinator, although she had to admit this planner could use a little finesse.

"Just do what she says," Ciera scolded Hadley. "We don't want to ruin Georgia's day."

The wedding coordinator had lowered the booming volume of her voice to a more conversational level, but she still could be heard over all of the other beach noise even at the distance where they were.

"I'm going to need the rings so we can practice putting them on," the bossy coordinator said to Georgia. "It can be tricky in the humidity, and I need to see how they fit so we don't have any issues tomorrow." While Paige agreed about practicing with the rings, it was the kind of thing most planners would have asked instead of demanded.

"I didn't know we would need them. They're in the house. Do you want me to run up and get them?" Georgia jerked her thumb at the house.

The wedding coordinator let out a sigh. "We don't have time for that. It will delay the whole timeline."

Hadley stepped forward. "I know where they are. I'll get them." She jogged for the stairs before anyone could stop her.

The wedding coordinator shook her head, clearly annoyed by the disruption in her schedule. "I guess we'll have to come back to the rings. Let's discuss the vows. Have you written your own?" Before Georgia could answer, the coordinator coughed and waved her hand in front of her face.

"I'm sorry. I can't work like this. What is that horrific smell?" Eager to help keep the rehearsal moving as smoothly as possible,

Paige searched the beach to try to locate anything that might be offending an offending odor. Her gaze swept from the water up the beach and eventually landed on the cloud of smoke drifting down from the wide front porch of the house. Jacob Merrick and the four investors all stood next to the rail with cigars in their hands. Aiden, cigar-less, stood in the middle of them, chatting. It looked like maybe they hadn't exhausted their lunch conversation after all.

Paige pointed to the house and raised her voice. "I'm so sorry about that. Friends of the father of the groom. I'll see if we can move them downwind."

Paige started for the steps, but Ciera caught her arm. "That's a lot of steps for your ankle. You stay here. I'll go." Before Paige could protest, Ciera was off, leaving Paige standing there all by herself.

Or maybe not so by herself. Brody stepped up next to her and slid his hands into the pockets of his navy shorts.

"They should've asked you to do this wedding. You would've done a better job."

"I offered, but Georgia didn't want me to feel like I was at work at her wedding. This lady came highly recommended from local vendors. She's not so bad."

They watched for a second as the wedding coordinator lectured Georgia and Lane on the importance of memorizing their vows and not having to read them off an index card.

Brody gave her a questioning look. "Not so bad? I've seen drill sergeants with more compassion."

He brought up a valid point. "She could stand to work on her people skills, but this part is always stressful."

This easy conversation was the first time Paige had been alone with Brody since they broke up. Sure, they had chatted a couple times since he'd returned, but it was more of exchanging pleasantries in passing. They hadn't stood like this, just the two of them having a real conversation, in over a year.

Standing here with him felt normal in a comfortable sort of way. And yet, she had the vague feeling that something was missing.

"I've been so busy this weekend that we haven't had a chance to catch up. I want to hear about your time in Luxembourg." She turned to look at him. His hair, his smile, the way he stood, everything looked exactly the same. Standing here among their friends in a place where they had all vacationed before, it appeared as if nothing had changed in the year he'd been gone. And yet everything felt different.

"Luxembourg was fun. I did a ton of traveling, lived in a tiny apartment with the smallest refrigerator you've ever seen." He shrugged. "It was good to be on my own for a while, but there's no place like home."

"Hilltop is a special place." She, too, had traveled all over the world. Her mother's career had kept them bouncing back and forth between North America and Europe. She had more stamps in her passport before she was five than most people had in their entire life and had stayed in some of the finest hotels in the world. But she'd never fallen in love with any place the way she had with Hilltop. It had felt like home from the first time she drove in to visit Ciera's family.

"It is," he agreed.

Wait. Somehow, she had managed to accidentally stumble on the moment she'd been waiting for. Here she was, alone with him, talking about the past. They were in stage three of her plan. All she had to do was remind him how she played a major part in his past being so great. She searched her memory for one of their favorite moments together.

"Remember that time we went hiking in Elm Ridge State Park to see the leaves changing and got lost?"

Brody chuckled. The familiar sound caused memories to flood into her mind the same way hearing an old song did. Suddenly, she could remember exactly how it had felt to stand with him. To laugh with him. To dream about the future with him. The memories were comforting but at the same time seemed strangely distant.

"There was a moment there where I thought we were going to have to learn how to live in the wilderness. Those trail markings needed to be more prominent."

"They were kind of hard to see," she agreed.

"I don't think I've been hiking since."

The statement shocked her and pulled her out of reliving the past. "Really? I thought you loved being outdoors."

Brody shrugged. "I like being outside, but not so much in the wilderness. I'm more of a sophisticated outdoorsman."

Paige pictured being among the dolphins in their natural environment yesterday or standing in the middle of that forest where the only sound was the wind rustling through the trees and the birds singing. Those were the moments that spoke to her soul. She couldn't imagine anyone not wanting to experience it.

"But seriously, how have you been?" he asked.

She could tell by the way he looked at her that something had shifted between them. It was a more intimate look, more reminiscent of how he used to look at her when they were together. She waited for the butterflies to kick in the way they used to when she melted under his adoring gaze, but today they were quiet.

"Being the head wedding coordinator at the resort has kept me busy, but it's been good. I'm doing what I love. I can't ask for more."

He studied her, as if he were trying to see inside her head. Or inside her heart. She held his gaze, remembering in vivid detail how much she loved to look at his eyes. They were an intoxicating shade of deep blue. The air between them...well it didn't quite sizzle the way she remembered. It was comfortable, though, which was a good starting place.

"You seem happy," he said finally.

Without meaning to, she glanced up at the house where Aiden

was standing on the porch in the middle of the fog of cigar smoke. He was gesturing and laughing, fully engaged in the conversation around him. Even in the middle of a situation he didn't want to be in, standing amid the smoke she knew he hated, he found a way to have fun. He caught her eye and flashed a smile meant just for her. It hit her right in the chest, the brightness radiating outward until it settled as a smile on her own face.

"I am." She realized she was happier on this trip than she'd been in a long time. She had credited it to being at the beach, watching one of her best friends marry the love of her life, and the chance to reconnect with Brody. But what if it was something else? Something she hadn't planned for?

Ciera walked up the stairs to where Aiden was standing on Jacob's front porch.

"The mean lady on the beach has not so kindly demanded y'all move downwind so she doesn't have to be offended by your stinky cigars."

Aiden glanced down at the action on the beach. The bride and groom looked serious as the wedding coordinator lectured them about something. "That lady has a lot of opinions."

"You're telling me." She nodded at the house. "I'm going to help Hadley find the rings. I think it might take us a while." She winked and disappeared into the house.

"Hey fellas, the wedding party has requested we move down to this end of the porch."

Aiden had one professor in college who told them, one rainy day close to finals, most business deals weren't made in an office with the help of the theory they learned in school. They were made through relationships. Successful business men and women knew the art of conversation, were well read and up to date on social happenings. And it never hurt to have a great golf swing. Aiden took that as permission to skip studying for a round of golf.

And here he was, more than ten years later, trying to close a multimillion-dollar restaurant deal by comparing cigars on the front porch of his partner's beach house. Perhaps the business college needed to look into adding The Art of Schmoozing to their required classes.

"Aiden, tell us again how you came up with the concept of Cedar Break." The investor Aiden had dubbed the ringleader leaned his elbow on the rail and puffed on his cigar.

"An unlucky game of darts, boys." Aiden chuckled and slapped the man on the back, ready to retell the story they'd already heard several times. Jacob gave him a look that told him he really needed to sell it.

"I was complaining to my buddy that Hilltop needed a restaurant that made good comfort food so I could stop making it."

"Were you cooking for your buddy?" another investor asked.

"You bet I was. Everyone wants to eat great food in a place where they feel comfortable. That place for my friends had become my kitchen. If the restaurant thing hadn't worked out, I was thinking about starting to charge them."

That part was one hundred percent true. He'd started cooking all the time. He loved creating new recipes in his kitchen, and since recipes were rarely made for just one person, he was always looking for someone to share it with.

"You should see his place. It's the bachelor pad of your dreams," Jacob added.

Aiden did his best to look modest. If by "dream bachelor pad" Jacob meant giant empty house with a pool table in his dining room, then yes. That's what he had. "I might have a few toys."

"You needed someone to cater for you," the first investor added. Aiden pointed at him. "Exactly. Which is what I told my buddy.

And he said if I thought I was such a good chef, why didn't I open my own restaurant?"

So the actual conversation might have been a little less confrontational, and it was something they'd talked about several times before the infamous dart game. But the basic concept was the same.

"So he challenged me to a round of darts. He won, I'd open my own restaurant and keep feeding him. I won, he had to cook for me for a change."

"Best out of three?" the first investor asked.

"No. This was win or go home. And I gotta tell you, I thought I was about to be out a boatload of money when I watched him throw that final bullseye." Aiden crossed his arms in front of his chest and stared at the ground, shaking his head as if contemplating a tragedy. The whole porch got quiet, enthralled by his theatrics. Then Aiden looked up and grinned. "Luckiest bet I ever lost."

The porch erupted in laughter.

"And the rest, as they say, is history," Jacob closed.

Aiden nodded. "That was the last dinner I cooked for anyone in the kitchen at my house. I got Jacob on board the next day and we opened the doors to Cedar Break a month later."

He left out the part that Jacob came on board very reluctantly and that he didn't cook at his house again because he had to work around the clock in order to get his new restaurant open that quickly. In fact, he was the first head chef because he couldn't afford to hire anyone else in the beginning.

"And now you have your bachelor pad back to yourself."

Aiden nodded and draped his arms over the railing. "Absolutely," he drawled out.

The truth was he missed the days when his house was full of the laughter and company of his best friends, and random freeloaders, sitting around his island. Now, when he came home from the restaurant, the only thing that met him was the empty pool table.

The investor squeezed his shoulder. "You're living the dream."

Padded bank account, thriving business, tricked out bachelor pad. It should be the dream, right?

His gaze drifted down to Paige.

The third investor nodded his head in Paige's direction. "And what about her? Was she around during the bet?"

"No. She's fairly recent."

The investor nodded as if he understood. "You don't look like the type that can be tied down."

Right. He wasn't the type to be tied down. Except, what if being in a relationship wasn't being tied down? What if falling in love was what gave him wings?

It sounded crazy, he knew, but being with Paige this weekend had ignited something inside him he'd never felt before.

The crew kept talking but he tuned them out, all of his attention focused on Paige. The sun glimmered off her hair, making her look as if she was sparkling. Her wide smile spread all the way across her face and radiated through her whole body. Kindness danced in her eyes and her adventurous spirit bounced in every step she took. She was radiant. Just one glance drew you in, made you want to be around her. At least it had for him.

A familiar excitement surged through him, bringing him to life. Being around her had always had that sort of reaction, but on this trip it had been heightened. That Brody character had been a fool. Aiden couldn't imagine being able to move across the globe and leave her behind. But, judging by the way Brody was leaning into her as she was talking to him on the beach, he was going to change his tune very soon. Paige's three-step plan was about to be successful. She was getting what her heart desired, and he was happy for her.

The thought of her with Brody settled like a rock in the pit of his stomach. Soon he would have to give her up. True, she had never really been his to begin with. This whole relationship had been fake, but what he felt when he was around her was real.

She looked up at him for a second time and their eyes met. Even from this distance he could see the golden flecks dancing in her hazel eyes. He had the urge to wrap his arms around her and pull her close to him.

Pretty soon he was going to be a free man. The restaurant would be gone, and he'd go back to being single. But he wasn't tonight, and maybe that was a good thing.

Chapter Twelve

W HEN JACOB MERRICK WANTED TO impress someone, he pulled out all the stops. The rehearsal dinner was no exception. He proclaimed it a night of celebration, and it was clear he'd spared no expense. While Aiden was sure most of the extravagance was intended for his son, at least part of the over-the-top night was meant for the four couples sitting at his table.

Round tables draped in tablecloths with flickering candles in the center had been set up on the beach. A formally dressed waitstaff served made-to-order meals from the Cedar Break's menu. Since there wasn't a kitchen anywhere near the beach, Aiden wondered how they pulled it off. But he had to admit, the chef had done a great job with what he and Paige had both ordered. He would have tried the other entrees at the table, but he thought eating off the investors' plates might be too familiar. Maybe later he would find the kitchen and give his compliments to the chef.

After dessert had been served and the toasts were finished, Jacob got up to thank everyone.

"The night is just getting warmed up. We have a great band and dancing is required." On cue, the small stage just in front of the cliffs lit up and the band started playing. "And stick around because we have plenty of surprises left. You're not going to want to go to bed early tonight."

As soon as he finished speaking, the lead singer launched into a song. The space in front of the stage filled with people dancing.

All of Paige's friends were already out there, and she was moving to the beat in her chair, but she didn't get up. Sitting here making conversation with people she would probably never see again after this weekend was a huge sacrifice for her, but he appreciated every minute of it. She was a fantastic partner and worked a dinner table like a boss. Tonight wouldn't have been as successful, or as enjoyable, if she hadn't been there.

"Who's ready for some dancing?" Aiden rubbed his hands together.

The ringleader leaned back and signaled for their waiter. "I think another round of drinks is required first."

The rest of the table agreed. Paige tried to refresh her smile, but Aiden could tell she was disappointed. Enough. She'd put in her time with these people. It was his job to entertain them, but they would be fine for one drink without him.

"Y'all enjoy that drink. I'm going to take this lovely lady dancing." He stood and held his hand out to Paige. "Shall we?"

She took his hand and followed him to the wooden dance floor set on top of the sand. "Thanks for that."

"I think it's time to play with kids our own age for a while."

She maneuvered her way to the middle of the crowd, among her friends. It didn't matter that there were people moving all around and them, it was as if a spotlight shone directly on her. In the sea full of bobbing, jiving people, she was the only person he could see.

She moved with carefree abandon. She wasn't the best dancer he'd ever seen, but she might have won the award for having the most fun, a trait she spread to everyone within her vicinity. And by the end of the third song, everyone was covered in sweat and smiles.

The band slowed it down and the crowd cleared, some finding a partner, some headed back to their tables. Aiden stepped in front of Paige.

"May I have this dance?" He offered her his hand.

She slid her delicate hand into his. "I thought you'd never ask."

He spun her once, then his hand settled in the spot where her waist met the small of her back. Energy soared through his arms and swirled around his chest, leaving him feeling vibrant and alive. He'd been waiting all day to hold her in his arms. In fact, it felt like he'd been waiting a lot longer than that, although he couldn't quite pinpoint how long. Since they got to Seacrest? Since they decided to start their fake relationship? Did it go even farther back than that?

It didn't matter. He was holding her now. They fell into an easy rhythm with the song.

"Thanks again for tonight. I couldn't have entertained the table without you."

"My pleasure."

"Your stories of growing up in the fashion industry made the night. I had no idea."

"Most people don't. I'm not exactly the poster child for high fashion."

True, she didn't wear the bizarre creations he normally associated with Fashion Week, but that didn't make her any less stunning. She was strong, brave, and adventurous, qualities that drew people to her. They were the qualities that drew him to her. Every second he spent with her left him wanting more. More time with her. More conversations with her. More laughing with her.

"If you ask me, they'd be lucky to have you as their poster child."

She laughed, not taking him seriously. "Hmm. Which part do you think they'd like best? My windblown, messy hair, or the fact that there's not a trace of my lipstick left and I forgot to bring the tube with me to refresh it?"

"Let me see."

He added some space between them and pretended to study her with a mock seriousness.

Her soft lips were pulled up in an infectious grin. He didn't know a thing about lipstick shades, but he did know that her lips were inviting. He was overcome with the urge to press his own lips against them, to feel for himself how soft and sweet they were. He moved on quickly before he got lost in the impulse.

Her hair was swept up on top of her head, showing off her long neck and the creamy skin around her collarbone, which wasn't helping his urge to kiss her. At all.

He moved on to her eyes, which, perhaps, he liked the best. They were compassionate and kind, not to mention the most alluring color he'd ever seen. It was as if someone had taken the richest shades of blue, green and brown and swirled them together.

His breath caught in his chest and the rest of the world faded away. It was as if he were seeing her, truly seeing her, for the first time. And now that he had, it was impossible to look away. An emotion stronger than any he'd ever felt pulsed through him.

There weren't even words to describe how captivating she was, so he went with the best one he could think of.

"You are perfect." His voice came out in a husky whisper.

Her expression changed from her playful smile into something more serious, as if she'd been caught off guard. He wanted to explore her expression some more, but he couldn't stand it any longer. He had to hold her closer.

He slid his hand around the small of her back and pulled her into him.

Aiden's words swirled around Paige, blocking out everything else happening around them.

Perfect? There were a lot of things she *did* that were perfect. She'd graduated college with a perfect 4.0 GPA; she had a perfect driving record. It might be subjective, but she would argue that, with Aiden's help, she'd constructed the perfect ice cream flavor earlier today. But *being* perfect? Never in her entire life had she ever been in the running for that.

She was glad he'd pulled her close so he couldn't see the way his words made her face flush. An emotion danced in her chest, filling her with brightness. In his arms, she felt like she was floating, and she had to glance at the sand to make sure they were still standing on the ground.

"Thanks," she managed to squeak out. Why did it feel so right to be in his arms?

She searched her memory for a time when she'd danced with Aiden before, but she came up empty. She'd known him for years, been at hundreds of events with him, probably spent thousands of hours with him, but she couldn't remember a time when he'd held her. At least not like this. And now that she knew what it was like to be in his arms, her body ached for all the years she'd missed this.

They swayed and spun under the light of the twinkling stars, yet it felt they were twinkling insider her. The melody of one of her favorite songs drifted through the air behind them. It was as if she were in a dream. Reality seemed worlds away. She knew there were other people around them. Last she checked, there were many couples on the dance floor, but right now she would've sworn they were the only two people on the beach.

She thought about saying something, coming up with some clever comment that would spark the witty banter they usually shared, but right now she didn't want to. Right now, all she wanted to do was to be held in his arms, let the world fall away and soak in the feeling of being cherished.

Closing her eyes, she melted in to his embrace. She did her best to memorize every single sensation. She wanted to remember the way his woodsy scent mixed with the salt air, the way his rough cheek felt pressed against hers, the way the gentle touch of his hand on her back sent shivers straight up her spine. Most of all, she wanted to remember the way his heart seemed to beat in perfect rhythm with hers.

The song ended and she drew in one last breath, trying to hold on to the feeling as long as possible. Aiden stepped back and she stared into his eyes. The air between them crackled.

"Who knew Aiden Pierce was an amazing dancer? Any other hidden talents I should know about?" It was a weak attempt at a joke, but it at least earned her one of his charming crooked grins. The band launched into another fast song and the dance floor filled up again. Any second now the spell Aiden had cast over her would break and she would come back to reality.

"You question my dancing ability? Baby, you ain't seen nothing yet." He winked, sending another wave of excitement crashing over her. He grabbed her hand and pulled her into the middle of the crowd, spun her once and then broke into a spirited rendition of disco fever. He did the moves with such passion that everyone circled around to watch, including Paige, who couldn't help but notice she was still very much under his spell.

When he got through one rotation, he held out his hand to her.

"Come on, Smoochems, show 'em what you got."

"I'm not sure I got those kinds of moves."

"Not with that kind of attitude." He grabbed her hand and pulled her toward him. "It's all in the hips."

"Don't say I didn't warn you." She stood next to him and waited for the beat. Then they started dancing. She followed his lead, keeping her gaze locked with his. She did the first move with a bit of hesitation, the way she normally would when all eyes were on her. Being in the spotlight was not her gift. She kept expecting the elated feeling from their shared dance to fall away, stealing her newfound confidence. But instead, a strange thing happened.

There was this way he looked at her, a hint of some expression she couldn't quite identify, that ignited something inside her. The warm, tingling feeling in her chest spiraled through her until giddy excitement filled her whole body. She tipped her head back and laughed. For the moment, she let go of every insecurity holding her back and danced like no one was watching. The crowd around them clapped to the beat. She wasn't even sure who was in the crowd, if it was her friends, or his investors, or even Brody. Her eyes never left Aiden and she remained fully submerged in whatever spell she was under.

Eventually they danced themselves out of the circle, letting someone else take a turn showing off moves. One song faded into the next, which faded into the next. Somewhere along the way, she was aware of the throbbing in her ankle, but she didn't want to stop the magic, so she did her best to dance with all her weight on her good leg. Aiden seemed to notice and stood on her bad side, allowing her to lean on him.

There were two more slow songs, each more magical than the one before it, and more fast songs than she could count. She was dripping with sweat when Lane's parents took the stage.

"We have one last surprise before we break this party up and send everyone home to get their beauty rest for tomorrow. To celebrate this momentous occasion, we're going to light the night sky with eco-friendly wish lanterns."

Jacob handed the microphone to his wife. "Lanterns are lined up along the water. Choose one and write a wish for the wedding couple on one side and a wish for yourself on the other. When everyone is finished, we'll light the candles and send them floating up into eternity."

All along the shore, just above where the waves rolled to a stop, the white paper lanterns were set out in a neat line with three or four feet between each one. The band played softly while each of the guests spread out to claim one. Paige leaned on Aiden's shoulder and limped down the beach. Since it took them longer, they had to walk all the way to the last ones.

It was darker and quieter down here. The light from the tiki torches and twinkle lights strung around the party area faded away, and laughter that had surrounded them on the dance floor drifted out to sea. Down here, at the end, the sound of the waves became more predominant.

"Tonight has been magical. The Merricks have outdone themselves." Paige picked up the lantern and examined the blank paper sides.

"It's Jacob's goal to outdo everyone." His voice sounded jaded, and even though his attention was on his lantern, he had the same worried expression he got when they were talking about the restaurant deal. Something was bothering him.

She looked up at him, studying his expression in the moonlit darkness. "Is everything going okay with the investors?"

He fiddled with the candle in his lantern, his jaw tight, seemingly lost in thought. Then he looked up and his expression softened.

"It's great. But let's not talk about business. Tonight is about Georgia and Lane. What do you wish for them?"

Paige pulled off the marker that was attached to the top of the lantern and tapped it against her chin. "Not sure. It needs to be something as amazing as they are."

"Live long and prosper?" He offered.

"Hummm. Maybe something a little more encouraging."

"May the force be with you."

She tried to give him a stern look, but she couldn't help but crack a smile. "How about something more optimistic?"

"To infinity and beyond."

This time she giggled. "You're hopeless." She stared out over the water and thought.

"Oh, I got it." She pulled the cap off the marker with her teeth and wrote out the beautiful wish, pausing to make sure she got the wording just right. When she finished, she looked up.

Aiden was watching her with an expression she could only describe as adoring and it made her pulse quicken.

"What?"

"After all the weddings you've had to attend, you still treat every one of them as if they're the most special."

"Every wedding is the most special. There's nothing more beautiful than seeing a couple promise their forevers to each other in front of their friends and family." Her heart swelled at the thought of it. "Getting to be part of it, no matter the role, is an honor."

"You want to read me what you wrote?"

Paige reread the words she'd written on her lantern and shook her head. "No. These words are just for them."

She looked up and met his intense gaze, and he took a step closer. She swallowed hard in an attempt to keep her surging emotions under control.

"What kind of wish do you have for yourself?" His low, deep voice reverberated through her and it felt like there was a magnetic force pulling her closer to him, perhaps even back into his arms. She took a tiny step closer, not sure how much longer she could fight it.

"I can't tell you. If I do, then it won't come true."

She wanted to focus on his eyes or his hair or the collar of his shirt. Really, she would've settled for looking at anything that could've fallen in the friendly category. Since that was what they were. Friends.

Instead, the only thing she could focus on was the way his crooked grin caused her heart to do flip-flops. The magnetic pull strengthened and she positioned her lantern between them in case she lost the battle with it.

"I'll tell you mine if you tell me yours." He waggled his eyebrows. She was overcome with the desire to kiss him, to be kissed by him. To be lost in his embrace. She had to grip the lantern with both hands to keep herself from moving.

"Nope. Doesn't work that way. Wishes are very particular."

Aiden shrugged and turned his focus to his lantern. "Just offering."

Brody. This whole weekend, the only reason she was standing here with Aiden, was to get back what she had with Brody. Her wish was for a happily ever after with Brody. Wasn't it?

She turned her lantern over and stared at the blank space where her wish was to go. There was only one thing that needed to go in that space. In her heart of hearts, she'd known all along what she wanted to write there. Excitement sparkled through her as she scribbled the words across the paper.

"It must be a good wish," he said.

"It is." The thought of it made her overflow with joy. She hugged the lantern against her chest, guarding the words and clinging with all her might to the last thing standing between her and Aiden. The magic of the night had cast a spell over her, one so powerful she couldn't resist it.

"Your turn," she said. "You have to write your wish."

He pulled the cap off with his teeth, then his gaze turned away from her for the first time during this whole conversation. She'd hoped it would break the force pulling her into him, or at the very least lessen it. Instead it strengthened.

He wrote without hesitation but only a few letters, maybe three or four. His gaze returned to hers and remained locked on her as he put the cap back on the pen. The heat in the air between them sizzled all the way through her.

"You didn't write much." She could hardly breathe.

"Didn't need to." His smirk made it look as if he knew a secret. One she was dying to know. She swallowed hard, again.

"More movie quotes?"

He shook his head. "Can't tell. Wishes are very particular."

She was in trouble. Alone, on a dark beach with nothing but

two paper lanterns stopping her from finding out exactly what it would feel like to kiss Aiden Pierce.

"Can I light your candles?" The assistant wedding director appeared beside her, holding up a candle lighter. Both of them turned to looked at her. Paige couldn't decide if she was thankful for the distraction or if she should tell her to walk away, immediately.

"Light her up." Aiden held his lantern out to her.

"Hold on to them until we get everyone lit. We'll do a big countdown and launch at the same time."

Paige nodded her understanding and glanced down the beach to see the wedding coordinator lighting the lanterns at the other end where most of her friends had ended up. Slowly the beach began to glow.

Jacob's voice over the microphone broke the silence as he counted down from five. Paige took a step closer to the water in preparation to launch.

Four.

The cool waves washed over her toes and her feet sunk in the sand. For the first time, she didn't care if her sandals got wet. In fact, there was only one thing she did care about right now.

Three.

Aiden stepped up next to her. Close enough that his shoulder grazed hers in a way that sent shivers through her whole body.

Two.

As hard as she tried, she couldn't keep her focus on her lantern. She had to look at him. His gaze burned through her, the magnetic pull strengthening to the point where she couldn't resist it any more.

One.

They mouthed the words in unison. Her eyes stayed locked with his. They held out their lanterns. A gentle ocean breeze blew through her hair, skimming over her skin. With a slight toss upwards, she took her hands off of her wish. Aiden did the same.

The heat from the candles and the sea breeze lifted the lanterns up and into the night.

All along the beach, the lanterns floated out over the waves, twinkling against the dark sky. The soft music from the band drifted around them. The whole scene seemed to be out of a dream, especially whatever was happening between her and the man standing next to her.

Aiden slid his hand around her waist. It was warm and confident. Without the lanterns, there was nothing standing between them now, not that it mattered. The force pulling her to him was so strong there wasn't anything that could stop it. She took a tiny sidestep closer to him.

He turned to face her, his eyes searching hers.

"What an amazing sight."

She couldn't say for sure if he was referring to the view of the flickering lanterns floating into the darkness or if he was talking about her. What she did know for sure was that while the night sky was nice, the sight she was enamored with was the man standing in front of her.

Aiden slid his free hand behind her neck and his thumb gently caressed her cheek. Exhilaration shot through her. He was going to kiss her. She leaned into him and closed her eyes in eager expectation of his lips pressing against hers. Maybe wishes did come true.

"Paige."

The sound of her name coming from behind her jarred her back to reality, forcing her eyes open. Startled, she stepped away from him and turned to the voice. Aiden caressed the side of her cheek with his thumb one last time before he pulled his hand away. As if by reflex her hand covered her lips, which were still tingling with anticipation.

She turned to see that Ciera was walking toward them with Jacob Merrick on her heels. Paige hoped she didn't have the guilty look of a kid with her hand in the cookie jar. Although in this particular situation, her hand had never actually been in the cookie jar and she wished she could shoo away the intruders so she could finish what she started.

Or maybe it was a good thing they were interrupted before they got carried away. This was only a fake relationship, after all. The only reason she was even standing in this spot with tingling lips and surging emotions was because of her wish to be kissing Brody again. Right?

"Georgia's ready to head back. She wants to get plenty of rest before tomorrow." Ciera's questioning look went from Paige to Aiden and back to Paige.

"Right. Let's go, then." She had every intention of walking away from Aiden, but her feet didn't move. Perhaps it was because the cool waves felt so good against her ankles and she liked the way her toes felt sunk down in the soft, wet sand. But more than likely, it was because standing next to Aiden just felt right. So right, she wasn't sure she wanted to leave.

"It's pretty dark out here. Why don't I drive the four of you back?" Aiden offered.

"Actually, I just invited the investors up for a nightcap at our house. I need you to get them started while I finish up here." Jacob shot Aiden a look that left little room for questioning.

"Georgia wants to walk back anyway. One last time for us all to be together." Ciera's voice might have sounded sweet, but she gave Jacob a look that said no one bossed her brother around like that. Except for maybe her.

"That works out, then." Aiden lightly kissed Paige's cheek. It wasn't exactly the kind of kiss she'd been hoping for, but it sent electricity racing through her anyway. She needed this long, moonlit walk on the quiet beach to help break whatever spell she was under.

"Be safe," he said to Paige, then he turned his gaze to his sister. "And Cici, text me when you get there."

He took three large steps until he was away from Paige and standing next to Jacob. "Let's go pour some drinks."

Jacob slapped him on the shoulder, looking quite pleased with himself, and they headed up the beach to the stairs. Paige walked with Ciera along the shore to where their friends were waiting for them.

"Looks like you and my brother are taking your roles seriously."

"Trying to make it look authentic." Paige avoided looking directly at her best friend, the one person who was able to tell if she was hiding something. Not that she was hiding anything.

"That's good, because you know Aiden doesn't do commitments. Like, ever."

"I know," Paige said, forcing herself not to glance over her shoulder in his direction. The excitement of tonight still pulsed through her.

"I mean, I love my brother and all, but the guy never even had a favorite stuffed animal growing up."

"Yep, he always says he likes to keep his options open." She tried to bring herself back to reality, to remember that she was walking on the sand and not in the clouds, but she couldn't help it. Being around Aiden filled her with the kind of joy that made her feel buoyant and she wasn't quite ready to come down.

"His average relationship lasts one date. He's the king of keeping things casual, if it even gets that far."

"Mm-hmm," Paige agreed. Of course she knew Aiden kept things casual, but tonight hadn't felt casual. The way he looked at her tonight and the way her spirit soared when she was in his arms felt real. It felt like it could've been the beginning of something that could last. Maybe…

"Forever isn't in his vocabulary," Ciera continued.

Forever. The words Paige wrote on her lantern flashed into her mind. A heaviness tugged at her chest, forcing her back to reality. Of course Aiden didn't do forever. Everyone who knew him could testify to that. One great evening wasn't going to change that, regardless of what was or wasn't written on a wish lantern.

"Ciera, I know." Paige said the words more forcefully this time, but she had a feeling the frustration in her voice was meant more for herself than for her friend.

Ciera stopped walking and faced Paige. Her voice was gentle and understanding. "My brother is a great guy, but he makes a really lousy boyfriend." She laid her hand on Paige's arm, a look of genuine concern written all over her face. "You're my best friend, and I know the kind of all-in relationship you're looking for. I just don't want to see you get hurt."

Paige let her friend's concern wash over her, hoping it would dull her aching disappointment. So maybe Paige had allowed herself to get a little carried away. Twinkle lights and slow dances sometimes had that effect.

"We're just friends," she said. Friends who, perhaps, had gotten a little caught up in the romance of a wedding. But absolutely nothing more.

Chapter Thirteen

I F ANY OF THEM WERE still floating on the elation from the rehearsal dinner the night before, it was quickly squashed as soon as Georgia's phone rang at exactly nine a.m. the next morning.

Paige hadn't paid any attention to the phone conversation, as she assumed it was some well-wisher calling to offer happy sentiments on the morning of her big day. It wasn't until Georgia hung up that anyone realized there was a problem.

After she clicked off, Georgia sat motionless in her chair. She stared straight ahead, her face void of any expression, and she clutched her phone in her hand.

"Honey, what's wrong?" Ciera asked.

"The hairstylist has food poisoning," she reported. "She can't come."

The whole balcony got quiet for a second as they all considered this news. Ciera and Hadley both looked to Paige with wide-eyed, worried expressions.

"I know that's a disappointment, but we'll find a way to fix it." It was Paige's wedding planner tagline for any problem that came up. She delivered it with the same calm confidence she used with all her brides, only this time it took a lot more effort. Georgia wasn't just any bride, she was one of Paige's best friends. Her wedding deserved to be more perfect than any other Paige had been a part of.

"She was supposed to be here in four hours." Tears were starting to well up in Georgia's eyes.

"That's plenty of time," Paige added. So maybe plenty was a stretch, but they still had some time, which was positive. "We'll figure this out."

Ciera sprang into action. "Absolutely. Paige is the best at this kind of stuff. You have nothing to worry about." She took Georgia's phone from her hands and laid it on the table before she wrapped her arm around her friend's shoulders. "Why don't you go take a long, hot shower. By the time you're done, we'll have a new plan."

"I guess a shower was next on my list," Georgia muttered. She reluctantly pushed her chair away from the round patio table on the balcony. "You sure you've got this?" She looked at Paige with pleading eyes.

"Of course she's got this, and Hadley's here to help her. Have you ever seen Hadley on one of her job sites when a contractor hasn't gotten his job done? The woman doesn't take no for an answer. She always gets her projects completed on time." Ciera opened the sliding glass door and waited for Georgia to go in before her. "I have total confidence in those two."

Hadley waited until the door closed behind Georgia and Ciera before she turned to Paige. "I don't have confidence in us. Making sure my cabinet guy gets his installs done on time is not even in the same ball park as finding a new hair and makeup person. Tell me you have a plan."

Paige chewed on her lip, trying not to let her panic take over. "I don't know anyone in this town. No one here owes me any favors."

"So what do we do?"

Paige picked up her phone and started tapping. "Google every hairstylist in town and hope we can find someone who's available."

After thirty minutes and more than twenty names, Paige waited for Hadley to finish up her conversation with the last stylist on their list.

"Any luck?" she asked when Hadley clicked off.

Hadley shook her head and drew a line through that name. "Nope. Looks like our only maybe was the one who could fit her in at three if we drove to her salon that's forty-five minutes away. Georgia would be late to her own wedding." She tossed the pen on the table and leaned back in her chair with a frustrated huff. "How are you at doing hair?"

Paige buried her face in her hands. "This is a disaster."

"Is it time to panic yet?"

Paige had already started to panic. In a few short hours, Georgia would walk down the aisle surrounded by her friends and family to...

"Wait." Paige looked, a new idea forming in her mind. "Georgia's cousin is staying in the condo right below ours, right? The one who snores?"

Hadley's face scrunched up with confusion. "I think so. Why?"

"Her last-minute roommate, Sasha, went to cosmetology school."

"You're going to ask Sasha to help us out?" Georgia questioned.

Paige grabbed her phone off the table and headed for the front door. "Desperate times call for desperate measures. Wish me luck."

She jogged down the steps, typing a quick text message as she went. This had to work. It was the last option. She paused to catch her breath, then knocked on the door.

After a painfully long wait, the door swung open to reveal Georgia's cousin, still wearing her pajamas.

"Morning, Elle," Paige said in her most cheerful voice. "Is Sasha here?"

Elle shot her a questioning look. "Sasha?"

"Mm-hmm." Paige tried to stay optimistic, although she was starting to second guess her plan. "I need a favor. Well, technically, Georgia needs a favor."

"What does Georgia need from Sasha?" Elle asked, sounding confused and perhaps a little offended.

Paige wanted to tell her she should feel blessed to be left out of helping with this little dilemma. But before she got the chance, Sasha passed by the door clutching a coffee cup in her hands. A glimmer of hope cut through some of Paige's tension. Maybe this disaster was going to work out after all.

Paige waved to her. "Good morning, Sasha. I have a huge favor to ask you."

"Sure. What do you need?"

She appeared to be dressed to go somewhere. Her long hair fell in perfect auburn waves. She wore a sundress that seemed to be custom tailored for her. The only indication that she wasn't about to walk out the door were her pink bunny slippers. Paige hoped she was willing to change whatever plans had prompted her to get ready.

"The stylist Georgia hired to do her hair and makeup is sick. We've called everyone in the area, but no one has any availability."

"That's awful," Elle said. "What's she going to do?"

Nervousness fluttered in Paige's gut and she clasped her hands in front of her to keep herself from fidgeting.

"Well, since Sasha has experience doing hair and makeup, I was hoping she could help us out?" She shifted her gaze to Sasha. "Georgia would be incredibly grateful. We all would be." She bit her lip and held her breath. This was their final long shot to get someone to help them. If Sasha declined, Paige, Ciera, and Hadley would be in charge of Georgia's hair. Paige didn't even want to think about what it would look like.

"Just Georgia?"

The question made Paige's spirits soar. The door hadn't been slammed in her face, which she was embarrassed to admit she was fearing. Sasha had no reason to want to help them out. In fact, she had every reason to want to avoid Paige. But she hadn't said no.

"If you take care of Georgia, the rest of us can do our own."

"Right now?"

Paige couldn't decide if that was a positive response or not.

"She has to be ready for the wedding at three-thirty. So whenever you think you need to start is fine. We'll work around your schedule."

Sasha shrugged and sipped her coffee. What did that mean? Was that a yes shrug or a you're-on-your-own shrug? Paige was too afraid to ask. Vision of the coiffure disaster she would be responsible for if this task was left to her flashed in her mind.

"We'll get you anything you need," she begged. "Well, at least anything that you can find at the closest Walmart. Make us a list and Aiden will be here any second to go get everything on it." She was desperate. Nervousness twisted in the pit of her stomach and she shifted her weight from one leg to the other, unable to stand still.

Sasha stared at the sky as if she were thinking about something. Finally, she took a sip of her coffee. "It would probably be easier if I just went with him. Does she have a picture of what she wants?"

Paige froze. "You're saying yes?"

"Sure. I don't have anything else to do today, Brody—"

"Thank you, thank you, thank you." She threw her arms around Sasha. She wanted to sing or to jump around, but since Sasha seemed a little caught off guard at the embrace, she forced herself to let go and step back. "You're a life saver. Georgia will be so relieved."

Sasha sipped her coffee again as if this was just another normal morning for her. Paige's phone buzzed in her hand, diverting her attention.

"Aiden is on his way and you're more than welcome to go with him. Do you want me to text you when he gets here?"

Sasha glanced down at her clothes. "Sure. I probably need to get ready. I can't go out looking like this."

Besides the bunny slippers, Sasha looked more than ready to show up at any event. With some blinged-out jewelry, she could have even passed as ready for the wedding. Paige tried not to think about the wildly messy bun that sat on top of her own head or the fact that the only beauty regimen she'd done so far this morning was brush her teeth.

"Take all the time you need. Why don't you text us when you're ready?"

Sasha flashed a friendly smile, one that made Paige wonder if they had misjudged her in the beginning. She tried to push away the thought before it made her think about Brody and what that would mean for trying to win him back. "What time should Georgia be ready for you?"

"She needs to be camera-ready at three-thirty."

Well, wedding-ready, but Paige didn't feel the need to correct her. Sasha pursed her lips together and looked up at the sky again. "If we start at one I'll have plenty of time to do everyone's hair and both hair and makeup for Georgia. Will that work?"

"That would be amazing. We'll be ready at one o'clock."

"Oh, and can you text me a picture of what she wants? That will help me know what I need to get."

"I'll go get it right now."

Paige almost ran into Aiden when she left the condo.

"You rang, my dear?" His crooked grin made her heart do the strange flip-flop thing again. Or perhaps it was the intense relief of not having to spend the afternoon trying to help Georgia fix her hair for the most important day of her life.

"Thanks for getting here so fast. Am I keeping you from something?"

He followed her up the last flight of stairs to her condo.

"Only sitting in a cabana with a bunch of dudes trying to remind everyone else that they're masters of the universe."

"Have you told them how you are cornhole champion of Hilltop, Texas? Surely that would put you in the running."

Aiden faked a look of disappointment. "I was just about to when I had to leave. Now they may never know."

"On the bright side, you get to take Sasha to Walmart to buy her anything she needs in the beauty department."

"Considering the alternative, it sounds amazing. But may I ask why?"

She stuck her head in the door to make sure all of her roommates were fully dressed before she opened it all the way for Aiden to follow her in. "There was a slight hair and makeup emergency, and Sasha is going to get us out of it."

An hour and two hundred dollars later, Aiden delivered Sasha and a car full of hair products back to the condos. Ciera and Paige met them at the door.

Ciera grabbed Sasha's hand. "We're so glad you're here. Come on in. Hadley just got lunch and you have to eat first." The two girls disappeared into the condo.

Aiden was left standing on the front porch holding blue bags full of Sasha's purchases. He held them out to Paige.

"You now have things I didn't even know were things."

She took one of the bags from him and peeked into it.

"I probably don't know what most of this stuff is." She pulled one contraption out of the bag and held it up to examine it before she dropped it back in the bag. "Thanks for taking her to run the errand. I owe you big-time."

"My pleasure. But I think you're the one who saved the day."

Paige waved off the compliment as she continued to rifle through the contents in the bag. "Georgia deserves for her day to be perfect. And apparently that requires buying one of these." Paige held up something that looked like a strange mix between a curling iron and a hair dryer.

Aiden held up his hand in defense. "I don't even pretend to know what kind of contraptions you ladies need."

Paige pulled a lipstick out of the bag and read the label on the bottom. "As my mom would say, it's all in the name of beauty."

She dropped the lipstick back into the bag and took the other bag from him. "Thanks for stepping up to help us out of this mess."

"Playing Uber driver was nothing. You're a good friend to set this all up."

Paige rifled through the contents of the second bag. "Georgia, Ciera, and Hadley are my best friends. This is a small thing compared to what any of them would do for me."

Finally, she looked up from the bags. "I better get these inside. See you at the wedding?" With a smile, she disappeared into the condo.

He spent the rest of the afternoon at the beach club with the investors, trying to not think about Paige. But the more he tried to not think about her, the more he did. Everything reminded him of her. No one smiled the way she did or listened with the same attention as she gave. The conversations seemed a little duller without her around. Even the ocean's sparkle didn't seem as radiant.

She'd even given friendship a different meaning. The investors claimed to be friends. They claimed they started working together because of their friendship, but they didn't have the kind of friendship Paige talked about. Aiden had the feeling that any one of them would throw any other under the bus if the money was right. It was a depressing thought.

He had a lot of friends. He liked to think of himself as a nice guy who was fun to be around. He never was short on invitations to do things or lacked people to call to hang out with him, but did he have someone who thought of him as his best friend?

His college buddies promised a good time when they were

around, but he could go months without talking to them. He saw his golfing buddies at least once or twice a week, but he didn't know much about them other than their favorite brand of ball and what kind of beer they drank.

A year ago, shoot, even last week, he would've said he was okay with that. It was the way he liked it. His life was about having fun, enjoying experiences, being active. Maybe it meant he never got too involved. He never had a business he couldn't let go of. He never found himself in a relationship he couldn't walk away from. If having fun meant keeping things casual, he was okay with it.

But this week he'd begun to rethink that decision. Paige had him wondering if keeping things casual was making him miss out.

It had been a day of chaos, but thanks to Sasha and Aiden, Paige thought everything was going to work out for Georgia's perfect day. Both Ciera and Hadley had gotten their hair done, and then Sasha had taken a break from hair to do Georgia's makeup. That way, according to Sasha, her face would be done when the photographer showed up to take pictures of her getting ready.

Now it was Paige's turn.

"You're up," Sasha said and patted the swivel bar stool they had moved in front of the sliding glass window as their salon setup.

The thought of sitting in the "salon chair" had made her uncomfortable all day, mostly because she would be alone with Sasha. While they weren't exactly enemies, they were certainly on opposing sides. Sasha had what Paige wanted, and this whole weekend had been about taking it back. Naturally, that made things a little awkward between them.

But she'd avoided it as long as possible. Paige reluctantly slid into the chair. The sooner they got started, the sooner she could get it over with. Plus, she had the lovely view of the ocean to focus on. Sasha picked up a brush from the console table they had moved over to hold all her supplies and pulled it through Paige's hair. Since the other three girls had all gone downstairs to greet some of their friends who had just arrived, the condo was extra quiet. The silence between them made Paige feel more uncomfortable than she already was. She needed to say something.

"Thanks again for doing this."

"No problem. I was glad to have something to do today."

There was silence again as Sasha continued brushing Paige's hair. She fidgeted with the hem of her shorts, trying to think of some common ground they could talk about.

"I hear you got a major role in a TV series. Congratulations."

"Thanks." Sasha didn't sound as excited as Paige would have expected. "It turns out it's not quite the big deal my agent made it out to be. It's for a small network, and so far they've only picked up the first eight episodes." She picked up one of the curling irons and wrapped the first section of Paige's hair around it.

"Still, you're doing what you love, which is a great accomplishment."

"In a way, I guess." Sasha moved to the next section of hair.

"Did you always want to be a wedding planner?"

Out of instinct Paige shook her head no, not remembering that she was connected to a scorching hot iron. It pulled her hair and burned her scalp. She froze in her place to avoid any more harm. Sasha released her hair from the wand.

"Oops. Sorry about that. I've never been very good at playing beauty shop. I'm guaranteed at least one burn every time the curling iron comes out," Paige said.

Sasha giggled. "I had that problem when I was in school. I never realized how much I move my head when I talk until I had a curling wand attached to it." She brushed out the piece of hair she had been working on and rewrapped it around the wand.

Paige realized it was the first time she'd heard Sasha laugh all weekend. It was an interesting fact that begged to be explored deeper, but today Paige didn't want to go deeper—especially when it came to Sasha Kane. Or while she was sitting in this chair.

"To answer your question with words, no, I didn't always want to be a wedding planner. I started off in the accounting department of guest services, but it turned out that I had a knack for planning events. And since I love weddings, this job was a perfect fit."

Talking about the thing she loved to do lifted her spirits and she started feeling more confident in the salon chair. Just a smidge.

"You're very good at it. You did a great job on my friend's wedding, especially dealing with her impossible mother. Please tell me she was the most difficult woman you've ever encountered."

Memories of some of the most difficult brides and mothers floated to the front of her mind. "She would make the list, but I have some stories."

"After some of the actresses I have worked with, I can only imagine. I once worked with an actress who demanded that all her water be exactly forty-eight degrees. They had to bring in a wine cooler just to chill her water bottles."

Was she starting to connect with Sasha? The idea was jolting and comforting at the same time. Instead of fighting it, she gave in to it and launched into one of her favorite demanding bride stories.

"I once had a bride who forbade any of her guests to carry loose change because it might jingle and distract from the wedding. We had to stand outside the doors with labeled baggies and collect it from everyone." Paige visualized the decorated lockbox the bride had provided them to store the money. There was a picture of it in their office just to remind her that no request was too ludicrous.

"Seriously? People forked over their change?" Sasha sprayed sections of her hair and wrapped it around a different kind of curling wand.

"All but two old crotchety men. Wedding guests are surprisingly compliant."

"It's probably because the atmosphere of love puts everyone in a good mood."

"Love is a powerful thing." Love had certainly caused her to do crazy things this weekend. Fake relationships. Three-step plans. Sitting in a chair letting "the other woman" do her hair for her best friend's wedding.

Paige was so caught up in her own thoughts that she almost missed that Sasha got unusually quiet as well. The silence made her uneasy.

"I was hoping the love of this wedding would work its magic for me this weekend," Sasha said.

It felt like the beginning of a deep, personal conversation. As the person working to end Sasha's relationship, was she allowed to be part of this kind of conversation? It seemed like it should be illegal, like insider trading or something. Paige's first instinct was to jump out of their makeshift salon chair and race out the door. But since she was connected to the storyteller by a hair-pulling, scalp-burning stick, she was forced to stay where she was and offer the most non-committal response she could think of. "Oh?"

Sasha let out a big sigh and twisted the next section of hair a little tighter than she had before. "When we first met in Europe, I thought we really connected. We were only together for a couple of days, but I felt like there was something there, you know?"

There was a pause as she released the pressure from the curl she was on and moved to the next strand. "Then when I found out I would be moving to the same area where he lived, I assumed it was kismet. He took me out on our first official date the same day I pulled into town."

There was a pause, as if Sasha was considering what to say next. Or even if she should share anything else.

Do not engage, do not engage, do not engage.

While Paige could appreciate Sasha's struggle, it wasn't her job to help her ex-boyfriend's new fling figure out why their relationship wasn't working. Surely Sasha had other friends to talk this through with, didn't she? Paige was only there to get her hair done, and all she had to do was sit still and stay quiet for just a little longer.

But apparently it didn't matter what Paige's brain thought was the best way to avoid an awkward conversation she felt sure she shouldn't be a part of. Her mouth did what it wanted.

"And when you officially started dating that initial connection didn't seem to be there anymore?"

Sasha exhaled, as if she'd been waiting to share this with someone. "No. At least not like it was in Europe. So when he asked if I wanted to come this weekend, I agreed, thinking maybe a trip to the beach would help us find our spark."

"A beach wedding is a great place to rekindle a romance." She should know. It had been her plan, too.

"That's what I thought. But honestly, I didn't factor in being here with you."

Had Sasha caught on to her plan? It was naive to think that she wouldn't. Getting one's old boyfriend back was a lot easier when you didn't know the other woman.

Not sure what to do, she decided to play dumb. "Me?" Perhaps it was a cowardly move, but she did need Sasha to fix Georgia's hair. She was a despicable human being. Georgia better have the most amazing wedding pictures ever.

Sasha finally put down the curling iron and started twisting her hair up, securing it with bobby pins.

"It's one thing being compared to the memory of you. But side by side in person? It's been hard to measure up."

Was she joking? This knockout beauty with the perfect figure and graceful movements was nervous about being compared to Paige?

"Hard to measure up to me?"

Paige had no idea what was being done to her hair. It felt like there were pins all over her head, but she didn't dare move. This conversation had her frozen in place.

"You're smart and funny and kind. Everyone loves being around you." She paused and stuck what felt like fifteen more pins in Paige's hair. "It's hard to compete with all that."

Paige was stunned. After all the things that she had done to look ridiculous, Sasha was jealous of her?

"Hold this over your face, I'm going to spray your hair."

Sasha handed her a small towel, which Paige held over her face. Never had she been so thankful for hairspray in her whole life. Hiding behind the cloth gave her the perfect excuse to not say anything, which worked out since she couldn't think of anything to say.

Sasha sprayed, stopped to fiddle with a few pieces of Paige's hair, then sprayed again. She took the towel back and laid it on the side table, stepping in front of Paige to examine her. Paige sat absolutely still.

She fixed a few stray pieces of hair before she stepped back, a proud smile lighting up her face.

"All done. You look great, if I do say so myself." She gave Paige a handheld mirror.

Paige took a deep breath before she looked into the mirror. She barely recognized the reflection that stared back to her. Somehow, the way her hair was piled on her head with curls falling down changed the shape of her face.

"You know, if you used a brown eyeliner, it would really make your eyes pop. I think I have some in my bag if you want to try it."

Paige seemed to have entered some sort of alternate reality. One where Sasha was jealous of her. And they were friends.

"You're very talented." Paige tried to angle the mirror so she could see the back of her hair, amazed at what a few bobby pins and a curling iron could do.

"You have great hair. Since it's so straight, it's fun to work with." Sasha busied herself with tidying the supplies on the console table. "Plus, I've been in a lot of low-budget productions, so I've had a lot of practice."

Paige wanted to say something else, but the front door swung open and her three friends walked in.

"Oh, wow! Paige, you look gorgeous!"

"I love your hair!"

"You know it's not polite to overshadow the bride."

And just like that, Sasha shrunk to the background and Paige was swept into the center of the mix.

Sasha had given up her entire afternoon to do them a favor. She was the one that got them out of a jam. And even though she didn't have to, she gave up her time to make Paige look beautiful, when Paige had spent all weekend trying to outshine Sasha.

Who was the talented, kind one now?

Chapter Fourteen

FOR THE FIRST TIME HE could remember, Aiden showed up to a wedding early. He liked to think that it was because he was trying to be responsible. According to the famous lecture his mom gave any time he was late, being on time was an important way to show people they mattered. Maybe promptness hadn't been his strong suit in the past, but it was about time to turn over a new leaf.

Some might argue that he'd headed to the beach to avoid talking numbers and strategy with Jacob or trying to be friends with people he didn't care for just to make more money. While that wasn't a completely false accusation, he liked to think it wasn't entirely true either.

He walked down the long flight of wooden steps to the beach, listening to the soothing sound of the waves and the laughter of the members of the wedding party who had already started to gather. The real reason he was early, the one he preferred not to think about, was that he felt lost.

Rows of white chairs proudly waiting for guests sat in neat lines on either side of an aisle outlined by white rose petals. An arbor with flowers woven through it stood at the front waiting for the bride and groom to exchange vows and proclaim their love. A wide space at the front stood vacant just waiting for the attendants to stand and bear witness to their friends' happiness. And he stood there wondering where he fit in the mix.

This wasn't a feeling he was used to. He had always considered himself to be somewhat of a chameleon. Adapting to his circumstances was his thing. He was known for rolling with the punches. But he was starting to think that always being ready for the next best thing wasn't all it was cracked up to be.

Sure, it was fun. His life was full of adventure and excitement. He moved from one great thing to the next, like a giant game of musical chairs. The result was a ton of memories and a contact list in his phone full of friends, but was that enough? Part of him wondered if he would be the one without a chair when the music ran out.

He strolled across the powdery sand to where the wedding was set up. Where to sit was example number one of his new hypothesis. The whole reason he was at the wedding was to seal the big business deal. He should sit with the investors, but he didn't belong with them. Honestly, he only mattered to them as long as he was making them money. He didn't want that to be his place. He didn't want to become one of the self-centered sharks whose primary concern was the bottom line. Was that the path he was on?

Later tonight, his name would be on a place card at the head table because he was one of the bridesmaid's dates. That in itself made him important, but not because of who he was. It was because of who she was. And since it was a fake relationship, he wasn't even sure he belonged there.

Noise from the top of the stairs diverted his attention. The three bridesmaids stood on the top step. The photographer was a few steps down, taking pictures of them.

Before this weekend, Aiden had never considered Paige to be anything other than his little sister's best friend. She'd been hanging around their house since Ciera first brought her home from college when they were freshmen. She'd become a regular at most family holidays and rarely did he ever see Ciera without her. But she was always just the friendly girl who didn't have her own family.

Lately, something had changed.

She stood between his sister and Hadley, talking and laughing. They all wore long dresses in the same blush color, but each of them was a different style. Aiden didn't know the official name of the type of dress Paige had on, but it was stunning. It was sleeveless, with the neckline going down in a slight V. The floor-length skirt flowed around her, making her appear as if she were floating. Between the afternoon sun bathing her in light and the way her joy lit her from within, she glowed. His breath caught in his chest.

The girls made their way down the steps to where Lane was standing with his groomsmen at the bottom. Aiden couldn't help it any longer. He had to walk over to her. Paige caught sight of him and waved. She finished telling Lane something, and when he started up the steps, she came over to meet Aiden.

"Look at you being early for a change. I knew you had it in you." She had a playful twinkle in her eye and he wanted to have some sort of witty banter to toss back at her. But the truth was, she'd rendered him speechless.

He shrugged, well aware of the goofy grin spread across his face. "I'm trying out something new."

She reached up and tightened his loosened tie, smoothing it down against the front of his shirt. She did this often, at almost every tie-worthy event they attended together. In fact, he'd stopped bothering to do it himself with the anticipation that she would make it look perfectly straight as soon as she saw him. But this time her touch reached him in places he'd never anticipated.

Before she finished with the tie, he wrapped his hand around hers and held it against his chest. She stared at their hands for a second before she looked into his eyes.

"You look amazing." His words had a breathless quality to them that seemed appropriate, since he was breathless. He watched the compliment register on her face, and he wished he could have found the words to express exactly how amazing she looked. It was as if he were looking at an angel, and it was impossible for him to look away.

"Thank you." Her fingertips wrapped around his hand and the gesture sent electricity racing through his body. And he knew.

He'd had plenty of friends get married, stood next to many of them at their weddings. Every time he asked them why they decided to do it. Was the timing right? Did it seem like a logical next step? Was there some sort of relationship ultimatum? Every one of them had the same answer: When you meet the right one, you just know.

Aiden always nodded and played along, never really believing them. It sounded as mythical as Santa Claus. But here he was, standing on the beach, staring into the eyes of a woman he was in a fake relationship with, and he *knew*.

The realization blew through him like a strong ocean breeze, leaving exhilaration in its wake. He had to resist the urge to pull her into his arms and kiss her.

He let go of her hand and rocked back on his heels, sliding his hands into his pockets. "What are you up to now? Being the wedding expert you are, I thought you could help me find the perfect seat." His confidence had returned, because when he was in her presence, he didn't feel lost. He felt vibrant and alive, like there was nothing he couldn't accomplish.

"The bride and groom are having ten minutes alone so the intimate moment of him seeing her for the first time could be shared between just the two of them instead of in front of a crowd." She nodded her head up at the Grand Cabana where they had their business lunch. The top of Lane and Georgia's heads just peeked out over the top. "So I have a few minutes."

He wanted more than a few minutes. When he looked at her, he saw forever, and for the first time in his life that didn't terrify him. In fact, it did the opposite. It breathed life into places that had felt cold and empty for a long time.

She snagged her bottom lip with her teeth and took a step back to examine him. "Humm. Let's see." She had the playful twinkle in her eye that he loved. The one that he'd admired the very first time they met. "You're here as a guest of the groom, so that puts you on the right side. You're too good to sit with the freeloaders who are here for the free food and drinks, but you aren't quite family. So I'd say… " She paused, her gaze returning to his. Love swirled in his chest.

Then something happened. Her playful expression fell away, like she'd noticed something for the first time. She drew in a shallow breath, her gaze burning into his. He took a small step toward her. Was she feeling the same thing he was? Had whatever ignited in him ignited in her too?

He wanted to slide his hand behind her head, like he did last night, and finish the kiss they didn't get to start. He wanted to breathe in her intoxicating scent. He wanted her in a way he'd never wanted anything before in his entire life.

But before he could do any of that, she closed her eyes and shook her head slightly. When she opened them, the look was gone and her playful grin had returned.

"I'd say you're a third row inside aisle kind of guy."

Aiden looked at the seat in question, welcoming the excuse to look at something other than her. He needed to get his thoughts under control before he did something stupid. Like drop to his knee and propose right there.

"Can't argue with an expert." Plus, if she was standing next to the bride, it would give him a clear view of her.

"Paige, they want to get a few more pictures of the attendants."

His sister's voice broke his trance.

Paige shrugged. "Dury calls."

Unable to keep his lips off her any longer, he slid his hand behind her back and brushed a kiss across her cheek. "I'll see you after the wedding."

She looked dazed for a split second, then she flashed a coy grin before turning to where the rest of the wedding party waited.

He watched her glide across the sand, cherishing the feeling of exhilaration that made him want to fly. But there was also a sinking feeling starting to seep in. Love was a two-person game, and Aiden wasn't sure she wanted to play with him.

Paige had witnessed a lot of weddings, but this was the first time she'd watched one of her best friends get married and it was more beautiful than anything she'd seen before. Normally, she got swept away in the romance, but this wedding took it to a whole different level. Georgia was getting the happily ever after she'd always wanted, and it made Paige's heart swell with happiness.

After the couple was pronounced husband and wife, the guests made their way up the stairs to the community's clubhouse, where cocktail hour and the reception would take place. The wedding party hung out on the beach where they could take more pictures. Since the actual wedding was over and most of the pictures had been taken, there was less pressure this time to keep Georgia's dress from getting dirty from the sand and surf. Between the freedom of not caring about her dress and the elation of already being married to the love of her life, Georgia glowed.

Paige stood back on the sand and watched the photographer take pictures of the happy couple standing where the waves just washed into the shore. The setting was perfect. The sun hung low in a clear blue sky, casting a golden glow over everyone. The ocean was clear and gentle waves rolled onto the powder white sand. And as if the setting wasn't perfect enough, the entire mood of everyone involved was joyful. Her wedding coordinator brain marveled at how it was the perfect recipe to capture awe-worthy pictures. Her best friend brain cherished the privilege getting to witness this display of true happiness.

"I don't think I've ever seen Lane this exuberant." Brody stepped up beside her.

"They're perfect together." She watched as Lane whispered something in Georgia's ear. The expression on Georgia's face was priceless. A picture of true love. The photographer clicked away. Brody nodded. "That they are."

They stood there, side by side, in silence, watching the scene for a moment. Paige was lost in the happiness of it all.

"I've missed you," Brody said, breaking the silence.

It took Paige a second to register that he was talking to her, and then another second to understand what he said.

"Missed me?" Her words came out more hostile than she'd intended, but she was shocked. Missed her? He left her behind when he moved to a new country, hadn't talked to her since, and then showed up with a new girlfriend. What part of that said he'd missed her?

Brody didn't seem fazed by her tone. He just stood there, looking as confident as always. "I miss when we were happy." He thrust his chin in the direction of the happy couple. "Like that."

Paige, still dumbfounded, turned her head to look at Georgia and Lane. She stared at them, almost gaping, trying to make sense of what Brody was saying to her.

In all of the couples she'd watched exchange vows, this had to be one of the most in-love couples she'd ever seen. Yes, there had been a time when she and Brody were happy, but had they ever looked like that?

"You're with Sasha now." She whispered the words, as if to remind herself as much as to remind him. It didn't matter if they had been perfect or not if there wasn't any possibility for it to happen in the future.

"Yes." He shoved his hands into his pockets and stared at the sand. "But what if I wasn't?"

They were the words Paige had hoped he would say since she

first saw him walk into Aiden's cousin's wedding. This conversation, right here, was the one that had inspired her to wear the shoes that almost broke her ankle last weekend. She wasn't sure how she was expecting to feel when she heard them, but she was pretty sure it should have been more than just...confused.

"What do you mean?" she asked.

"I'm not sure it's going to work out. She came along this weekend to see if there was anything there. But the only thing this weekend reminded me was that I no longer had you."

This is the part where butterflies flying at mach speed should have stormed her body. But she didn't feel even one single flutter.

"We can't be having this conversation. Not while you're still in a relationship with someone else."

Surely that was it. She just needed to know that she had all of him, no strings attached. No messy baggage to stand in the way of true happiness.

"Of course. You're absolutely right. It isn't fair to you or her." Interesting. He wasn't even using her name any more.

They were silent for a second, both watching the photo session in front of them. Or, in her case at least, pretending to watch while trying to sort out the mess of thoughts twisting around in her mind.

"But if there wasn't anything standing in our way, would you want to talk about us?" When he finished the question, he met her gaze with one of his charming looks. It was the same look that made her fall in love with him two years ago. But this time it did nothing for her. If anything, it only heightened the confusion swirling in her mind.

Since he left town, she'd been hoping for a chance to walk down memory lane with him. She was convinced they belonged together, convinced that he'd made a mistake by leaving her behind. All she had to do was remind him of what they had. One walk down memory lane and she was sure they would get back to a place where they had the kind of blissful happiness Georgia and Lane shared. Okay, maybe not quite *that* happy, but it would be good enough.

So why did his offer leave her feeling twisted up inside instead of wanting to break into a happy dance?

"Now can I get all the bridesmaids out here with them?" the photographer called.

Paige had never been so grateful for an interruption. She flashed an apologetic smile and took a step toward the water. Before she got too far, he caught her hand. "I'll find you later. When I have the freedom to say everything I've been wanting to."

Paige's heart lurched. It seemed prompted more by nervousness than excitement, which didn't feel quite right. But at least it was some sort of reaction. He missed her. He wanted to walk down memory lane. There were more things, good things, he wanted to say to her. She was finally getting the second chance with Brody she had been wishing for. She should be feeling something, even if it was a nervous lurch.

"Okay." It was a dumb response, but it was all that would come out of her mouth. Somehow, she'd imagined this moment going very differently. Maybe fireworks going off or a choir of angels singing the hallelujah chorus was a bit over the top, but she expected there to be some sort of grand feeling that swept them both away.

She joined her friends and smiled for the camera, realizing that for the first time that day, her smile was forced.

Chapter Fifteen

"Can we get the bride and groom to the dance floor? It's time for the father-daughter and mother-son dance." The DJ's voice interrupted the laughter at the head table.

Georgia pushed back from the table and wiped the tears from under her eyes. "I'm being paged, but only serious talk until we get back. I don't want to miss anything funny."

The whole reception dinner had been so filled with laughter that Paige's sides ached. Part of it was due to a good group of friends celebrating together, but at least some of it had to do with Aiden. He had the kind of infectious energy that turned any event into a party, or in this case, elevated any party to an epic level. It wasn't that he demanded all the attention or put on a one-man comedy act. No. He worked the table, bringing out the best in everyone.

"We promise to observe without saying a thing. We'll sit here like statues." Hadley sat up straight and folded her hands on the table in front of her.

Lane gave her a suspicious look. "I'm not sure I believe you."

"I'll keep them under control. Scout's honor." Aiden held up three fingers.

Lane took Georgia's hand to walk to the dance floor and pointed at Aiden with the other. "I know I don't believe you."

They made their way to meet their parents, and for the first time during the dinner, the head table got quiet to watch the iconic dance.

Paige turned her chair around, so she could see the dance floor that was directly behind her.

The DJ cued the music, and Georgia and her dad two-stepped around the floor while Lane and his mother sort of rocked side to side in the middle.

Aiden casually draped his arm over the back of her chair, a gesture that had become more and more comfortable over the past few days. "I have to admit, this is not one of the more exciting parts of a wedding."

Paige leaned into his embrace. While even she had to agree the father-daughter dance could be a little slow, she was still entranced by it. "It's a special memory for them. I think it's sweet."

She stole a glance at Aiden. His eyes were scrunched up in consideration as he watched the dancers. "I guess, but they could make it a little more entertaining."

"Like what? You want them to add some jazz hands?"

Aiden shrugged. "I mean, it wouldn't hurt."

Paige giggled. "Well, when it's your turn, you and Mama Pierce can stage a show-stopping Broadway number with all the jazz hands you want."

Aiden gave a short, dismissive snort of a laugh. Oh, right. Aiden didn't do forever, which meant dancing with his mother at his own wedding wasn't something he'd ever considered. Or ever planned on doing.

The realization sent an icy streak of disappointment crackling through her, which she did her best to ignore. This moment was about Georgia and Lane and their parents, not whatever was or wasn't going on between her and the guy next to her. She shifted in her seat, hoping the extra physical distance between them would help her distance herself from whatever she was starting to feel. He was only her *fake* boyfriend, after all.

The song came to an end and Georgia reunited with her new husband in the middle of the dance floor, the observing parents joining their spouses.

"The newlyweds want to open the dance floor tonight by celebrating everlasting love with a couples' dance. We need all couples to join us on the dance floor," the DJ announced.

Young couples at the beginning of their journey joined older couples, like Georgia's grandparents who had just celebrated their sixtieth wedding anniversary. Seeing love that stood the test of time encouraged Paige. Happily-ever-afters did exist in real life.

"Smoochems, you coming?"

She'd been so consumed in her own thoughts, she hadn't realized Aiden had stood up.

"Oh right. We're a couple. I almost forgot." She wasn't sure a pretend relationship of four days qualified them to be out there, but since sitting it out would raise too many questions, she took his hand and followed. "You going to pull out some of those show-stopping moves right now?"

"Tempting." They stepped onto the dance floor. He spun her once and then pulled her into him. "But tonight is about dancing with you."

The world blurred around her until the only thing in her focus was him. Fake relationship or not, being in Aiden's arms felt right.

Four days ago she was content to promise Brody forever based on a memory of being happy enough. Their relationship had checked all the boxes, or so she thought. But this weekend had changed that. Even on their best days, the time in their relationship when everything was going exactly how it should have been, she never felt the way she did when she was with Aiden.

"Tonight has been a welcome break from business. Thanks for giving me an excuse to not sit at the investors' table."

"Happy to help, although on behalf of wedding and event

planners everywhere, you're going to have to stop changing the seating assignment at the last minute."

She kept their conversation light and friendly because that's how they always kept things, but she wasn't feeling light and friendly. She felt like everything was starting to fall apart. She was supposed to want Brody and Aiden was just a friend, but what if she'd gotten it backwards?

"Follow the assigned plan? Now where's the fun in that?" He pulled her closer and together they spun around, weaving through the couples dancing in a more traditional flow, until they were on the other side of the dance floor. Paige's head spun, but it had more to do with the man whose arms she was in than the actual turns. She struggled to grasp onto something familiar, something that made sense.

"What's wrong with following plans? Sticking with a well-thought-out plan is how you know you'll get where you want to go."

Of course, it helped to have an end destination in mind. Before this weekend, she had been so sure that a life with Brody was her end goal. But why? Because he fit some list she'd made up and they were happy enough? What kind of person entered into forever because they were happy enough?

"I've got nothing against plans, but sometimes you gotta change it up. If you're always hanging out at the same table, you'll never meet anyone new." He spun them again. Quick steps with the world spinning around and around, until they were in the opposite corner, away from most of the crowd and dancing by themselves.

She looked up into his eyes and wondered how she'd missed it. How had she not noticed that she wasn't in love with Brody? She was in love with Aiden.

The revelation didn't come as a shock. It was as if she'd known it all along. He was nothing like what she thought she wanted but everything she needed, and here, in his arms, she felt like she had finally found home. And the thought terrified her.

The one thing Aiden didn't do was commitment. Ciera had reiterated that last night. He was the king of keeping it casual. The one-date wonder. He never stayed with any one thing too long. Falling in love with Aiden was like falling in love with a dream; beautiful in the moment but never meant to last.

"But if you're always changing seats, you never get the chance to really know the people at your table. Don't you ever want to stick with your group?"

It was just a playful conversation about where to sit at a wedding, but the meaning behind her question was anything but playful. What she wanted to ask was "Is there any chance you could love me back? Or is falling in love with you a futile venture?"

"Stay in the same place? Where's the fun in that?" He spun her once more and all of a sudden she realized they had spun out of the crowd to a quiet spot where they were all alone. "If you get tied down in one spot, you'll never know what it feels like to be out here, where there's nothing to distract you from the beauty of the stars." Laughter danced in his eyes, as playful as always, but his words caused a heaviness to tug on her heart.

"The night sky is pretty great." She rested her head against his chest and swayed to the song. If it was only a dream, at the very least she could hold on to it until it was time to wake up.

"Let's start narrowing this down by eliminating all the couples who aren't married. If you haven't said 'I do' yet, then you have to get off the dance floor," the DJ called.

Several couples made their way back to their tables. Paige stepped away from Aiden, wondering if this would be more than just the end of a dance for them.

"That's us. I guess our time is up." She gazed into his eyes one last time. She couldn't help wishing he would stop her with the three little words she realized she had always wanted to hear him say. But he couldn't help who he was, and she wouldn't hold it against him. She turned for the table.

He caught her hand. "Paige." He said her name in his low, smooth voice.

She stared at his hand holding hers before she looked up into his eyes. Gone was his playful expression, and in its place a more serious one. One she had never seen on Aiden before, but it made her pulse race. Hope fluttered inside her. Maybe he wasn't a dream after all. Maybe—

"Paige, can I talk to you?" Paige had been so preoccupied by the drama going on in her own mind that she hadn't noticed Sasha walk up next to her. She had to blink a few times to bring herself back to reality.

"Sure." She looked back at Aiden. "You don't mind, do you?"

He dropped her hand and slid his into his pocket. "Not at all. I gotta find the investors anyway. I've been neglecting them all night. I'll catch ya later."

She watched him walk back into the mass of people slapping shoulders and making jokes. Yep, just a dream.

With a sigh, she turned back to Sasha. "What's going on?"

"I wanted to say thank you before I go."

"Go? Go where?"

Sasha glanced down the beach in the direction of their condos and Paige noticed there were tears in her eyes.

"I broke up with Brody, so I think it's best if I leave and give him some space."

"Oh, Sasha, I'm so sorry." It didn't surprise her that they had broken up. Both of them had hinted their relationship was headed in that direction. But it did surprise her how she felt; plagued with guilt and genuinely sympathetic. Technically, this had been part of Paige's original goal, but now, nothing about that felt right.

"Thanks, but it was the right thing to do. He's a nice guy and I hoped we could make it work." She looked around, as if examining where they'd ended up. "But I realized that if I was having to work that hard to try to find a spark, maybe I was looking in the wrong place to begin with. The right guy is out there somewhere, it just wasn't Brody."

She took a breath and wiped away the single tear sliding down her cheek. "Anyway, I wanted to say thanks for being so kind to me this weekend. You, of all people, had every reason not to be, and you were the one who reached out and included me. It means a lot."

Paige didn't deserve any credit at all. "I'm the one who should be thanking you. Georgia looked radiant on her wedding day because of you. You'll always have friends in us." As she said it, she realized she truly meant it.

Sasha flashed a sad smile, then turned and made her way down to the beach. Paige watched her until she faded into the darkness.

As usual, everything had gone according to her perfectly orchestrated plan. Here they were at the end of the weekend and every goal had been accomplished. Georgia and Lane got married, Brody was no longer with the other girl, Aiden's multimillion-dollar sale was all but a done deal, and their fake relationship was coming to a close. All the boxes had been checked and her life, as usual, appeared to be in perfect order.

Yet Paige couldn't help but feel that everything was falling apart around her.

Being in love made Aiden feel like Superman. He could leap over tall buildings in a single bound, he could stop speeding bullets, he could entertain a table of the most self-absorbed people he'd ever met and like it. Nothing was out of his reach.

"What a night." He slapped the first investor on the shoulder as he walked off the dance floor after couples married less than five years were eliminated. "I could get use to the beach life."

The investor sank into his chair and grabbed for his drink.

"Maybe your next venture? Beachside boutique hotel? Or luxury condos, maybe? Do you dabble in real estate?"

He'd never considered real estate, but maybe it was time to build his own tall building to leap over. "Not yet. But you never know."

The investor swirled the ice around in his glass. "I like your style. You remind me of a younger version of myself." He took a sip. "I assume everything's in order for tomorrow's closing?"

"Contracts are printed and I have shiny new pens perfect for signing."

"And I have some cigars for the post-signature celebration."

Normally, the thought of being trapped in a haze of smog while trying to enjoy their self-acclaiming conversation sounded like torture, but he was in such a good mood tonight he didn't let it bother him. "Sounds like we're all set."

He tried to maintain eye contact, or at the very least, keep his eyes in the general direction of the person he was conversing with, but he couldn't help himself. If Paige was anywhere in his field of vision, his gaze was drawn to her.

She wasn't doing anything special, just talking with Georgia's grandmother on the other side of the courtyard, but it was impossible for Aiden to look away. She was radiant and he wanted to be where she was.

"She's a keeper. You're one lucky man." The investor leaned back in his chair and crossed his ankle over his knee. "I find the best way to hold on to ones like that is with big diamonds. Particularly the ones fitted for a specific finger."

Aiden had always considered himself an eternal bachelor. He didn't have anything against marriage in general, it just wasn't for him. Forever was a long time to be tied to anything. But at the moment, forever sounded like a long time to be without her.

Although, if he were being technical, she wasn't really with him now.

"I don't think we're quite there yet."

As if she could sense him, she looked up and their eyes met across the room. Excitement jolted through him, making him feel as though he was levitating. Maybe she wasn't his yet, but there wasn't anything holding him back from trying.

"When you get there, I have a guy who will take care of you." He slapped Aiden on the shoulder. "But don't hang around here with me. Nights like this are meant for young lovers."

He wandered off, probably in search of another drink, leaving Aiden alone. He hadn't acted on his feelings for Paige because he was honoring the fact that she was with someone else, a fact he now realized wasn't true. They hadn't gotten back together yet.

Sure, she thought she wanted to be with Brody, but she couldn't deny there was something between them when they were dancing. Truth be told, there had been something between them for a long time. It was the reason he especially loved the family holidays she came to and why he always looked for her when he was at the resort. He was in love with Paige, and, unless he'd misread all the signs, she was pretty comfortable around him as well.

Georgia's grandmother walked away from her, and Paige was left standing alone watching the action from the far side of the dance floor. Her hips moved in rhythm to the beat. The twinkle lights strung around the perimeter of the courtyard softly lit her features. His heart leapt inside his chest.

Maybe she would still choose Brody. Maybe she really was meant to be with that pompous ladder-climber. And if that was what she wanted, he would wish her well. He would even dance at her wedding. But he at least deserved a chance. She deserved to know how he felt about her.

Exhilaration prompted his steps. He'd never uttered the three sacred words he was about to say, but he never felt more equipped to say anything in his entire life.

Five tables stood between where he was and where he wanted to be. He passed the first one in what felt like one giant step.

Maybe he should've rehearsed some sort of speech. Or, at the very least, he could've thought through what he wanted to say, but he didn't want to wait one more second. He needed to say it now.

He almost tripped over a chair turned the wrong way at the next table, but he caught himself before he fell. She made a face to show her concern and then laughed. He loved her laugh. It lit her entire body. Adoration so bright and shiny surged through his entire body until he wondered if it made him glow. He'd never felt so alive.

"Aiden! We're headed to the dance floor. Bring your crazy moves," one of the groomsmen called as he walked past. Aiden took his eyes off Paige just for a second so he could answer.

"I'm there. I just have to take care of something first." Although as he rounded the next table, he considered breaking into a dance right there. Or singing, or shouting, or attempting to fly. Never in his whole life had he been consumed by a force as powerful as love. He stopped to pick up a handbag that had fallen on the ground before he returned his attention to Paige.

But something had captured her attention, too. Or should he say someone? Brody, seemingly unaware of Aiden, stepped in between them.

A chilling disappointment took the edge off his elation and made him pause. He set the handbag on the table and watched the scene in front of him, trying to interpret what was being said.

The smile that had lit Paige's lovely face only a second ago had faded. She fidgeted with her hair as she listened to whatever he was saying to her. Brody's head was hung low, his shoulders stooped forward, in the posture of an apology.

Aiden fought the urge to continue on. He also had something he wanted to tell Paige, a truth he needed her to hear. He considered playing dumb as he stepped in the middle of what appeared to be a personal conversation, or even shouting the words to her from where he was.

But this wasn't just about Aiden. It was also about her.

The thought made him hesitate and a heaviness descended over him. She'd already told him what she wanted. In fact, she'd made it crystal clear all weekend what her intentions were. She wanted Brody.

Brody made her happy. A life with Brody was what she saw in her future. Although she never specifically told him the wish she wrote down last night, she'd hinted that it was to get Brody back. Before this weekend started, before he had his life-changing revelation, Paige had already chosen Brody.

The realization didn't steal any of the love that was illuminating every inch of his being, but it did make him hesitate. Of course, he wanted to be the one that made her smile, to fill her life with the kind of love that gave her wings. But even more than that, he just wanted her to be happy.

And if Brody was what truly made her happy, then he couldn't mess that up for her.

Paige looked over Brody's head at him. He gave her a thumbs up and mouthed the question "All good?"

With a sly smile she gave him a discreet nod and mouthed the word "perfect."

He stood there and watched for one more excruciating moment while Brody looked up at Paige and took her hands into his. Only moments ago he had felt like he could leap tall buildings, and now he felt as if he barely had enough energy to pick his feet up to walk.

He could still have told her the way he felt. He could have proclaimed his love for everyone to hear then stood next to Brody, shoulder to shoulder, and made her choose between them. But that wouldn't have been fair to her.

She was perfect and beautiful and a thousand other wonderful things, but she wasn't his. With one last look, he turned and walked away.

So Paige had gotten what she wanted. Good for her. No one deserved happiness more than she did.

It was all good because Aiden was getting what he wanted, too. He was about to sell his prized restaurant for crazy money, and he was on par to live his uncommitted, carefree, bachelor life forever.

Lucky him.

Paige hadn't actually listened to a word Brody said after he told her it was over with Sasha. It was some sort of half-hearted excuse for an apology and an explanation of why leaving her alone and heartbroken all those months ago was a good thing—for him at least.

She tried to listen, honestly she did, but she was distracted by Aiden.

It had looked like he wanted to tell her something, and from the happiness radiating from him, she guessed it was good news. Blame it on the romance of the wedding or her own romantic heart, but she had hoped he was coming to say what she wanted to hear. That while he hadn't done commitment in the past, she was different. She made him want to do those things he said he never would.

But as soon as he asked if everything was okay, he had walked away.

Paige silently scolded the disappointment that descended on her as she watched him leave her and rejoin the party. It was the right thing for him to do. He was only in this as a pawn. Nothing more. Because Aiden Pierce didn't do relationships.

"We were good together, Paige. So what do you say? Can we give us another chance?" For the first time since he started his sorry-not-sorry speech, Brody looked up into her eyes.

Nothing. She felt nothing.

It was all going according to her perfectly executed plan, even down to the "I want you back" speech at the end of the weekend. Next, if she were checking things off the imaginary list in her head, she should say yes. Absolutely. Her response should probably be followed by some sort of passionate kiss and possibly fireworks.

She licked her lips, trying to get her mouth ready to say the word she was supposed to say.

"Thanks, Brody." *Thanks? What did that even mean?* Her brain was not doing a great job.

She could see the confusion register on Brody's face as well. She searched the crowd again for Aiden and found him on the edge of the dance floor, laughing with Ciera and Georgia.

"I, er, think I need a little time to try to sort through all of this."

The answer shocked her almost as much as it seemed to shock him.

"Right. Take all the time you need. I'll catch up with you later."

He wandered off into the night and she stood there trying to make her thoughts make sense. This was what she'd dreamed about, wasn't it? This was what she'd waited for. Saying yes to Brody would set her up for the life she thought she wanted. Happily ever after and happy enough weren't all that different, were they?

She closed her eyes and let the cool breeze wash over her, trying to realign her heart with the plan her brain had come up with. Unfortunately, three little words echoed in her mind like a drum beat. They were the same dreaded three little words that always threatened to undo any plan.

But what if...

Chapter Sixteen

THE RECEPTION ENDED WITH GEORGIA and Lane making their exit through a tunnel of guests waving sparklers pointing toward a decorated golf cart. It was a tip they had taken from Paige, who had done that many times at the resort. Her couples wanted the finality of a grand exit, but since they were staying at the other side of the resort, getting in a car and driving off was a bit much. In this case, Georgia and Lane were driving just down the block to an oceanfront bed and breakfast.

Paige, Ciera, and Hadley stood closest to the golf cart.

"You are the best bridesmaids ever!" Georgia squealed. She hugged Hadley, then Ciera. When she hugged Paige, she lowered her voice to whisper and leaned her mouth right next to Paige's ear. "And go get your man."

Confusion twisted around inside Paige, but she did her best to keep it from showing on her face as the golf cart disappeared from sight.

Ciera let out a happy sigh. "What a perfect day."

"May I have your attention, please?" The wedding coordinator clapped her hands, standing in the place where the golf cart had just been.

Hadley glared at the woman. "Seriously, isn't her job over?" she whispered.

Paige giggled.

"The bride and groom would like to thank you all for being

here to celebrate with them. The reception is now concluded. However, there are a few members of the wedding party and family who have been tasked with returning various items." She pointed at the three girls. "That includes all of you. Please see my assistant to confirm your job."

"That includes all of you," Hadley mocked as they made their way through the crowd to find the assistant. "If I hire someone like that to do my wedding, Paige, you have my permission to fire her on the spot."

"Please don't ever clap your hands at your clients. It's just rude," Ciera mumbled.

"It's now on the top of my list of things to avoid." Although the way she could project her voice was a cool little trick. If Paige could master that, the entire Hilltop Resort would be able to hear her when she needed something. Of course, she would have to use a much kinder tone.

The assistant checked something off her list when they approached. "I have three piles of things for you to take home. There is a bag in the club's dressing room, her veil and pre-wedding bag are at the Merricks' house and some things left over from the ceremony are under the staging tent on the beach."

The house wasn't exactly someplace Paige wanted to be right now. Both Brody and Aiden were staying there. There was a good chance she would encounter one or both of them on her errand, perhaps even at the same time, which might inspire a conversation she wasn't ready to have.

The beach wasn't much better. Luckily, her friends stepped in for her. "Paige, you can get the dressing room, I'll run down to the beach, and Ciera can go to the house. We can meet at the car."

Since most of the wedding guests had taken off in the direction of the parking lot or the Merricks' house, the courtyard and clubhouse were quiet. Other than vendors cleaning up, Paige was the only person there. She welcomed the few minutes alone.

Perhaps away from all the people and the craziness, she could get her thoughts together.

She owed Brody an answer, and in theory it should be an easy one. For over two years, she had convinced herself he was the one she should end up with. Getting back together with him had been her whole goal. This was what she wanted.

She grabbed the bag and headed out to Aiden's SUV that they had borrowed for the day. Before this weekend, everything had been so clear, but now she wasn't sure.

She opened the passenger side door and Aiden's familiar scent drifted over her. It smelled like cedar, worn leather and fun. His favorite tattered sun visor hung from the rearview mirror and there was an old football on the floor in the backseat. The SUV looked like him, felt like him, and she slid into the passenger seat feeling closer to him.

She leaned her head against the head rest and breathed in deeply, hoping for a little clarity. It didn't work. With a solid plan and clear objectives, how did she manage to get herself so far off track?

The sound of the trunk opening startled her, and she shook her head slightly, trying to hide the conflicted emotions that were playing through her.

"It is crazy down at that house." Ciera's cheery voice rang through the car. Paige turned to watch her in time to see her heft a large, hard-sided suitcase into the back. "Lane forgot to take his suitcase. Apparently the wedding planner extraordinaire wasn't on top of everything."

Hadley appeared, walking across the parking lot holding two bags. "Who knew it took so much stuff to get ready for one wedding?" She tossed her bags into the back of the SUV and took the veil from Ciera. "I'll lay this out in the back seat with me so it won't get crunched. I'm not sure what Georgia is planning on doing with it, but I don't want to be the one responsible for messing it up."

Once everything was situated, Ciera shut the doors and climbed into the driver's seat.

"We have to run by the bed and breakfast and drop off Lane's bag. Aiden told me he needs his car first thing in the morning, but he said we can drive it home and he'll walk down to get it as soon as he finishes saying goodnight to everyone."

At the thought of Aiden, excitement danced through Paige. She had to bite her bottom lip to keep it from spreading into a huge, goofy grin across her face.

"Any idea what time that'll be?" she asked. Not that it mattered, of course. She was simply asking to make sure the plan had been thought through.

"No clue, but knowing my brother, it could be a while." Ciera pulled out onto the main street, headed in the direction of the bed and breakfast.

"I ran into Brody on my way back from the beach," Hadley reported, with a hint of scandal in her voice. "He all of the sudden seems very interested in you. He asked what your plans were for the night."

"Oh." It was all Paige could think to say because just hearing the mention of his name caused a different, not quite as pleasant emotion to roll through her. She tried to tell herself a few nerves were normal when considering an offer that might lead to forever, but she feared icy apprehension stealing her joy was more than normal nerves.

She was a tangled-up mess. The thought of Aiden made her spirit soar and the thought of Brody filled her with dread. Seriously, what was wrong with her?

"He wanted me to tell you to check your phone. It's *very* important." Hadley rolled her eyes. "I'd told him you'd check it if you had time. Any idea what he thinks is so urgent all of the sudden?"

Paige did her best to try to look innocent. "No idea." Which was mostly true. While she could guess at the topic, getting back together, she wasn't sure what was so important that he needed to text her right now. Her fingers tingled, wanting to climb over the backseat and pull her phone out of her clutch. But since she didn't want to dive into the long, drawn-out conversation about the internal battle raging in her mind, she made herself refrain.

Ciera turned into the bed and breakfast's parking lot and Paige nearly jumped out of the car. "I'll run the suitcase in."

"You sure? Is your ankle up for it?"

Paige was already around to the trunk before anyone else had the chance to get out. "It feels much better today." That wasn't entirely true, but she was willing to take any distraction from the drama in her head.

With the suitcase in her hand, she started up the steps. She had every intention of telling Hadley and Ciera about what happened, but she needed to be able to express it in coherent sentences first.

Brody's new girlfriend broke up with him because they couldn't find their spark. And now he wants me back, only I'm not sure because I might be in love with your brother, who, just like you warned me, doesn't do commitment. It didn't exactly seem like the best way to dump this on her best friends.

Paige ducked her head in the front door of the bed and breakfast and rolled the suitcase next to the check-in desk. If only hers was a simple love story like Georgia and Lane's. One where… She smiled at the memory of how Georgia and Lane started. Well, maybe love stories weren't meant to be simple. They were just meant to end well.

After handing off the bag to the owner of the B&B, Paige trotted back down to the car. "Mission accomplished."

"Thanks. The wedding boss said to please text her when it was delivered," Ciera said as she pulled out on the main road.

Hadley took out her phone. "I'm sending it now. And including the clapping emoji."

Ciera let out a snort of a laugh. "You're so bad."

Paige might have laughed, too, if she didn't have a hundred other thoughts occupying her mind.

Traffic on the main highway was unusually light just after midnight, and it only took them a couple of minutes to drive the short distance to their condos. Ciera's phone dinged as soon as they pulled into the parking lot, but she didn't bother to check the message until they had parked and unloaded everything from the car and were walking up the stairs.

"Wow, that was fast. Aiden said he's on his way."

The flurry of excitement dashed through Paige again, but she adjusted the bag on her shoulder to try to keep herself in check.

"How's he getting here?" Not that it really mattered, but it seemed like a more appropriate question than "Did he ask about me?"

"He said he's walking on the beach. It's after midnight. Is that safe? I'm not sure that's safe."

Walking alone in the dark anywhere at midnight wasn't the best call, but probably the only real threats this beach held were tiny crabs getting out of his way or accidently stepping on one of the baby sea turtles trying to make its way to the water.

"I'm sure he's fine, but I can meet him down there with the keys if it would make you feel more comfortable."

"You don't have to," Ciera said. "I can go."

"I don't mind at all. In fact, I was wanting to walk down to the beach one last time to get a better look at the moon anyway." Paige prayed there was actually a moon worth looking at tonight and it wasn't covered by clouds.

Hadley studied her for a moment with a look Paige couldn't

quite place. Then she held out her hand. "Sounds lovely. Want me to take your bag up for you?"

Ciera just shrugged and handed her the keys.

Paige didn't hesitate. With the keys in one hand and her clutch in the other, she took off for the stairs. "I'll be up in a bit."

An almost full moon lit the night sky in front of her as she rounded the building for the stairs that lead to the beach. True, it wasn't what she was coming to see, but she stopped to admire the sight anyway. It was a perfect night.

A warm breeze blew past, sending her full skirt fluttering behind her as she stepped slowly down each weathered, wooden step toward the beach. She probably should have been thinking up some sort of game plan, or at the very least, some idea of what she wanted to accomplish during this moonlight meeting with the man she might be in love with. Instead, with every step closer to the sand, she let go of her control. Her fears and worries floated away on the wind, until she stopped on the final step.

Here she was. Forever stretched out before her in a soft darkness. It wasn't as defined as she normally would've liked it to be. In the darkness, the inky waves seemed to blend seamlessly into the velvety sky. She'd never been a fan of vagueness, yet here there was a certain beauty to it.

She sunk down onto the final step, her toes dug into the cool sand, and she pulled her phone out of her clutch.

She sucked in a deep breath, letting the calmness of the night filter through her before she opened the text message from Brody.

Give us a chance, babe. We were happy before and now that I'm back, we'll be happy again.

Had they been happy? She would be the first to admit they'd been happy enough, but was that the same thing as happy? She'd imagined life with Brody would be good, but this weekend she'd started wondering if there was something better.

"You waiting for me?" The familiar lazy drawl floated around her like a warm hug. She closed her eyes and breathed it in before she opened them to look up at the dark form walking toward her. The silvery light of the moon lit his crooked grin and ignited something inside her.

"A trek in the darkness by yourself? I wanted to make sure you made it." She barely recognized the husky voice that floated into the darkness, but it didn't seem to faze Aiden, who stopped right in front of her and leaned on the railing.

"I hear your part of Operation Wedding Weekend was successful. Are congratulations in order?"

"Nothing has been finalized yet." She left off the part that she was the one holding things up.

"I guess you do still have one roadblock in the way. Even fake relationships have to come to an end. Is that why you're waiting for me? Is this our break-up moment?" He chuckled at his own joke, but she realized that was exactly why she was there. She needed to know if a relationship with Aiden was even a possibility.

"Something like that."

"I'm usually on the other side of this conversation, but it's always good to embrace new experiences." He straightened up, circled his shoulders and few times and stretched his neck from side to side. "Okay, I'm ready. Lay it on me." He braced himself as if waiting for a punch to the gut.

"Seriously? You've never been dumped?"

He rubbed his jaw with one hand. "Maybe once in junior high, but she did it in a note her friend gave me. I'm not sure it counts."

"If you're such the expert on being the breaker-upper, maybe you should do it."

"In that case…" He pulled his phone out of his pocket. The bright screen lit up his playful face and something inside her soared. How did this happen? How did she let herself fall in love with Aiden Pierce?

A smirk tugged on the corner of his mouth and he said the

words aloud as he typed a message. "Thanks for the memories but we're over." He pressed send and then looked up to meet her eyes. The phone in her hand dinged, but she didn't bother reading the message. She didn't want it to be over.

"Classy," she joked, trying to keep the mood light. But she didn't feel light. She felt heavy and a knot twisted in the pit of her stomach.

Aiden gave a nonchalant shrug. "I know." He dropped his phone back in his pocket. "Now that we've gotten that out of the way, you've got nothing holding you back."

"Guess not." Maybe their fake relationship was no longer standing in her way, but there was still something holding her back. It was a problem she didn't anticipate, and now that she found herself here, she wasn't sure how to solve it. Or even if it could be solved. Love would be so much easier if it just played by the rules.

Aiden sank down onto the step next to her. "It has been quite the weekend." He squeezed her knee in a friendly way and then his hand lingered there. The sea grass on the hill behind them rustled in the warm breeze.

"It has." The waves rolled into the shore and she let the memories of the past few days roll through her. In theory, this whole weekend with Aiden had been a fabrication. Merely an illusion created for other people to see. At the end of it, she was supposed to be able to walk away without a problem because there wasn't really anything to walk away from. There shouldn't have been anything to miss.

But it didn't matter what theory said; she was going to miss this. Maybe even a lot.

"Brody's a lucky man," Aiden said.

She replayed the words from his text in her mind. They were to the point but not exactly swoon-worthy. "Let's hope he feels the same way."

"He'd be a fool not to." Aiden removed his hand from her knee and settled it in his lap. The distance between them seemed to grow along with the dull ache in her chest.

She sat there next to him in silence until she found the nerve to ask the one question she came there to ask. "Is there any reason I shouldn't do this?"

She held her breath while she waited for him to respond. He was still for a second, so still that she almost regretted asking the question, but then he looked up. His gaze met hers with a look that made the air between them crackle.

She hadn't imagined it. There was something very real between them, and from the way he looked at her, he felt it, too. The realization tingled through her.

But the attraction between them wasn't what was in question here. In her heart of hearts she knew he felt the same way. The way he held her, the way he looked at her, the way he made her feel when it was just the two of them, with no one else watching. Whatever was happening between them was real, at least for right now.

The problem was that Aiden didn't do commitments. He didn't like to be tied down. Forever was one of his least favorite words, which was a problem since forever was all Paige was willing to settle for.

The magnetic force between them tugged her toward him and something glimmered in his eyes. For a moment she thought he was going to say the words she had hoped he would say. She wanted him to tell her that she couldn't be with Brody because she belonged with him, and that he was no longer afraid of forever, or whatever was even longer than that.

But then the glimmer faded, his intimate look faded away and his normal, relaxed expression returned.

"I can't think of any."

The ache in her chest intensified until it felt like a vise grip was squeezing her heart. Tears stung her eyes and she squeezed them shut before they could spill out over her cheeks.

Ciera had warned her about this very thing so she wouldn't get hurt. And it wasn't like Paige didn't listen. She had. She knew this was who Aiden was before they started this whole charade. But knowledge wasn't enough to keep her from falling in love and warnings didn't make this moment hurt any less.

"You deserve all the happiness in the world. Go and get it."

She let his words swirl around her like a warm ocean breeze and kept her eyes closed for one more glorious moment while she enjoyed the beautiful dream. Then she felt him back away and she opened her eyes.

She had to dig deep to find her playful tone. "You have been the best fake boyfriend a girl could've asked for." She tossed him the keys.

He caught them and twirled them around his finger. "I only hope it was as good for you as it was for me. I'll see ya back at home."

He trotted up the stairs and she turned away just in time to let the first tear roll down her cheek.

It would have been polite if he had walked up the stairs with her instead of leaving her alone on the beach in the dark, but he was running out of self-control and on the verge of doing something he would regret. Well, maybe he wouldn't regret it. It was something he'd been wanting to do for a long time, but it wasn't what she wanted. And in the end, what was best for her was his ultimate goal.

Aiden stopped at the top of the stairs to look back one last time. She stood in the sand, a few steps away from where they had been sitting, looking out over the ocean. The way the moon lit her and the way her long dress fluttered in the breeze made her look like an angel.

That warm feeling flowed through him again. He had finally fallen in love, something he wasn't sure would ever happen, and it just happened to be with the one person he couldn't have. It seemed unfair.

But it was also unfair to her to make her choose. She'd asked him, as a friend, for a favor to help her get back the man she loved. He didn't want to make her life more complicated. If Brody was who truly made her happy, who was he to stand in their way? No matter how much it hurt to walk away from her.

Heaviness filled him, making even walking sound like and effort, but he forced himself to turn and take a step anyway. It was time to let her go. Time to let her grab the happiness she so deserved.

He climbed into his SUV and started the ignition. He'd arrived here four days ago with a plan, and he felt confident to say the weekend had been one hundred percent successful. Paige got her one true love and Aiden was about to get millions.

This was what he had wanted. His goal was to be free, no strings attached, so he could move on to the next great thing. He was available for whatever adventures awaited just beyond the horizon.

But being free felt much emptier than it did before he knew what it was like to be with the one his heart desired.

Chapter Seventeen

THE NEXT MORNING PAIGE WHEELED her packed suitcase out of her room and left it by the front door. She slumped down on the bar stool next to Ciera.

"I'm going to drive back to Hilltop with Brody." She announced it the same way she would've have announced that she was making a trip to the grocery store or she had to swing by the bank. "Anything in particular you're going to talk about during your ten-hour car ride?"

Paige reached for the bowl of grapes and plucked one off. "I don't know. His favorite place to visit in Europe, how fluent in French he's become, if we should get back together."

She popped the grape in her mouth and chewed. They had texted back and forth last night until the wee hours of the morning, but nothing had been decided. She told him it was because she didn't want to rush into anything. In light of their history, she wanted to make sure they were both making the right choice. It seemed like a responsible thing to say.

Ciera took a bite of her cereal. "Sounds like riveting conversation. I take it Sasha won't be joining you."

Paige popped another grape in her mouth. "They broke up."

Before Ciera could respond, Hadley walked out of her room, her own packed suitcase rolling behind her. "I just had an interesting phone call." She dropped her bag in the entryway and then walked around the island into the kitchen to pour herself a cup of coffee.

After her first sip, she leaned back against the counter. "It seems Sasha is looking for someone to drive her to the airport this morning. Would you happen to know anything about that, Paige?"

"They broke up," Ciera reported and took another bite of her cereal.

"Humm." Hadley sipped her coffee.

The room got uncomfortably quiet. Paige knew she should tell them everything that was happening, but even after a whole night of lying awake and thinking about it, she still didn't know what to say. Or how she felt about it.

"Sasha and Brody broke up last night and now he wants to get back together with me." Again, Paige reported the facts like she was reporting the weather.

Hadley nodded. "And Aiden?"

Ciera paused, spoon midway to her mouth, and stared at Paige.

Aiden. This whole thing would be so much easier if he wasn't involved. She was supposed to want Brody. Her happily ever after was supposed to be with Brody. That was the plan. Yet the only thing she wanted was the one thing she couldn't have. Aiden.

"I'm not sure when he's going home. I think he has his big contract signing today, but he didn't need me for that. My job is over."

Her connection with him was over. Sure, she would see him at family holidays and events she went to with Ciera, but would she still do family holidays with Ciera when she was with Brody? For the first time it dawned on her that her entire relationship with Aiden, even as a friend, might be over.

Ciera stared at her one more second, then put her bite in her mouth. "She's riding home with Brody," she told Hadley through a mouthful of cereal.

Hadley nodded thoughtfully. "Good. That leaves an open seat in our car to take Sasha to the airport."

Hadley had driven out to Seacrest with one of the groomsmen

and she and Ciera were supposed to ride back with them since Aiden had to stay another day. Now, she was glad she wasn't going to have to sit in a car with her two best friends answering all of their questions for ten hours. Although, the thought of ten hours in a car with Brody didn't sound much more appealing. She broke off another grape, hoping the long road trip would bring her clarity.

The phone next to her buzzed. A text from Brody lit up the screen.

"He's here. I gotta go."

She hugged each of her friends, then headed outside to meet him. He waited in his car while she struggled down the stairs with all of her luggage. After she loaded her things into the trunk, she climbed into the passenger seat next to him.

"I would've helped you with your bags, but I didn't want to leave the car double parked." He didn't look overly torn up about it as he kept his attention on the back-up camera.

"No problem." She was capable of taking care of herself, after all. She was a strong, independent woman. Still, she wouldn't have minded if he'd at least offered.

They drove out of town, leaving the beauty of the beach behind them and pulling onto the freeway. They'd been traveling for about forty-five minutes when he finally brought up the subject she had actively been avoiding.

"So, are we back together or what?"

Romantic. It sent chills…well, nowhere.

"I think it's a little more complicated than that."

Brody propped his elbow on the door and cocked his head to the side as if he had never considered this response. "Huh. I thought the two of us together was an obvious choice. We make sense."

She'd thought that, too. For a long time she'd even been convinced of it. But questions had started to form in her mind, ones that probably should've formed years ago when they first started dating.

"What do you love about me?" Most of the time she would consider this a needy question. It was one she had seen self-consumed brides ask their doting fiancés when they were looking for a little self-assurance. She'd promised herself, after the second or third time she saw a bride pull this stunt, that she'd never stoop to this level. Although right now, she had a different reason for asking.

"Well…" He shifted in his seat, looking uncomfortable and ill-prepared to answer the question, which didn't surprise Paige. She was expecting this response.

"You are good at your job." He paused. She could almost see the wheels turning inside his head. "You're good at planning stuff."

His lacking list should've caused her spirit to droop, but instead it had the opposite effect. It gave her confirmation.

"What did you like about us? When we were together?" This time she asked the question with more confidence.

He was quiet for a second. "We had fun together, didn't we?"

Two weeks ago, she would've given the same answer. But as she thought about it over the last week, she wasn't sure it was true. Maybe they had fun in the beginning, but for the majority of their relationship they were simply comfortable with each other.

She'd missed the distinction at first, confusing acceptance with love. He accepted who she was, she would even be willing to say he loved her as a person, but he wasn't in love with her. It was possible he never had been.

And she'd never really been in love with him. She loved the consistency of a committed relationship. In a childhood that was anything but stable, she'd never experienced that before. It was like a breath of fresh air to know that kind of commitment existed. It was her first glimpse that the life she'd always dreamed about existed.

And, if she were really being honest, she loved the way he looked. Who wouldn't? She'd still argue that he was one the most attractive men on the planet, in a pressed and groomed sort of way. There might have been a sense of pride that came from being desired by someone like that. But that wasn't love.

Paige already knew everything she needed to know. But she kept going, hoping he would catch on before she had to spell it out for him.

"Sasha told me you were happy, too. When you were in Europe?"

Brody shrugged. "It's easy to fall in love when you're surrounded by art and culture and good food."

Funny, she thought it was easy to fall in love when she was in the middle of the ocean surrounded by a pod of dolphins. "How did we get this so wrong?"

From the look on his face, Brody hadn't caught up with her yet. But he would. She settled into her seat, ready for the long drive ahead of them.

"It's a great day for doing business, boys," Jacob Merrick said as he leaned back in the wide leather chair in the boardroom at his neighborhood's club house.

"Indeed, it is." Aiden unzipped his backpack-style briefcase and pulled out five folders. Ones that did not have the Cedar Break logo on them. Energy, the positive kind that he hadn't experienced in a while, charged through him as he set one folder in front of each investor. He dropped the final one in front of Jacob.

This wasn't the presentation Jacob was expecting. The printed pages inside those folders did not hold the contracts they were supposed to. Aiden was well aware that Jacob didn't like surprises, but he did like money. And as long as everything went the way he thought it would over the next hour, there would be plenty of that.

Aiden strode around to the front of the table and hit the remote in his pocket that controlled the PowerPoint. The first slide appeared on all three flat-screen TVs mounted around the room.

"The investment you're making is not in a restaurant. It's in an experience, a lifestyle, a place where people belong. But what if that experience can last longer than a simple meal?"

From the corner of his eye, Aiden caught Jacob tense. His brows furrowed and he froze in his chair. But Aiden didn't let his dark gaze stop him. He flipped to the next slide.

"What if that experience could be prolonged into a more than just a place to eat? What if we could build that experience into a place where memories were made? A place so precious that it became a tradition. Part of a legacy."

By the content looks on their faces, he could tell he had the investors' attention. Aiden wasn't surprised. Over the course of the weekend he'd talked about oceanfront real estate and boutique hotels with all four of them. It was something their firm seemed interested in, even if they weren't verbally expressing it yet. All he had to do was convince them that this was the property they wanted to start with.

He studied Jacob's expression as he flipped to the next slide.

"What if you didn't buy Cedar Break, but rather, invested that money in an oceanfront boutique hotel with a five-star restaurant that will create an experience friends and families will come back to season after season, holiday after holiday, year after year?"

Every muscle in Jacob's neck tensed. Aiden knew he wasn't happy, but he didn't care. Last night, as he drove away from Paige, he decided he couldn't do it. He couldn't walk away from everything he loved on the same weekend. Being free was overrated. He was ready to be part of something.

Cedar Break was his baby from the beginning. It had become like his home. The staff had become like his family. This time, he wasn't willing to walk away from it because someone told him the price was right.

The first investor leaned forward and studied the picture on the screen. "A hotel, huh? Interesting."

"Not just a hotel. A vacation experience."

"And what kind of investment would this require?" another investor asked.

"If you open your folders, you will find all of the financial information on page two. Proposed investments, detailed budgets and estimated returns."

The sound of papers turning filled the room and everyone got quiet. Aiden forced himself to stand still and look comfortable, even though this was the most uncomfortable he'd ever been during a pitch. There was always a healthy dose of nervousness that went along with any big meeting, but normally it was the kind of nervous excitement that energized him. This morning, however, it felt different, as if he had more riding on this presentation than he ever had before.

"And you already have a piece of property in mind?" One of the investors asked.

Aiden flipped to the next slide. It was a beauty shot of the property Aiden had first seen on one of his morning jogs.

"I do. It's an oceanfront gem not too far down the beach from where we are now. I spoke with a realtor this morning. The owners are eager to sell and available for a quick close. You'll find the spec of the property along with a proposed construction timeline in your dossiers."

More pages rustled. The ringleader tapped his pen against the heavy wooden table as he read the pages in front of him. Seconds ticked by.

Aiden shoved his hands in his pockets to keep himself from fidgeting. He actively avoided eye contact with Jacob. A lot was riding on this decision. If it went south, there was a good chance their partnership would too. There was a decent chance he could walk away from this meeting with nothing. But that was a risk he was willing to take.

Finally, the ringleader stopped tapping and looked at the

investor at the end of the table, the one who had been the quietest all weekend. "Davis, what do you think?"

All eyes turned to Davis. He scribbled something in his folder, studied it, then stroked his jaw. "It's intriguing."

Intriguing was good, although Aiden had a pretty good idea that they would be intrigued. This proposal wasn't just some random plan he threw together in the middle of the night. Over the weekend, the investors had done a lot of talking and most of the subjects revolved, in some way, around themselves. That meant Aiden had done a lot of listening. Bits and pieces of this idea had slowly formed with each new conversation until he had a plan for a new business that excited him.

But the idea was rough. He hadn't had time to bounce the concept off anyone else to find and iron out any possible issues. Shoot, he hadn't even had enough time to bounce it off himself. The numbers were raw and the timelines were an estimate at best, but he knew it would be intriguing. And what was even better was that it intrigued him, which was more than he could say about any other start-up idea he'd had in the past three years.

But he needed the investors to be more than intrigued. He needed them to be interested. To pull this off and to get them to walk away from Cedar Break, he needed them to be all in.

The ringleader looked at Jacob. "I like this guy." He turned back to Aiden. "I'm interested. Tell us more."

After what had to be one of the most awkward ten-hour car rides ever, Paige pushed open the door into her dark house and tossed her keys into the bowl. Her cat met her in the entry way.

"Hello, Lavender. I hope you've had a far more relaxing weekend than I did." She reached down to scratch the cat behind her ears before she struggled to pull the rest of her luggage inside and closed the door. The cat purred and rubbed against her legs.

"So, you want an update on Operation Wedding Weekend?" She left her bags in the dark entryway and wandered into the kitchen with the cat trotting along after her. "The Ger-Brody-Back section was a complete failure."

Her stomach rumbled as she opened the refrigerator door. After she outlined all the reasons they shouldn't be together, Brody seemed anxious to get home. They only stopped once to get gas. Not that she blamed him. She was pretty anxious to get out of that car as well. Maybe she should've thought through her plan of having that conversation at the beginning of a road trip a little better.

"It seems I wasn't really in love with him after all," Paige reported to the cat. "I was so worried thinking about how perfect our life could be I missed how perfectly wrong we were for each other."

She heaved out a sigh as she examined the contents in her fridge. Nothing but orange juice and half a stick of butter. It looked as empty and depressed as she felt. She closed the door before she had anymore time to think about it and went for the freezer instead. Given the circumstances, a pint of Strawberries and Cream ice cream seemed like a reasonable choice for dinner. Grabbing a spoon from the drawer, she plopped herself down on a stool at her island and dove right in. Lavender jumped up on the counter and sat next to her.

"The thing is, I'm not even upset about that part because, as it turns out, I'm in love with someone else." The thought of Aiden fluttered through her leaving and warm, tingling trail followed by a dull ache. She didn't want to be in love with him. He didn't check off any of the boxes on her perfect husband list, the biggest problem being that he didn't do commitments. Long term wasn't his thing, so a future with him was out of the question.

But none of that mattered to her heart.

"Perhaps some things were never meant to be." Like finding the end of a rainbow. Pulling off the perfect wedding. Spending forever with the one your heart desires.

The cat nudged her hand with her head. Paige scratched her ears while she spooned another large bite of ice cream into her mouth. After eating the outstanding custom berry and basil ice cream with Aiden, this store-bought stuff seemed flavorless. The vanilla base was boring and the strawberries were bland at best. Great. The weekend had even ruined what she'd previously considered to be her favorite kind of ice cream. She took another drab bite while she reminisced about some of the most impressive flavors—and moments—of the weekend. Experiencing perfection was exhilarating, but it made everything else seem mundane by comparison.

So maybe Aiden didn't love her back. Maybe a future with him was out of the question, but they were still friends. She could still hang out with him, still enjoy his company.

"It's not romantic, not the relationship that I want, but it's something." She wasn't sure if she was trying to convince herself or the cat.

True, it was something, and for now she was willing to settle for it. But how long could she stare at the one thing she could never have before the temptation got too great and she had to walk away?

"Later," she answered herself out loud. "We'll worry about that later."

She let out a defeated sigh and scooped up another large bite of bland ice cream. Her house was so quiet the hum of the refrigerator seemed deafening. Back to being alone. She put the bite in her mouth and chewed slowly.

She'd had the perfect plan to get her perfect future back on track. And, all things considered, she'd even executed it almost flawlessly. But none of it mattered because it wasn't what she really wanted.

Lavender pawed the ice cream container, tipping it over. Paige caught it just before it spilled on the counter. She took one more quick bite, then scooped a tiny amount onto the end of the spoon and held it up for the cat as she replaced the lid on the carton. "At least one of us should get what we want."

Chapter Eighteen

FRIDAY NIGHT AIDEN HEADED TO his parents' house for a family dinner. Every so often, Lottie Pierce would declare that her family had not sat down around the same table in way too long, and all four siblings were summoned. And as long as she was cooking for that many people, she usually invited a few others, too. By the end, there were so many people it always required more than one table, which, perhaps, defeated the purpose.

"Who wants some pie?" Aiden called as he stepped through the front door. He had to stop short to keep from tripping over his three-year-old niece who was running through the entry way into the room next to it. Close on her heels were the neighbor's little girl and the dog. Sounds of talking and laughing came from all over the house. Yep. Sounded like a family dinner.

Aiden found his mom in the kitchen along with his oldest sister and a family friend. "Hello, Mama." He kissed her on the cheek. "I brought you a pie."

"Is that peach?"

Aiden set them on the counter. "Absolutely. One for you and one for the rest of us to share."

"You know my love language." She beamed and kept chopping.

Aiden snagged one of the carrots off her cutting board. "I'm going to say a quick round of hellos and I'll be back to help."

His first stop was the small living area off the back of the house that had been dubbed "Gram's Den." As usual, Gram was in her favorite chair in front of the TV.

"Hey, beautiful." He kissed her cheek and took a seat in the chair next to her.

"You're just in time for the new episode." She patted his knee and turned up the volume on the TV to a nearly deafening level as the theme music filled the room. "We're about to find out if Larissa's baby is Greystone's or Jordan's."

"Greystone is still in the picture?" Over the years that Aiden had watched this show with his grandmother, the characters and the storyline had changed surprisingly little. It wasn't hard to go weeks or even months without watching an episode and still be able to pick up on what was going on.

"How was your business thing? Did you sell your restaurant?" Gram asked, her eyes still glued to the TV.

"No." He settled back in the chair and crossed his ankle over his knee. "I'm selling them a different idea instead."

It was the best of both worlds; he got to keep his restaurant and he got to start a new business that excited him. The future, his professional future at least, gleamed.

"And how about the girl? Did you get her?"

Gram's question caught him off guard. "The girl?"

"That Paige girl. She's precious. You know, I've always liked her."

Disappointment panged a deep place he didn't want to talk about. "Paige is with someone else, Gram, remember?"

"She's still with the doofus? Good heavens, that girl is as clueless as you are."

Aiden studied his grandmother. Perhaps her memory wasn't as good as it used to be. "You told her to fight for him, remember?"

She shook her head. "No. I told her to fight for love. Anyone with eyes could see she wasn't in love with the doofus. She's been mooning over someone else for ages." She turned the TV's volume up another two notches. "If you didn't see that, you're a slow as Jordan."

"It's not nice to call people names, Gram."

She waved off the comment. "I'm eighty-five years old. Rules don't apply to me anymore."

The show started again and Gram concentrated on the action—if you could call it action—on the TV. Aiden stared at the screen, too, trying his hardest to not think about the girl his grandmother thought was precious. The one he was in love with.

After two minutes, Gram looked over at him, her brows furrowed. "Why are you still here?"

"I'm waiting to see whose baby it is." That's why they were watching this show, right?

She studied him. "Maybe you're the doofus."

He started to ignore her words as the crazy ramblings of an old lady, but they struck a nerve. "Gram, we're—"

She cut him off. "You don't need to tell me something we both know isn't true. Your empty words aren't doing anyone any favors in this room."

Empty words? Favors? Didn't Gram understand that watching Paige choose some other guy wasn't his choice? He was doing the noble thing by letting her walk away. Wasn't he?

As if reading his mind, Gram wrapped her warm, withered hand around his. "She's never going to know how you feel unless you tell her. You have to fight for love. This is your shot, kiddo. Take it."

Aiden let the sage words simmer in him until they ignited a fire inside that launched him out of his chair. "I gotta go." Excitement buzzed through him. Maybe he'd missed his shot before. Maybe fear and disappointment had caused him to pass on opportunities he should've taken, but not anymore. He loved Paige.

"Now you got it," Gram said, returning her attention to the screen. "Tell that sweet girl I said hello."

"Will do. Thanks, Gram." He kissed her on the cheek and then bolted for the door. He'd never felt this good in his life, and he had the bounce in his step to prove it.

He almost ran into Ciera on his way out.

"Where are you going in such a hurry?" she asked.

"To tell Paige I love her." The thrill of saying it out loud made him want to break into a dance or belt a song at the top of his lungs. Ciera studied him for a second. "Huh, Hadley said she thought that was the case."

"Has been for a long time," Gram called from her chair. "He's a little slow on the uptake."

"Well, I'm saying it now." He pushed open the exterior door that led to the side of the house and announced his revelation to the world. "I love Paige!" And now he was on his way to tell her.

It wasn't until the heat from outside kissed his face that he paused and looked back at his sister. "Any idea where she might be today?"

Ciera shook her head and took the seat next to Gram in front of the TV.

"I think she has a wedding tonight. She's probably at the resort."

The resort. This was perfect. A plan started to form in his mind. It was a rough plan, but it didn't matter. Some of his most successful ventures had started as rough ideas. He stepped out of the house onto the long concrete driveway, wondering if the exploding anticipation inside him was what Neil Armstrong felt the first time he stepped on the moon. It was only a small step, but everything from here on out was about to be different.

"Tell Mom sorry I couldn't stay for dinner," he called over his shoulder as he broke into a jog for his car.

As always, Paige waited until the glowing bride on her father's arm was halfway down the aisle before she started to close the doors. So far, there had not been one hiccup in this storybook wedding, but tonight perfection didn't excite her the way it usually did. In fact, the wedding itself left her feeling a little flat. True, Friday weddings were generally more subdued than weekend weddings and this bride was more casual than most. But the main thing dragging her down was her disillusioned view on love after last weekend.

Instead of focusing on her couple's happiness, she allowed her mind to wander to mundane places like laundry and what errands she could run on her way home as she closed the second of the double doors, muting the romantic melody of the guitar solo processional. In fact, since she didn't care to gaze at the romantic moment when the happy couple promised their forevers to each other like she normally did, now would be the perfect time to make a grocery list. She'd just pulled up the app on her tablet when she was distracted by the footsteps echoing across the room.

Aiden strode across the room toward her. His long strides were strong and confident and his blue eyes danced against his tan skin. Just the sight of him made her spirit soar, filling every inch of her with a rosy glow that overflowed into a smile. It was hard to believe that she'd gone years without connecting this feeling to what it was. Being in love with him.

She hugged her tablet against her chest and watched him walk toward her. Eventually this sort of reaction to him would go away, or at the very least decrease, wouldn't it? Or was she destined to swoon every time he walked into a room? Love, even when it was one-sided, was a strange thing.

"You know, this fashionably late thing is becoming quite the problem." Also, his shorts and canvas sneakers were underdressed, even for this casual wedding. But she kept that tidbit to herself, especially since he looked better in it than most people looked in formal attire.

"I'm not here for the wedding," he said, not that she was paying attention. She was too busy admiring his dazzling smile and the way his infectious energy seemed to bring the entire room to life.

He stopped in front of her. "I'm here for you."

That time, his words caught her attention. "Me? You have another business meeting you need me to plan?" The familiar longing throbbed deep in her chest. Of course she'd love to work with him again because it would mean she would get to spend more time with him. But how long could she pretend being friends with him was enough for her?

"Not work." He shoved his hands into his pockets. "I didn't sell the restaurant, by the way."

This caused her to pause. Since selling Cedar Break was his goal, she expected this news to be delivered with disappointment or even a hint of regret, but at the moment Aiden looked the opposite of disappointed. In fact, if she had to label his current emotion, she would have called it exuberant. Something wasn't adding up here. She forced her thoughts off of her one-sided love situation and onto what he was telling her.

"What happened?"

He gazed into her eyes with a look so gentle it took her breath away. "I realized some things in life are too good to walk away from."

She knew it wasn't possible, but it felt as if he could see all the way into her soul. The warm rays of love radiated through her, filling every inch of her with light. It was intoxicating in the most delicious way. This was the way love was supposed to feel, and she stood for a moment, soaking it in.

"Cedar Break is a special place. I can understand not wanting to let it go." Of course, letting go wasn't her specialty. She knew at some point she would have to let Aiden go. Whatever was happening between them wouldn't last. It couldn't last. She'd already been over this in her mind more than once during the past week. But for the moment, with her pulse thundering in her ears and the warmth of love rolling through her, she allowed herself to revel in the fantasy.

Aiden nodded. "You made me reconsider my stance on commitment."

At least she'd made a lasting impact on his life. He had definitely made one on hers. Memories of dancing with him on the beach played through her mind, filling her with a yearning so strong she ached.

This was ridiculous. She needed to get control over herself. She couldn't get carried away every time he looked at her. Above everything else, he was a friend, one that she deeply valued, and he was there to tell her…Well, at the moment she couldn't remember what he was there to tell her, which was the problem. She couldn't let her crazy emotions steal her focus. There were things that needed to be done; she had a wedding to run. She needed to stop ogling him and walk away. Play time was over. Her tongue darted out to wet her lips in preparation to tell him she had to get back to work. Only, those weren't the words she blurted out.

"I'm in love with you."

And at the very same moment he said, "I love you."

She froze, unable to believe she'd just said what she did and that she'd heard what she did. The guitar processional outside stopped and everything around them got quiet.

"You what?" She whispered the words, equally afraid that she'd heard him wrong and that she'd heard him right.

He stepped closer to her, filling the gap between them, and gently took the tablet out of her hands, placing it on the table next to them. With nothing else between them she was left feeling open and vulnerable.

This was the moment where everything changed. From this point on, there were no more excuses of friendships or fake relationships. There was no more denying the way she felt about him. There was nothing left to hide behind. It was a strange sensation of joyful anticipation and prickling fear. She held her breath as she waited for his answer.

"I am in love with you." His fingertips trailed down her arms until he took her hands in his, a confident smile lighting his face. "I have been for some time. Maybe even longer than I realized."

Paige closed her eyes, letting his words resonate in her mind. If this was some sort of dream, she didn't want to wake up. But when she opened her eyes, he was still there, staring back at her with the same look of adoration that had taken her breath away earlier.

All the emotions swirling around her had stolen her voice, which was probably just as well. She couldn't think of anything to say in response. Never once had she brainstormed ideas for the perfect line for this scenario. So she just stood there, letting joy consume her and trying to take it all in.

Aiden continued. "No one compares to you. No one has your breathtaking beauty or your adventurous spirit or your kind heart. Even though our relationship was fake, being with you made me realize I've never wanted anything more. That night, when we had to write a wish on the lanterns, my wish was for you."

Giddy excitement danced through her. Aiden Pierce was in love with her, and hearing him say it out loud was even more glorious than she imagined it would be. "You know it's bad luck to tell someone your wish."

He shrugged, laughter crinkling his eyes. "I'm willing to take my chances."

A vision of what their life together could look like flashed before her. But there was still one problem.

She had a wish, too. Forever with Aiden. It was what *she* wrote on her lantern that night and the dream that had echoed in her heart every day since. She didn't just want to have fun with Aiden or be happy for now with Aiden. She wanted forever.

"So, this wish of yours. Is it a short-term deal or an 'as long as it makes sense' deal or..." She couldn't even make herself finish the sentence. Hope had sprouted deep within her, making her jittery with anticipation. But the fear of rejection, the fear of having to walk away from the one thing she wanted more than anything else, loomed over her like a boulder balanced on the edge of a cliff. One word and all of this happiness could be dashed.

Aiden slid his hand behind her head, his thumb caressing her cheek and his expression turned more serious than any she had ever seen on him. "I want you now and forever and for whatever comes after that."

The passion in his voice combined with the love in his eyes washed over her like a gentle wave. A happiness richer than anything she'd ever experienced bubbled up inside her. It caused tears to brim in her eyes and her smile to stretch so far across her face she could feel her muscles straining.

And then he kissed her.

His hands found her hips and he pulled her into him, before he wrapped his arms around her back. He held her against his strong chest and kissed her deeper. It was gentle and sweet, but so filled with passion she could feel it all the way down to her toes. Everything else faded away from her awareness and she focused on the moment. On him. On them.

When she finally took a breath and looked up at him, he had a silly grin plastered on his face. "Is it safe to assume there isn't anyone else in the picture?"

Paige shook her head. "Turns out I was in love with someone else the entire time."

Aiden's thumb caressed her cheek. "That's good news. For me, anyway."

"For all of us. I think everyone got exactly what they wished for." When they had time, she would fill him in on Brody. And he would have to tell her what happened with the investors and Cedar Break. Apparently, a lot had happened since he left her standing on the beach.

But all that could wait. Right now, she wanted to enjoy the moment.

"So, forever, huh? I thought you didn't believe in that word." She playfully snagged her lip with her teeth.

"I didn't, until I imagined forever without you." His expression turned more serious. "Walking away from you was the hardest thing I have ever done. Trust me, it will never happen again."

Standing on the beach that night had been one of her hardest moments, as well. Back then, with her heart broken, she would have never imagined they would end up here. "Promise?"

He gazed down at her with his warm blue eyes. "To steal a phrase from your profession, I do." He gently kissed her lips again. "From now until forever, I do."

Epilogue

SUMMER HAD BEEN SO BUSY for Paige that it didn't seem like twelve weeks had passed since she stood on this same beach with this same group of people celebrating a new beginning. Only this time, instead of wedding dresses and tuxes, the stars of the day wore hard hats and carried silver tipped shovels. And instead of standing on the sand, they were standing on the fresh dirt of a newly cleared construction site.

"I know we're here to be supportive and everything, but how long do you think this ground-breaking ceremony will take? We're only here for two days, so I need to maximize my beach time," Ciera said.

"Right? And we can't even stay out all day today. Sasha's show premieres tonight and I promised her we'd video-chat with her from the watch party." Paige glanced at her watch.

Ciera's eyes lit up. "Did you read the review of it in *Entertainment Magazine*? They called it the best new show of the fall! I can't wait to see it. But you're right. That doesn't give us much time."

Georgia glanced at her watch and nodded. "Which is the reason I'm wearing my swimsuit under my clothes right now. The second we're done up here, I'll be in the water."

"I'm right there with you," Paige said. "Unfortunately, there's no staircase to the beach here yet. We either have to find a rope and rappel down the bluff or find public access." If there was any way to climb down the steep embankment to the beach, Paige would have done it this morning. She needed to get her toes in the sand.

"That's a problem," Georgia said.

"What's a problem?" Hadley walked up on their group. She lifted up her shiny new white hardhat with the new resort's logo emblazoned on the front and wiped away the sweat that was beading up on her forehead in the humid September morning.

"Your beach access situation," Georgia reported.

Hadley nodded, looking thoughtful. "I'll make that priority number one in the project." She looked out toward the water. "But you can't beat that view. It almost makes my tiny trailer in the middle of a construction zone worth it."

Paige turned to admire the turquoise water that stretched out all the way to the horizon. She snaked her arm around her friend's waist. "I can't believe you get to live here and look at this for the next eight months."

Hadley leaned her head on Paige's shoulder. "Right? I have your boyfriend to thank for that."

Paige shook her head. "No, you have yourself to thank."

Ciera nodded. "Aiden and Jacob asked you because there was no one else they trusted to be on location and manage this huge construction project."

"And I'm excited about a change, but..." Hadley glanced over her shoulder at the crowd gathering behind them. Concern clouded her normally confident features. "I've never done anything this big before. Eight months to build a fifteen-room boutique resort AND get all three proposed restaurants operational? Let's hope everything goes according to plan."

One thing Paige had embraced this summer was that life never seemed to go according to plan. She looked across the crowd of people gathering in the big dirt field. Aiden was talking with one of the investors. When he caught her gaze he flashed her a smile, the intimate one that she knew was just for her. As always, it filled her with giddy excitement. Maybe life didn't follow her plan, but sometimes the unexpected turns took her to the most rewarding places.

"It won't. But there's nothing they can throw at you that you can't handle." Paige gave her a gentle squeeze.

Hadley drew in a deep breath, then refreshed her confident smile and stepped away from Paige, readjusting her hat. "Thanks for being here, guys. It means a lot. You're going to come visit me all the time, right?"

"I'm going to be here so often, you're going to have to kick me out," Ciera said.

"I hope your tiny trailer is big enough for all of us," Paige added.

"And you know you're always welcome to my dad's beach house if you need a break from the construction site. It's only a couple miles down the road and we're hardly ever there."

Hadley beamed at her friends. "Sounds like we have quite the adventures waiting for us." Just then, Jacob Merrick, who was talking with the town's mayor, waved her over. "Looks like I'm being summoned. I'll catch up with you later."

Less than fifteen minutes later, all the folding chairs they had set up were occupied and a solid row of video cameras and photographers stood behind them. After Aiden welcomed everyone and Jacob gave them a preview of what could be expected, the investors, along with Aiden, Jacob and their new project manager, Hadley, posed in their business suits and hardhats with their silver-tipped shovels.

Paige stood in the back among her friends and watched, pride beaming within her. It had been fun to watch Aiden work over the past three months, fun to see his passion and ideas take shape, and today all of that hard work was being brought to life. True, the building process had already been underway for a few weeks when they started clearing the land and the preliminary structures like Hadley's trailer and the temporary office building were put in place. But today made it feel official, and she could tell by Aiden's extra chipper attitude that he was basking in the excitement as well.

After the photo op was over, the crowd dispersed and each of them went to congratulate a different person. Lane and Georgia went to talk to his father, Ciera trotted over to hug Hadley, and Aiden headed directly to where Paige was standing.

"It's official. Pictures of the resort have been blasted all over social media. There's no going back now." He kissed her lips. "Thanks for being here."

"The man I love is the owner of the most amazing boutique hotel on 30A. I wouldn't have missed this moment for anything."

Aiden raised an eyebrow and turned his attention to the area where they'd just been digging. "Right now, I'm the partial owner of a pile of dirt and some pretty fancy drawings of what could be a hotel."

"Yeah, but your dirt comes with a great view."

"True." He took her hand and they strolled over to the edge of the bluff, looking out at the sparkling water that stretched out to the horizon. "Even if I live to be a hundred, I hope I never get to a point where this view gets old."

Paige drew in a deep breath, letting the salty air penetrate every inch of her body. "I don't think that's possible."

He turned and looked at her with gentle adoration. It was the same expression she'd seen daily since he showed up at the resort declaring his true feelings for her. The one that touched her deep inside, reminding her how loved she was. She knew, even if she lived to be older than a hundred, she would never tire of that view.

"Actually, I have an idea of how we can put this stunning setting to good use for one of our first events here. I was hoping you could help me with it."

Paige tore her attention away from the ocean and focused on him. "Sure. What kind of event?"

"That depends on you." He reached into his pocket and pulled out a tiny blue box. Dropping down to one knee, he opened the lid. "But I was hoping for a wedding."

The sunlight hit the ring, making a thousand different colors dance on the surface, but even that couldn't distract Paige from the brilliance of Aiden's smiling face. She didn't know if it was possible for her to love anyone more than she loved this man.

"Paige Westmoreland, will you marry me?"

She took a moment to let the question resonate through her. She wouldn't deny she had hoped this day would come, but hearing the words in real life was even more beautiful than she imagined. She was getting her wish. Forever with Aiden. A smile spread across her face and joy warmed her from within. "I thought you'd never ask."

Aiden arched an eyebrow, giving her that playful look she loved. Life with him was going to be fun. "That means yes, right?"

"Yes. A thousand times, yes."

He pulled the sparkling ring out of the box and slid it on her finger. Then he stood up, wrapped his arms around her and, lifting her off the ground, spun around and kissed her. The world swirling around her never felt so right.

When he set her down, she held her hand out to admire how the ring looked on her finger. "It's stunning."

He tucked a flyaway strand of her hair behind her ear. "It doesn't even come close to comparing to you." He kissed her forehead. "You, my love, are perfect."

"So, any news you'd like to share?" Ciera's voice broke up the moment. Paige looked over to see all their friends had gathered around them with goofy, expectant grins on their faces.

Aiden held out her hand to put the ring on display. "She said yes."

"Woo hoo!" Hadley popped the top of the champagne bottle, letting the cork fly over the bluff onto the sand below. "Looks like we have a lot of things to celebrate today."

She filled the flutes Georgia and Lane were holding and they passed them out. The six friends stood in a circle and held the glasses up for a toast.

"To shiny new beginnings," Hadley said.

"And happily-ever-afters," Aiden added.

Paige looked around the circle at the faces that she loved more than any others in the world. The faces that had become her family.

"And to friendship."

"To friendship," they all repeated.

They clinked their glasses together and drank to their sparkling futures.

BBQ Brisket Tacos with Sunshine Slaw

Aiden's improvised brisket tacos become a house specialty at his restaurant, and he serves them to investors who might buy the place. Both he and Paige have big decisions to make about what parts of their past to hold onto...and what to leave behind. Our recipe for BBQ brisket tacos is both casual and impressive, perfect for a summer gathering you'll always remember.

Yield: 12 brisket tacos (6 servings)
Prep Time: 20 minutes
Slow Cooker Time: 12 hours
Total Time: 12 hours plus 20 minutes

INGREDIENTS

Slow Cooker Beef Brisket:

- 2 tablespoons olive oil
- 2 tablespoons apple cider vinegar
- 1 tablespoon liquid hickory smoke
- 1 tablespoon Worcestershire sauce
- 2 tablespoons brown sugar, packed
- 2 tablespoons paprika
- 1½ tablespoons kosher salt
- 1 tablespoon garlic powder
- 1 tablespoon onion powder
- 2 teaspoons ground cumin
- 1 teaspoon coarse ground black pepper
- 1 (3 to 5 pound) beef brisket

Sunshine Slaw:

- 2 cups shredded cabbage slaw blend
- 1 cup thinly sliced red, yellow and orange bell pepper
- ½ cup thinly sliced red onion
- ¼ cup mayonnaise
- 2 tablespoons apple cider vinegar

Brisket Tacos:

- 12 street style (4-inch) flour tortillas, lightly grilled or heated until warm
- ¾ cup smoky BBQ sauce
- ¾ cup crumbled queso fresco
- as needed, fresh lime wedges
- as needed, f7resh cilantro

DIRECTIONS

1. To prepare slow cooker brisket: combine olive oil, cider vinegar, liquid smoke, Worcestershire and dry seasonings in

small bowl and mix to blend. Spread evenly over all sides of beef brisket.

2. Arrange rubbed brisket, fat side up, in slow cooker. Cook on low for 10 to 12 hours (based on size of brisket).

3. Preheat broiler. Carefully transfer brisket to sheet pan lined with foil (discard cooking liquid or save for another use). Heat brisket under broiler for 2 to 4 minutes, watching constantly, until surface is bubbly and golden brown and has developed a crispy "bark" on surface; let meat rest for 15 minutes before slicing (or refrigerate if making ahead). Thin slice brisket as needed for tacos. Reserve remaining brisket for another meal.

4. To prepare slaw: combine all ingredients in large bowl and toss to blend.

5. To prepare each taco: layer 2 slices beef brisket in center of warm flour tortilla; top with 1 tablespoon BBQ sauce, 1 tablespoon crumbled queso fresco and 2 tablespoons slaw. Garnish taco with cilantro. Serve with a fresh lime wedge.

For quick-and-easy week night taco assembly, use fully cooked smoked brisket purchased from a grocery store or BBQ restaurant in recipe.

Thanks so much for reading *Beach Wedding Weekend!*

You might also enjoy these other ebooks
from Hallmark Publishing:

The Secret Ingredient
Love on Location
A Dash of Love
Love Locks
Moonlight in Vermont
The Perfect Catch
Like Cats and Dogs
Dater's Handbook
A Country Wedding
Sunrise Cabin
October Kiss

For information about our new releases and exclusive
offers, sign up for our free newsletter!

You can also connect with us here:

Facebook.com/HallmarkPublishing

Twitter.com/HallmarkPublish

About the Author

Rachel wrote her first novel when she was twelve and entered it into a contest for young author/illustrators. Unfortunately, the judges weren't impressed with her stick figures, so she dropped the dream of becoming a world-famous illustrator and stuck to spinning stories. When she's not busy working on her latest book, she loves to travel with her family and friends. By far, her favorite destination is the beach, which tends to work its way into most of her stories. Between vacations, you can find her at home in The Woodlands, TX with her wonderful husband, their two adventurous kids and a couple of spirited pets.

Turn the page for a sneak peek of

A Down Home Christmas

LIZ TALLEY

Hallmark
PUBLISHING

Chapter One

I SHOULD'VE COME HOME BEFORE NOW.

The thought buzzed in Kris Trabeau's head as his car bumped down the winding drive that led to Trabeau Farms. New potholes and overgrown trees greeted him, causing the guilt he continually stowed in the back of his conscience to rocket to the forefront.

At the very least he should have hired someone years ago to help his aunt. The old homeplace was too big for such a slip of a woman to take care of by herself—especially one with a broken leg.

But he knew his Aunt Tansy well. The fiercely independent woman would have sent whomever he hired on their way before the ink was dry on the check. Which was part of the reason he'd driven almost three hundred miles to Charming, Mississippi. It was beyond time to convince his stubborn aunt to give up on living alone and come live with him in Nashville.

Just as Kris crested the hill that would bring the farmhouse into view, a chicken flapped across the drive.

A chicken wearing a sweater.

"What the—" The words died on his lips as a huge beast loped behind in pursuit of the squawking fowl. A leash trailed behind the dog that seemed single-minded in its pursuit of the chicken.

Next came a barefoot brunette, waving her hands and screaming.

"Heel, Edison. I said heel!"

Kris slammed on the brakes, the brand-new Mustang fishtailing before jerking to a halt. The woman's gaze flew toward him, her mouth dropping open, before she continued her mad dash to apprehend the dog. Kris unbuckled and climbed out of the car.

"Whoa, hey, you need help?"

"I got it," she called back, disappearing down the hill.

Kris lifted his eyebrows and mouthed, *Wow.*

Then his aunt came limping as fast as her crutches would allow. She wore a track suit circa 1995 and a medical boot around her leg. "Think he's gonna get my Loretta, does he? Well, he's got another thing coming, is what he's got."

Kris moved then, meeting his aunt who hadn't seemed to notice he stood in her driveway. "Whoa, now, Aunt Tansy. What's going on?"

"Oh, sugar, Edison's after Loretta Lynn again. That dog has taken a fascination with my chickens," his aunt said, her gaze fastened to the spot where the chicken, dog, and pretty brunette had disappeared. Then she jerked stunned eyes to him. "Wait, *Kris?* What are *you* doin' here?"

"Surprise," he said, throwing up his hands. "I thought I would visit for the holidays." *Even though I swore I would never come back.* Aunt Tansy closed her mouth and wobbled a little. "For the holidays?"

Here in front of him was the very reason he needed to convince her to make a change. Tansy hobbling around chasing a dog was dangerous. She could have tripped again and done even greater damage to her healing leg. Or what if she had a heart attack? Heart disease ran in the family. Or someone broke into the house and Aunt Tansy couldn't get to his great-granddaddy's shotgun in time? So many horrible things could happen to his closest living relative, things he hadn't considered until Thad Cumberland, editor of *The Charming Gazette*, had called his manager and relayed the news that Tansy had fallen, broken her femur, and was in surgery.

The panic at the thought that she could've died alone in that house with things still unsettled between them had sent a load of guilt so massive, Kris had trouble breathing. Guest appearances, tours, and promotional opportunities had occupied too much of his time lately, and he'd put his personal life on the back burner—including his Aunt Tansy. He couldn't put off addressing her situation any longer. Thanks to the new contract, now he could afford to take care of her the way she deserved.

But, of course, he couldn't tell her his plan just yet.

Tansy's dark eyes flashed with something that made the guilt he carried wriggle inside him. Tansy had taken him in at ten years old when his parents had died in a plane crash, sending a terrified Kris from the flat plains of Texas to the gentle Mississippi hills. Living at Trabeau Farms with a maiden aunt he'd barely known hadn't been easy. But Tansy was a determined woman and hadn't given up on him, even when he threw a brick through the front window of Ozzy Vanderhoot's Old-Fashioned General Store or when he drank a six-pack and spray-painted a choice directive on the Charming, Mississippi, water tower.

"Well, boy, I'm glad to see you, but I ain't got time to sit here jawin' when Edison's chasing my Loretta. He may not mean harm, but he might scare her to death. Wait here. I'll be right back," she said, starting toward the woods to his right.

"Hold up," he said, taking her by the elbow. She felt too thin. Looked too tired and old. How long had it been since he'd seen her? Three years? Maybe four? "You broke your leg. I'm sure you're not supposed to be running after chickens."

"I'm not running after chickens. I'm running after a dog."

"Let me get the dog…and the chicken," he said, carefully leading her to a flat patch where she could balance better. She looked so slight a stiff wind could likely blow her over.

Tansy didn't look satisfied. "You remember how to handle chickens? You're a fancy city boy now and all."

"I'm pretty sure I remember how to pick up a chicken," he

said, with a roll of his eyes. Fetching eggs had been one of his jobs growing up. Of course, back then, his aunt hadn't named her egg producers and dang sure hadn't dressed them in sweaters.

"I suppose it's like riding a bicycle," she conceded.

"Probably. I'll be back in a sec," Kris said, before jogging down the slope that led to a wooded copse that held a small creek and good climbing trees. He'd built a fort in those woods when he'd first come to live with Tansy, and the remnants were probably in there somewhere.

He followed the sound of yipping dog and squeaking brunette, pushing through the brush that should have been dead in December but wasn't. Because it was Mississippi and unusually warm for December. Heck, sometimes they even wore shorts at Christmas.

"Ouch, ouch. Please, Edison. Stop. Stop!" the woman yelled somewhere off to his left.

At that moment, the sweater-wearing chicken flew by Kris's head and the dog came bounding after it. Kris ducked as the chicken tumbled by, crashing into the underbrush. He snatched the leash that bumped behind the dog, making the beast's head jerk around when he reached the end of the tether. The huge fluffy dog immediately started yipping at the hapless hen. A few steps behind, the brunette emerged, panting, her curly hair displaying bits of leaf and twigs. With her pointed chin, big gray eyes, and flushed cheeks, she looked a bit like a woodland fairy.

"Oh, thank goodness," she breathed, pressing a hand against her chest.

Edison, who looked like a cross between a Saint Bernard and Chow Chow, whined and strained at the leash. The chicken's sweater had caught on a broken limb and the poor thing flapped and squawked. Kris extended the end of the leash to the woman. She took it and jerked her dog back toward her. "Sit, Edison. And hush! You're scaring Loretta."

The dog sat, tongue lolling out, panting, eyes still fixed on the

Rhode Island Red that flopped about pitifully in the brush. Kris went over to the bird and wondered how in the heck he was going to free the terrified Loretta Lynn without getting pecked to death. He started unbuttoning his flannel shirt.

"What are you doing?" the woman asked, sounding slightly alarmed.

"Trying to calm this chicken down."

"By taking your shirt off?" Her eyes grew wide as she looked from him to the chicken.

"I'm going to drape it over her so I don't get pecked. Then I'll try to free her."

"Oh," the woman said, tugging as her beast leapt against the restraint. "Good idea. Birds have a higher visual stimulus and covering her eyes should calm her down."

Visual stimulus?

He shrugged out of his shirt, glad he'd pulled on an undershirt to ward off the early morning chill when he left Nashville that morning. Then he approached the chicken, who grew even more agitated as he moved toward it. Carefully, he drew his shirt over Loretta, then slid his hands around her now-clothed body, pinning her wings to her sides. The hen went still. "There."

"Her sweater's still hung," the woman said unhelpfully.

"I got it," he said, pulling the royal blue yarn free from the branch and looking back at the woman and dog. "Why is this chicken wearing a sweater anyway?"

"That's Loretta Lynn. Miss Tansy's pet. She likes to knit sweaters for her hens. She got the idea off Pinterest."

"Pet? She calls them pets?" Kris arched a brow. "And people make clothes for farm animals now?"

"Haven't you seen the videos of baby goats in pajamas? They're so cute." She paused and then shook her head as if she knew she got off track. "For some reason, Edison really likes Loretta. I think it's because she's very flappy."

Kris couldn't stop his smile. "Flappy?"

"Miss Tansy sometimes gives Edison dog biscuits, and he remembers. So when he gets loose, he comes here. Unfortunately, the chickens intrigue him. Maybe he prefers Loretta because she makes the most noise."

"That makes sense. He's a dog, after all," he said, turning back to the chicken. He carefully lifted and tucked her beneath his arm. The hen, oddly enough, seemed to sink in relief against his side. Poor Loretta Lynn. "There now."

"I'm so relieved she's not dead. Miss Tansy would have killed me and Edison." The woman let out a sigh.

"And who are you exactly?" he asked.

The woman pushed back the hair curling into her eyes and held out her hand. "I'm Tory Odom. I live next door to Tansy."

"You're one of the Moffetts?"

"No, I live in the cottage on the other side of Tansy," she said as he took her hand. It was small and capable-looking, like she could smooth a child's fevered forehead or hoe a garden equally well.

"Oh, the Howards' old place?" Last time he'd been home, he'd predicted a strong wind could topple what was left of the Howard place.

"I restored the cottage. It's really nice now." Edison took that moment to spring toward the bundle under his arms. She tugged on his leash and pushed him into a sitting position. "And you are?"

"Oh, I'm Kris. Tansy's nephew."

"The country music singer?"

Kris felt pride stir inside. He'd waited a long time to be known as a country music singer. Being named CMA's New Artist of the Year just weeks ago had cemented his position in the country music scene. He'd placed his award in the center of his mantel and made sure the accent light hit it perfectly. The award was the first of many he'd use to decorate the downtown Nashville loft he'd purchased earlier that year with the royalties on his first album. *A Simple*

Dream had hit big last spring, but it had taken years of sweat, tears, and sore fingers from playing guitar for his dream to come true. He'd hit number one with two songs on his debut album and was in the process of putting together his second one. Of course, he still had to write some songs for it, but they would come. He prayed they would come. So, heck yeah, he was *the country music star*. "Star is kind of a strong word, but, yeah, I play country music."

"I didn't say star."

She *hadn't* said star. She'd said singer. He glanced away so she wouldn't see that he was embarrassed about the faux pas. He felt really stupid. "Right, right."

"I don't really care for country music. You could be a star and I wouldn't know it," she said, sounding like she offered an apology.

Her admission embarrassed him even more, and he found he hadn't a clue what to say to her. Maybe the sweater-bedecked chicken nestled beneath his arm paired with an ego smackdown had something to do with not being able to find the right words.

Or maybe it was the fact he'd not been able to find the words for the last few months.

And that was what worried him most.

Tory Odom was at her very essence a scientist, so she knew Kris Trabeau was exactly the sort of test subject that behavioral researchers would use to gauge the concept of attractiveness. People were more apt to trust others with symmetrical features as an indicator of being attractive. The man in front of her fit the description. Not only were his features symmetrical, but he also had broad shoulders, shaggy dark hair, and a scruffy beard. Normally she didn't care for a rough-around-the-edges look, but somehow it worked for this country music singer.

Then again, Tory also knew that good looks didn't amount to squat.

Kris's brow had gathered into a frown at her words about his not being a star.

That was rude, Tory.

"Uh, I don't listen to any music all that much, and when I do I like classics or Motown. No offense." She pulled Edison's leash as Kris pushed out of the underbrush. These woods extended toward a large lake on Salty Moffett's land. Salty and Tansy had a love-hate relationship and people said they always had. Tory had often wondered if it had to do with a relationship gone bad, but she'd never asked. Tansy was very private and not open to personal questions. Tory hadn't even known the woman had an injury until a week ago. Of course, that was mostly Tory's own fault. She'd been stuck in her own blue world and hadn't been out much herself.

"It's okay. I know not everyone listens to country music," Kris said, emerging into the clearing, holding back a limb so she could pass.

"Thank you," she said, studying the still green patch of clover covering the slope and praying there were no stickers. Her mad dash barefoot had been unwise, but when Edison had turned toward Tansy's and shot off like a rocket, she hadn't had time to go inside and put shoes on. She'd stepped on a pinecone and knew she'd scraped her foot.

Obviously, she and Edison needed to practice commands again. He'd done so well at obedience school but needed to have consistent practice. She'd slacked off over the last few months. Time for a refresher course on *sit* and *heel*.

They arrived back on the graveled drive where Tansy waited. When she saw Kris carrying the draped bundle beneath his arm, her shoulders sank. "Oh, no. Not Loretta Lynn."

"She's fine," Kris said, patting the hen beneath the shirt. "I covered her so she wouldn't see the dog and be scared."

"Oh, thank goodness," Tansy said, clasping a hand to her chest. Then she eyed Edison as he padded in front of Tory, tongue hanging, looking every bit as happy as a dog could look. Tory wished Edison would have the decency to be cowed, but no. Edison didn't seem to ever feel shame.

Tory shot Tansy an apologetic look. "I'm sorry, Miss Tansy. Edison has been doing so well at his obedience training that I let my guard down. He loves coming to visit you...uh, and the chickens. You know he would never hurt them intentionally."

Tansy sniffed. "He's a menace is what he is."

They all turned to look at the overgrown puppy with his shaggy coat, happy brown eyes, and smiling face. He looked nothing like a menace. In fact, he looked pretty adorable. He woofed and held up a paw.

"See? He's sorry," Tory said.

"Here, Aunt Tansy. Why don't you take your chicken back...to wherever you keep her." Kris handed the cloaked hen to his aunt.

Loretta flapped beneath his shirt but settled when Tansy cooed to her. "It's all right, Retta. You're safe now."

Kris shot Tory a look. She was fairly certain it was a "has my aunt gone bonkers?" look. Tory gave a slight shrug as Tansy hobbled off carrying the chicken. She'd also taken Kris's flannel shirt with her, leaving him clad in a thin t-shirt.

With Tansy gone and the drama of Edison chasing Loretta over, Tory started toward her house. Her left foot hurt from the pine cone scrape and she tried not to hobble. A person had to have some dignity after running like a wild woman after her adorable but obedience-challenged mutt. "Better get Edison back home. Nice to meet you."

"You need a ride?" Kris called after her.

"No. Edison would get your car dirty. He sheds a lot and that car looks—" she turned and glanced at his gleaming, granite gray Mustang GT, "very well taken care of."

He narrowed his eyes as if pondering what the dog hair would actually do to his leather interior. "It is, but you're barefoot."

"I made it here. I can make it back. But thank you for asking." Tory started across the large expanse of shaded yard, trying not to wince each time her foot struck the hard earth.

"Looks like you hurt your foot," Kris said, jogging to catch up with her. Edison's tail thumped and he grinned up at the country music singer like he'd found his new best friend. Edison was fickle that way. He loved everyone, and life was big fun. Chasing a squawking, flapping Loretta, Tammy, or Dolly around the farm was a great game. Maybe Tory needed to adopt a new friend for Edison. Perhaps he'd stop thinking about playing with Tansy's chickens if he had another pup to tug a rope with.

"I'm fine. Probably a thorn or a little scrape." She didn't want to put this man out any more than she already had. She was embarrassed of her disheveled hair, ratty sweatshirt and bare feet in serious need of a pedicure. Ever since Patrick had dumped her, she'd let her beauty routine slide. Chipped toenail paint aside, she didn't want to climb inside his fancy car with her hairy, drooling mutt.

"Let me drive you back. I insist." He placed a hand on her elbow, halting her.

"No. I can make it. It's less than half a mile."

"I know you can make it, but let me play the gentleman," he said, with a smile that made her stomach do a loop-de-loop.

Stop it, Tory.

"It's really not necessary."

"My Aunt Tansy would have my hide if I let you walk back barefoot. Come on. I can clean the seat if I need to."

Tory sighed. "Fine."

She hobbled beside him, praying Edison didn't do something ridiculous like tear the leather seats or barf on the floormat. He was notorious for having bad timing. Once he'd done his business in the middle of the vet's office right when the pastor of Charming United Methodist had asked her about her parents who lived a few towns over.

Edison had been adopted from a local rescue. Tory had fallen in love with his exuberance and sloppy kisses on first meeting, but Edison's past as an untrained puppy sometimes reared its head. Still, even polite dogs had accidents…and drooled.

"You sure your foot is okay?" Kris asked, opening the passenger door for her. Her ex, Patrick, had never opened the door for her. He'd told her he believed in equal rights for women and that her arm wasn't broken, was it? Of course, opening the door for a lady didn't mean a man thought she couldn't do it herself. It meant he was raised to be respectful. But in this case, it might be merely because she had a thorn or something in her foot and was trying to manage her overgrown canine who just happened to adore a car ride.

"It's fine," she said, wincing as Edison bounded into the small backseat with the enthusiasm of a toddler at a playground. Kris clicked the front seat back and she lowered herself into the seat. The interior of the car smelled new and gleamed in the weak winter sunlight.

Kris jogged around and slid into the driver's seat. When he closed the door, the intimacy level went to threat-level ten. Tory shifted toward the passenger door to give herself some room. Kris smelled like pine trees and expensive cologne, both strangely inviting. She tucked her frizzy hair behind her ear and tried to make sure her elbow on the middle console was positioned beneath her dog's drooling mouth without invading Kris's space.

He backed up, the car thrumming with power.

"This is quite a car," she said, trying to make conversation and catch the drool with her arm.

"Yeah, I thought about a pickup truck. You know, country music bad boy and all, but I used to covet these bad boys when I was a kid. My parents had a ranch hand who had a vintage GT he liked to soup up and race all over the county. I thought that was the coolest thing I'd ever seen."

"It's nice," she said. Then she made a face. "You call yourself a bad boy?"

He laughed. "No, but I liked the idea of the image. Like I was tough. That sounds lame, doesn't it?"

"I guess everyone wants to portray something."

They fell into silence as he pulled out onto the highway. The farm across from Tansy's had multiple blowup Christmas lawn ornaments at the entrance. The festive balloons bobbed in the afternoon breeze. Edison barked as the towering Santa dipped toward them. Kris made a neat right into her place and roared down the graveled drive.

"Oh, you did do a great job with the house," Kris said when her small farmhouse came into view. Tory was rather proud of the fresh bright white paint and black shutters. A swing hung on the front porch and she'd put bright patterned pillows in it. Ferns hung in between the rustic beams she'd used to support the porch. "But where are your Christmas blowup decorations?"

His question had been teasing, but her response was the one she'd given everyone who had commented on the absence of her Christmas decorations. "I don't have any. I'm not doing Christmas this year."

With that, she opened the door, flipped back the seat to let Edison bound out, and said, "Thanks for the ride."

CPSIA information can be obtained
at www.ICGtesting.com
Printed in the USA
LVHW042049110419
613904LV00001B/1

9 781947 892682